THIS BOOK BELONGS TO

Ginger Hall

Grifters
&
Swindlers

Grifters
&
Swindlers

Stories from *Ellery Queen's Mystery Magazine* and *Alfred Hitchcock Mystery Magazine*

Edited by Cynthia Manson

Carroll & Graf Publishers, Inc.
New York

First Carroll & Graf edition 1993

Carroll & Graf Publishers, Inc.
260 Fifth Avenue
New York, NY 10001

Library of Congress Cataloging-in-Publication Data

Grifters & swindlers : stories from Alfred Hitchcock mystery magazine and Ellery Queen's mystery magazine / edited by Cynthia Manson. — 1st Carroll & Graf ed.
    p.   cm.
   ISBN 0-88184-931-6 : $18.95
    1. Detective and mystery stories, American.   2. Swindlers and swindling—Fiction.   I. Manson, Cynthia.   II. Alfred Hitchcock mystery magazine.   III. Ellery Queen's mystery magazine.
   IV. Title: Grifters and swindlers.
PS648.D4G74   1993
813'.087208—dc20   92-46726
                                                                CIP

Manufactured in the United States of America

Robert L. Fish, copyright © 1977 by Robert L. Fish, reprinted by permission of Robert P. Mills, Ltd.; **THE CACKLE BLADDER** by William Campbell Gault, copyright © 1950 by Popular Publications, Inc., © renewed 1977, reprinted by permission of the author; **THE WESTERN FILM SCAM** by Francis M. Nevins, Jr., copyright © 1980 by Davis Publications, Inc., reprinted by permission of the author; **HOW TO TRAP A CROOK** by Julian Symons, copyright © 1972 by Julian Symons, reprinted by permission of Curtis Brown, Ltd.; **JUST THE LADY WE'RE LOOKING FOR** by Donald E. Westlake, copyright © 1964 by Donald E. Westlake, © renewed 1991, reprinted by permission of Knox Burger Associates; all stories previously appeared in **ELLERY QUEEN'S MYSTERY MAGAZINE** published by **DELL MAGAZINES,** a division of **BANTAM DOUBLEDAY DELL MAGAZINES.**

CONTENTS

INTRODUCTION

☐ MYSTERY READERS, CRIME BUFFS, FANS OF TELEVISION DETECtive shows and movies have always been fascinated by swindlers, also referred to as "grifters." In the *noir* period writers like Jim Thompson, David Goodis, and John D. MacDonald portrayed the grifter as an oily rough drifter, almost always male, who might run, for example, a con game of cards that put his clever skills to the test. Before the victim realizes that he has been cheated the grifter is long gone. He may already be scoping out his next prey in some other town.

Writers of crime fiction today no longer rely on those stereotypes. Grifters and con artists, both male and female, as illustrated in this collection come from every strata of society and wield an assortment of ingenious scams. What these grifters have in common is that they are all cheaters, liars, and slick at their trade. The element of surprise is cleverly executed by this collection's strong line-up of professional crime writers. Fraud is wrapped up in all sorts of disguises. The readers are kept guessing the nature of the con or who is conning whom throughout the narrative until the surprise punch at the end.

To describe these stories in any detail would give away the con but suffice it to say, the authors, well known to most of you, are almost as skilled as the grifters they write about in leading their readers astray. They include Jim Thompson, Robert L. Fish, David Morrell, Julian Symons, Simon Brett, Donald E. Westlake, and William Campbell Gault. It is fitting that Westlake be included alongside Thompson. Thompson wrote the book *The Grifters* on which Westlake based the screenplay for the popular and recent film of the same name. Keep your guard up and enjoy this entertaining collection of colorful grifters who manipulate their victims with cunning ploys in diversified settings.

—Cynthia Manson

THE FRIGHTENING FRAMMIS

by Jim Thompson

☐ For perhaps the hundredth time that day, Mitch Allison squared his shoulders, wreathed his face with an engaging grin, and swung his thumb in a gesture as old as hitchhiking. And for perhaps the hundredth time his appeal was rudely ignored. The oncoming car roared down on him, and past him, wiping the forced grin from his face with the nauseous blast of its exhausts.

Mitch cursed it hideously as he continued walking, damning the car's manufacturer, its owner and finally, and most fulsomely, himself.

"Just couldn't be satisfied, could you?" he grumbled bitterly. "Sitting right up on top of the world, and it wasn't good enough for you. Well, how do you like *this,* you stupid dull-witted moronic blankety-blank-blank!"

Mitch Allison was not the crying kind. He had grown up in a world where tears were more apt to inspire annoyance than sympathy, and a sob was likely to get you a punch in the throat. Still, he was very close to weeping now. If there had been any tears in him, he would have bawled with sheer shame and self-exasperation.

Less than a day ago, he had possessed almost twenty thousand dollars, the proceeds from robbing his wife, swindling the madam of a parlor house and pulling an intricate double double-cross on several "business" associates. Moreover, since it had been imperative for him to clear out of Los Angeles, his home town, he had had a deluxe stateroom on the eastbound Super Chief. Then . . .

Well, there was this elderly couple. Retired farmers, ostensibly, who had just sold their orange grove for a five-figure sum. So Mitch had tied into them, as the con man's saying is, suggesting a friendly little card game. What happened then was figuratively murder.

The nice old couple had taken him like Grant took Richmond. Their apparently palsied hands had made the cards perform in a manner which even Mitch, with all his years of suckering chumps, would have declared impossible. He couldn't believe his own eyes, his own senses. His twenty grand was gone and the supposed suckers were giving him the merry ha-ha in a matter of two hours.

Mitch had threatened to beat them into hamburger if they didn't return his dough. And that, of course, was a mistake, the compounding of one serious error with another. For the elderly couple—far more practiced in the con than he—had impeccable references and identification, while Mitch's were both scanty and lousy.

He couldn't establish legitimate ownership to twenty cents, let alone twenty grand. Certainly, he was in no position to explain how he had come by that twenty grand. His attempts to do so, when the old couple summoned the conductor, had led him into one palpable lie after another. In the end, he had had to jump the train, sans baggage and ceremony, to avoid arrest.

So now, here he was. Broke, disgusted, footsore, hungry, hitch-hiking his way back to Los Angeles where he probably would get killed as soon as he was spotted. Even if no one else cared to murder him, his wife Bette would be itching to do so. Still, a guy had to go some place, didn't he? And having softened up Bette before, perhaps he could do it again. It was a chance—his only chance.

A hustling man needs a good front. Right now, Mitch looked like the king of the tramps.

Brushing the sweat from his eyes, he paused to stare at

a sign attached to a road-side tree: *Los Angeles—125 Miles.* He looked past the sign, into the inviting shade of the trees beyond it. The ocean would be over there somewhere, not too far from the highway. If he could wash up a little, rinse out his shirt and underwear . . .

He sighed, shook his head and walked on. It wasn't worth the trouble, he decided. It wasn't safe. The way his luck was running, he'd probably wade into a school of sharks.

In the distance, he heard another car approaching. Wearily, knowing he had to try, Mitch turned and swung his thumb.

It was a Cadillac, a big black convertible. As it began to slow down, Mitch had a feeling that no woman had ever given him such a going over and seemed to like so well what she saw as the one sitting next to the Cad's driver.

The car came on, slower and slower. It came even with him, and the woman asked, "How far to El Ciudad?"

"El Ciudad?—" the car was creeping past him; Mitch had to trot along at its side to answer the question. "You mean, the resort? About fifty miles, I think."

"I see." The woman stared at him searchingly. "Would you like a ride?" she asked.

"Would I!"

She winked at Mitch, spoke over her shoulder to the man behind the wheel. "All right, stupid. Stop. We're giving this guy a ride."

The man grunted a dispirited curse. The car stopped, then spurted forward savagely as Mitch clambered into the back seat.

"What a jerk!" The woman stared disgustedly at her companion. "Can't even give a guy a ride without trying to break his neck!"

"Dry up," the man said wearily. "Drop dead."

"So damned tight you squeak! If I'd only known what you were like before I married you!"

"Ditto. Double you in spades."

The woman took a pint of whiskey from the glove com-

partment, drank from it, and casually handed it back to
Mitch. He took a long thirsty drink, and started to pass
the bottle back. But she had turned away again, become
engrossed in nagging at her husband.

Mitch was just a little embarrassed by the quarrel, but
only a little. Mitch Allison was not a guy to be easily or
seriously embarrassed. He took another drink, then another. Gratefully, he settled down into the deeply uphol-
stered seat, listening disinterestedly to the woman's brittle voice and her husband's retorts.

"Jerk! Stingy! Selfish . . . ," she was saying.

"Aw, Babe, lay off, will you? It's our honeymoon, and I'm
taking you to one of the nicest places in the country."

"Oh, sure! Taking me there during the off-season! Because you're just too cheap and jealous to live it up a little.
Because you don't want anyone to see me!"

"Now, that isn't so, Babe. I just want to be alone with
you, that's all."

"Well, I don't want to be alone with you! One week in a
lifetime is enough for me . . ."

Mitch wondered what kind of chump he could be to take
that sort of guff from a dame. In his own case, if Bette had
ever talked that way to him—*pow!* She'd be spitting out
teeth for the next year.

The woman's voice grew louder, sharper. The slump to
her husband's shoulders became more pronounced. Incuri-
ously, Mitch tried to determine what he looked like without those outsize sunglasses and the pulled-low motoring
cap. But he didn't figure long. The guy straightened suddenly, swerved the car off into a grass grown trail, and
slammed on the brakes.

Mitch was almost thrown from the seat. The husband
leapt from the car, and went stomping off into the trees.
She called after him angrily—profanely. Without turning,
he disappeared from view.

The woman shrugged, and looked humorously at Mitch.
"Some fun, huh, mister? Guess I rode hubby a little too
hard."

"Yeah," said Mitch. "Seems that you did."

"Well, he'll be back in a few minutes. Just has to sulk a little first."

She was red-haired, beautiful in a somewhat hard-faced way. But there was nothing hard-looking about her figure. She had the kind of a shape a guy dreams about, but seldom sees.

Mitch's eyes lingered on her. She noticed his gaze.

"Like me, mister?" she said softly. "Like to stay with me?"

"Huh?" Mitch licked his lips. "Now, look, lady—"

"Like to have this car? Like to have half of fifty thousand dollars?"

Mitch always had been a fast guy on the up-take, but this babe was pitching right past him.

"Now, look," he repeated shakily. "I—I—"

"You look," she said. "Take a *good* look."

There was a brief case on the front seat. She opened it, and handed it back to Mitch. And Mitch looked. He reached inside, took out a handful of its contents.

The brief case was filled, or at least half-filled, with traveler's checks of one-hundred-dollar denominations. Filled, practically speaking, with one hundred dollar bills. They would have to be countersigned, of course, but that was—

"—a cinch," the woman said intently. "Look at the signature. No curlycues, no fancy stuff. All you have to do is sign the name, Martin Lonsdale—just sign it plain and simple—and we're in."

"But—" Mitch shook his head. "But I'm not—"

"But you could be Martin Lonsdale—you *could* be my husband. If you were dressed up, if you had his identification." Her voice faded at the look Mitch gave her, then resumed again, sulkily.

"Why not, anyway? I've got a few rights, haven't I? He promised me the world with a ring around it if I'd marry him, and now I can't get a nickel out of him. I can't even tap his wallet, because he keeps all of his dough out of my hands with tricks like this."

"Tough," said Mitch. "That's really tough, that is."

He returned the checks to the brief case, snapped the lock on it, and tossed it back into the front seat. "How could I use his identification unless he was dead? Think he'd just go to sleep somewhere until I cashed the checks and made a getaway?"

The girl flounced around in the seat. Then she shrugged and got out. "Well," she said, "as long as that's the way you feel . . ."

"We'll get hubby, right?" Mitch also got out of the car. "Sure, we will—you and me together. We'll see that he gets back safe and sound, won't we?"

She whirled angrily, and stomped off ahead of him. Grinning, Mitch followed her through the trees and underbrush. There was an enticing roll to her hips—a deliberately exaggerated roll. She drew her skirt up a little, on the pretext of quickening her stride, and her long perfectly-shaped legs gleamed alluringly in the shade-dappled sunlight. Mitch admired the display dispassionately. Admired it, without being in the least tempted by it.

She was throwing everything she had at him, and what she had was plenty. And he, Mitch Allison, would be the first guy to admit that she had it. Still, she was a bum, a hundred and ten pounds of pure poison. Mitch grimaced distastefully. He wished she would back-talk him a little, give him some reason to put the slug on her, and he knew she was too smart to do it.

They emerged from the trees, came out on the face of a cliff overlooking the ocean. The man's trail clearly led here, but he was nowhere in sight. Mitch shot an inquiring glance at the girl. She shrugged, but her face had paled. Mitch stepped cautiously to the edge of the cliff and looked down.

Far below—a good one hundred feet at least—was the ocean, roiled, oily-looking, surging thunderously with the great foam-flecked waves of the incoming tide. It was an almost straight up-and-down drop to the water. About half-way down, snagged on a bush which sprouted from the cliff-face, was a man's motoring cap.

Mitch's stomach turned sickishly. Then he jumped and whirled as a wild scream rent the air.

It was the girl. She was kneeling, sobbing hysterically, at the base of a tree. Her husband's coat was there, suspended from a broken off branch, and she was holding a slip of paper in her hands.

"I didn't mean it!" she wept. "I wouldn't have done it! I was just sore, and—"

Mitch told her curtly to shut up. He took the note from her and read it, his lips pursed with a mixture of disdain and regret.

It was too bad, certainly. Death was always regrettable, whether brought on by one's own hand or another's. Still, a guy who would end his life over a dame like this one—well, the world hadn't lost much by the action and neither had he.

Mitch wadded the note, and tossed it over the cliff. He frisked the coat, and tossed it after the note. Then, briskly, he examined the wallet and personal papers of the late Martin Lonsdale.

There was a telegram, confirming reservations at El Ciudad Hotel and Country Club. There was a registration certificate—proof of ownership—on the Cadillac. There was a driver's license, and a photostat of Martin Lonsdale's discharge from the army. Mitch examined the last two items with particular care.

Brown hair, gray eyes—yep, that was all right; that matched the description of his own eyes and hair. Weight one hundred and eighty—right on the nose again. Complexion fair—okay, also. Height six feet one inch . . .

Mitch frowned slightly. Lonsdale hadn't looked to be over five eight or nine, so—So? So nothing. Lonsdale's shoulders had been slumped; he, Mitch, had only seen the man on his feet for a few seconds. At any rate, the height

on these papers matched his own and that was all that
mattered.

The girl was still on her knees, weeping. Mitch told her
to knock it off, for God's sake, and when she persisted he
kicked her lightly in the stomach. That stopped the tears,
but it pulled the stopper on some of the dirtiest language
he had ever heard.

Mitch listened to it for a moment, then gave her a sting-
ing slap on the jaw. "You've just passed the first plateau,"
he advised her pleasantly. "From now on, you won't get
less than a handful of knuckles. Like to try for it, or will
you settle for what you have?"

"You dirty, lousy, two-bit tinhorn." She glared at him. "I
just lost my husband, and—"

"Which was just what you wanted," Mitch nodded, "so
cut out the fake sob stuff. You wanted him dead. Okay, you
got your wish, and with no help from me. So now let's see
if we can't do a little business together."

"Why the hell should I do business with you? I'm his
widow. I've got a legal claim on the car and dough."

"Uh-huh," Mitch nodded judiciously. "And maybe you
can collect, too, if you care to wait long enough—and if
there aren't any other claims against the estate. And if, of
course, you're still alive."

"Alive? What do you—?"

"I mean you might be executed. For murder, you know.
A certain tall and handsome young man might tell the
cops you pushed Martin off of that cliff."

He grinned at her. The girl's eyes blazed, then dulled in
surrender.

"All right," she mumbled. "All right. But do you have to
be so—so nasty, so cold-blooded? Can't you act like—uh—"

Mitch hesitated. He had less than no use for her, and it
was difficult to conceal the fact. Still, when you had to do
business with a person, it was best to maintain the appearance of friendliness.

"We'll get along all right, Babe." He smiled boyishly,

giving her a wink. "This El Ciudad place. Is Martin known there?"

"He was never even in California before."

"Swell. That strengthens my identification. Gives us a high-class base of operations while we're cashing the checks. There's one more thing, though"—Mitch looked down at the telegram. "This only confirms a reservation for Martin Lonsdale."

"Well? It wouldn't necessarily have to mention his wife, would it? They have plenty of room at this time of the year."

Mitch nodded. "Now, about the clothes. Maybe I'm wrong, but Marty looked quite a bit smaller than—"

"They'll fit you," the girl said firmly. "Marty bought his clothes a little large. Thought they wore longer that way, you know."

She proved to be right. Except for his shoes, the dead man's clothes fitted Mitch perfectly.

Mitch retained only his own shoes and socks, and threw his other clothes into the ocean. Redressed in clean underwear, an expensive white shirt and tie, and a conservative-looking blue serge suit, he climbed behind the wheel of his car. The girl, Babe, snuggled close to him. He backed out onto the highway, and headed for El Ciudad.

"Mmmm . . ." Babe laid her head against his shoulder. "This is nice, isn't it, honey? And it's going to be a lot nicer, isn't it, when we get to the hotel?"

She shivered deliciously. Mitch suppressed a shudder.

"We'll cash the checks," she murmured, "and split the dough. And we'll sell the car, and split on that. We'll divide everything, even-stephen, won't we, honey? . . . Well, won't we?"

"Oh, sure. Naturally," Mitch said hastily. "You just bet we will!"

And he added silently: *Like hell!*

2.

El Ciudad is just a few miles beyond the outer outskirts of Los Angeles. A truly magnificent establishment during the tourist season, it was now, in mid-summer, anything but. The great lawns were brown, tinder-dry. The long rows of palm trees were as unappetizing as banana stalks. The tennis courts were half-hidden by weeds. Emptied of water, and drifted almost full of dried leaves and rubble, the swimming pool looked like some mammoth compost pit. The only spots of brightness were the red-and-white mailbox at the head of the driveway, and a green telephone booth at the first tee of the golf course.

Briefly, the exterior of the place was a depressing mess; and inside it was even less prepossessing. The furniture was draped with dust covers. Painter's drop-cloths, lumber, and sacks of plaster were strewn about the marble floor. Scaffolds reared toward the ceiling, and ladders were propped along the walls.

There was only a skeleton staff on duty; they were as dejected-looking as the establishment itself. The manager, also doubling as clerk, was unshaven and obviously suffering from a hangover. He apologized curtly for the disarray, explaining that the workmen who were refurbishing the place had gone on strike.

"Not that it makes much difference," he added. "Of course, we regret the inconvenience to you"—he didn't appear to regret it—"but you're our only guests."

He cashed one of the hundred-dollar checks for Mitch, his fingers lingering hungrily over the money. A bellboy in a baggy uniform showed "Mr. and Mrs. Lonsdale" to their suite. It consisted of two rooms and a connecting bath. Mitch looked it over, dismissed the bellboy with a dollar tip, and dropped into a chair in front of the air-conditioning vent.

"You know," he told Babe, "I'm beginning to understand your irritation with Marty. If this is a sample of his behavior, going to a winter resort in the middle of summer—"

"A double-distilled jerk," Babe agreed. "Scared to death that someone might make a play for me."

"Mmm-hmm," Mitch frowned thoughtfully. "You're sure that was his only reason? No matter how scared he was of competition, this deal just doesn't seem to make sense."

"Well—" the girl hesitated. "Of course, he probably didn't know it would be this bad."

The kitchens and dining room of El Ciudad were not in operation, but the bellboy made and served them soggy sandwiches and muddy coffee. He also supplied them with a bottle of whiskey at double the retail price. They had a few drinks, and ate. Then, with another drink before him, Mitch sat down at the desk and began practicing the signature of Martin Lonsdale.

For the one check—the one cashed by the manager—he had done all right. There was only a hundred dollars involved, and the manager had no reason to suspect the signature. But it would be a different story tomorrow when he began hitting the banks. Then, he would be cashing the checks in wholesale lots, cashing them with people whose business it was to be suspicious. His forgeries would have to be perfect, or else.

So he practiced and continued to practice, pausing occasionally to massage his hand or to exchange a word with the girl. When, finally, he achieved perfection, he started to work on the checks. Babe stopped him, immediately wary and alarmed.

"Why are you doing that? Aren't they supposed to be countersigned where they're cashed?"

Mitch shrugged. "Not necessarily. I can write my name in front of the person who does the cashing. Just establish, you know, that my signature is the same as the one on the checks."

"Yes, but why—"

"To save time, dammit! This is a forgery job, remember? We hold all the cards, but it *is* forgery. Which means we have to hit and get—cash in and disappear. Because sooner or later, there's going to be a rumble. Now, if you're afraid I'm going to lam out with these things—"

"Oh, now, of course I'm not, honey." But she stuck right with him until he had finished countersigning the checks. She was quite prepared, in fact, to spend the rest of the night. Mitch didn't want that. He shoved the checks back into the brief case, locked it and thrust it into her hands.

"Keep it," he said. "Put it under your pillow. And now get out of here so I can get some sleep."

He began to undress. The girl looked at him, poutingly.

"But, honey. I thought we were going to—uh—"

"We're both worn out," Mitch pointed out, "and there's another night coming."

He climbed into bed and turned on his side. Babe left, reluctantly. She took the brief case with her, and she locked the connecting door on her side of the bathroom.

Mitch rolled over on his back. Wide-eyed, staring up into the darkness, he pondered the problem of giving Babe a well-deserved rooking. It was simple enough in a way— that is, the preliminary steps were simple enough. After— and *if*—he successfully cashed the checks tomorrow, he had only to catch her off guard and put her on ice for the night. Bind and gag her, and lock her up in one of the clothes closets. From that point on, however, he wasn't sure what to do. Or, rather, he knew what to do, but he didn't know how the hell he was going to do it.

He couldn't scram in the Cad. A wagon like that would leave a trail a blind man could follow. For similar reasons, he couldn't zoom away in a taxi—if, that is, it was possible to get taxi service this far from the city.

How was he going to do it, then? Equally important, where would he hide out if he was able to do it? For he would sure as hell have to hide out fast after this caper. Babe would squawk bloody murder. It wouldn't make her anything, but she'd sure squawk. Her body was soft and lush but one look at that cast-iron mug of hers, and you knew she would.

So . . . ?

Mitch scowled in the darkness. Now, Bette, his wife, had a nondescript car. She could get him away from here, and she could hide him out indefinitely. She could—but it was preposterous to think that she would. Not after that last stunt he'd pulled on her.

Yes, he'd planned on pleading for forgiveness before his meeting with Martin and Babe Lonsdale. But the situation had been different then. There wasn't any fifty grand at stake. There wasn't the risk of a long prison stretch. If he appealed to Bette, he'd have to give her the full pitch on this deal. Which meant, naturally, that he'd be completely at her mercy. And if she wasn't feeling merciful, if he couldn't fast-talk her into giving him a break, well, that would be the end of the sleigh-ride.

Enter the cops. Exit Mitch Allison and fifty grand.

I'm going to have to stop crooking everyone, Mitch thought. *From now on I'm going to be honest, with at least one person.*

He fell asleep on this pious thought. Almost immediately, it seemed, it was morning and Babe was shaking him awake.

They headed into Los Angeles, stopping at a roadside diner for breakfast. As they ate, Mitch consulted the classified telephone directory, organizing an itinerary for the day's operations. Because of the time factor, his targets— the banks—had to be in the same general area. On the other hand, they had to be separated by a discreet distance, lest he be spotted in going from one to another. Needless to say, it was also essential that he tackle only independent banks. The branch banks, with their central refer system, would nail a paper-pusher on his second try.

Babe watched Mitch work, admiration in her eyes—and increasing caution. Here was one sharp cookie, she thought. As sharp as he was tough. A lot sharper than she'd ever be. Being the kind of dame she was, she'd contemplated throwing a curve to win. Now she knew that wouldn't do it; she'd have to put the blocks to him before he could do it to her.

She was lingering in the background when he approached the teller's cage at the first bank. She was never more than a few feet away from him throughout the day, one of the most nerve-wracking in Mitch Allison's career.

He began by pushing ten of the traveler's checks, a thousand bucks, at a time. A lead-pipe cinch with his appearance and identification. Usually a teller would do it on his own, or, if not, an executive's okay was a mere formality. Unfortunately, as Mitch soon realized, these thousand-dollar strikes couldn't get the job done. He was too short on time. He'd run out of banks before he ran out of checks. So he upped the ante to two grand, and finally to three, and things really tightened up.

Tellers automatically referred him to executives. The executives passed him up the line to their superiors. He was questioned, quizzed, studied narrowly. Again and again, his credentials were examined—the description on them checked off, item by item, with his own appearance. By ten minutes of three, when he disposed of the last check, his nerves were in knots.

He and Babe drove to a nearby bar where he tossed down a few quick ones. Considerably calmer, then, he headed the car toward El Ciudad.

"Look, honey," Babe turned suddenly in the seat and faced him. "Why are we going back to that joint, anyway? We've got the dough. Why not just dump this car for a price and beat it?"

"Just go off and leave our baggage? Start a lot of inquiries?" Mitch shook his head firmly.

"Well, no, I guess that wouldn't be so good, would it? But you said we ought to disappear fast. When are we going to do it?"

Mitch slanted a glance at her, deliberating over his reply. "I can get a guy here in L.A. to shoot me a come-quick telegram. It'll give us a legitimate excuse for pulling out tomorrow morning."

Babe nodded dubiously. She suggested that Mitch

phone his friend now, instead of calling through El Ciudad's switchboard. Mitch said that he couldn't.

"The guy works late, see? He wouldn't be home yet. I'll
call him from that phone booth out on the golf course.
That'll keep anyone from listening in."

"I see," Babe repeated. "You think of everything, don't
you, darling?"

They had dinner at a highway drive-in. Around dusk,
Mitch brought the car to a stop on El Ciudad's parking lot.
Babe reached hesitantly for the brief case. Mitch told her
to go right ahead and take it with her.

"Just don't forget, sweetheart. I can see both entrances
to the joint, and I've got the keys to this buggy."

"Now, don't you worry one bit," Babe smiled at him
brightly. "I'll be right inside waiting for you."

She headed for the hotel, waving to him gayly as she
passed through the entrance. Mitch sauntered out to the
phone booth and placed a call to Bette. Rather, since she
hung up on him the first two times, he placed three calls.

At last she stayed on the wire and he was able to give
her the pitch. The result was anything but reassuring. She
said she'd be seeing him—she'd be out just as fast as she
could make it. And he could depend on it. But there was
an ominous quality to her voice, a distinctly unwifely tone.
Before he could say anything more, she slammed up the
receiver for the third and last time.

Considerably disturbed, Mitch walked back across the
dead and dying grass and entered the hotel. The manager-
clerk's eyes shied away from him. The elevator-bellboy
was similarly furtive. Absorbed in his worry over Bette,
Mitch didn't notice. He got off at his floor and started
down the hall, ducking around scaffolding, wending his
way through a littered jungle of paint cans, plaster and
wallpaper.

He came to the door of his room. He turned the knob,
and entered.

And something crashed down on his head.

3.

It was dark when Mitch regained consciousness. He sat up, massaging his aching head, staring dizzily at the shattered glass on the floor—the remains of a broken whiskey bottle. Then he remembered; realization came to him. Ripping out a curse, he ran to the window.

The Cad was still there on the parking lot. Yes, and the keys were still in his pocket. Mitch whirled, ran through the bath, and kicked open the door to the other room.

It was empty, in immaculate order, sans Babe and sans baggage. There was nothing to indicate that it ever had been tenanted. Mitch tottered back into his own room, and there was a knock on the door and he flung it open.

A man walked in, and closed it behind him. He looked at Mitch. He looked down at the broken bottle. He shook his head in mild disapproval.

"So you are supposedly a sick man, Marty," he said gutturally. "So you have a great deal of money—my money. So drunk you should not get."

"H-huh? W-what?" Mitch said. "Who the hell are you?"

"So I am The Pig," the man said. "Who else?"

The name suited him. Place a pecan on top of a hen's egg and you've got a good idea of his appearance. He was perhaps five feet tall and he probably weighed three hundred pounds. His arms were short almost to the point of deformity. He had a size six head, and a size sixty waistline.

Mitch stared at him blankly, silently. The Pig apparently misunderstood his attitude.

"So you are not sure of me," he said. "So I will take it from the top, and give you proof. So you are The Man's good and faithful servant through all his difficulties. So The Man passes the word that you are to pay me fifty thousand dollars for services rendered. So you are a very sick man anyway, and have little to lose if detected while on the errand—"

"Wait a minute!" Mitch said. "I—I'm not—"

"So you are to transport the money in small traveler's

checks. So you cannot be robbed. So they can be easily cashed without attracting unwanted attention. So you have had a day to cash them. So"—the Pig concluded firmly—"you will give me the fifty thousand."

Mitch's mouth was very dry. Slowly, the various pieces of a puzzle were beginning to add up. And what they added up to was curtains—for him. He'd really stepped into something this time: a Grade-A jam, an honest-to-Hannah, double-distilled frammis. The Pig's next words were proof of the fact.

"So you know how I earned the fifty G's, Marty. So you would not like me to give you a demonstration. It is better to die a natural death."

"N-now—now, listen!" Mitch stammered. "You've got the wrong guy. I'm not Martin Lonsdale. I'm—I'm . . . Look, I'll show you." He started to reach for his wallet. And groaned silently, remembering: He had thrown it away. There was a risk of being caught with two sets of identification, so—

"So?" The Pig said.

"I—Look! Call this Man, whoever he is. Let me talk to him. He can tell you I'm not—"

"So," The Pig grunted, "who can call Alcatraz? So—" he added, "I will have the money, Marty."

"I don't have it! My wife—I mean the dame I registered in with—has it. She had the room next to mine, and—"

"So, but no. So I checked the registry myself. So there has been no woman with you."

"I tell you there was! These people here—they're hungry as hell, see, and she had plenty of dough to bribe them . . ." He broke off, realizing how true his words were. He resumed again, desperately: "Let me give you the whole pitch, tell you just what happened right from the beginning! I was trying to thumb a ride, see and this big Cadillac stopped for me. And . . ."

Mitch told him the tale.

The Pig was completely unimpressed.

"So that is a fifty-grand story? So a better one I could buy for a nickel."

"But it's true! Would I make up a yarn like that? Would I come here, knowing that you'd show up to collect?"

"So people do stupid things." The Pig shrugged. "So, also, I am a day early."

"But, dammit!—" There was a discreet rap on the door. Then, it opened and Bette came in.

This Bette was a honey, a little skimpy in the chin department, perhaps, but she had plenty everywhere else. A burlesque house stripteaser, her mannerisms and dress sometimes caused her to be mistaken for a member of a far older profession.

Mitch greeted her with almost hysterical gladness. "Tell this guy, honey! For God's sake, tell him who I am!"

"Tell him . . . ?" Bette hesitated, her eyes flickering. "Why, you're Martin Lonsdale, I guess. If this is your room. Didn't you send for me to—"

"*N-nno!*" Mitch burbled. "Don't do this to me, honey! Tell him who I really am. Please!—"

One of The Pig's fat arms moved casually. The fist at the end of it smashed into Mitch's face. It was like being slugged with a brick. Mitch stumbled and fell flat across the bed. Dully, as from a distance, he heard a murmur of conversation . . .

". . . had a date with him, a hundred-dollar date. And I came all the way out here from Los Angeles . . ."

"So Marty has another date. So I will pay the hundred dollars myself . . ."

There was a crisp rustle, then a dulcet, "Oh, aren't you nice!" Then, the door opened and closed, and Bette was gone. And The Pig slowly approached the bed. He had a hand in his pocket. There was a much bigger bulge in the pocket than a hand should make.

Mitch feigned unconsciousness until The Pig's hand started coming out of his pocket. Then Mitch's legs whipped up in a blur of motion. He went over backwards in a full somersault, landed on the other side of the bed, gripped and jerked it upward.

Speed simply wasn't The Pig's forte. He just wasn't built for it. He tried to get out of the way, and succeeded only in tripping over his own feet. The bed came down on him, pinning him to the floor. Mitch sent him to sleep with a vicious kick in the head.

Mitch realized he had been moving in a blur. But now his mind was crystal clear, sharper than it ever had been.

Where was Babe? Simple. Since she couldn't have ridden away from the place, she must have walked. And Mitch was positive he knew where she had walked to.

What to do with The Pig? Also simple. The materials for taking care of him were readily at hand.

Mitch turned on the water in the bathtub. He went out into the hall and returned with two sacks full of quick-drying plaster . . .

He left The Pig very well taken care of, sitting in plaster up to his chin. Then, guessing that it would be faster, he ran down the stairs and out to the Cadillac. Wheels spinning, he whipped it down the horseshoe driveway and out onto the highway.

He slowed down after a mile or two, peering off to his right at the weed-grown fields which lay opposite the ocean. Suddenly, he jerked the car onto the shoulder and braked it to a stop. He got out; his eyes narrowed with grim satisfaction.

He was approximately parallel now with the place where he had assumed the identity of Martin Lonsdale. The place where Martin Lonsdale had supposedly committed suicide. And out there in this fallow field was an abandoned produce shed.

From the highway, it appeared to be utterly dark, deserted. But as Mitch leaped the ditch and approached it, he caught a faint flicker of light. He came up on the building silently. He peered through a crack in the sagging door.

There was a small stack of groceries in one corner of the

room, also a large desert-type water bag. Blankets were
spread out in another corner. Well back from the door, a
can of beans was warming over a Sterno stove. A man
stood over it, looking impatiently down at the food.

Mitch knew who he was, even without the sunglasses
and cap. He also knew who he was *not*—for this man was
bald and well under six feet tall.

Mitch kicked open the door and went in. The guy let out
a startled "Gah!" as he flung himself forward, swinging.

He shouldn't have done it, of course. Mitch was sore
enough at him, as it was. A full uppercut, and the guy
soared toward the roof. He came down, horizontal, landing
amidst the groceries.

Mitch snatched him to his feet, and slapped him back
into consciousness. "All right. Let's have the story. All of it
and straight, get me? And don't ask me what story or
I'll—"

"I w-won't—I mean, I'll tell you!" the man babbled frantically.

"We—tied into Lonsdale at a motor-court. Figured he
was carrying heavy, so Babe pulled the tears for a ride. We
was just going to hold him up, you know. Honest to Gawd,
that's all! But—but—"

"But he put up a fight and you had to bump him."

"*Naw!* No!" the man protested. "He dropped dead on us!
I swear he did! I'd just pulled a knife on him—hadn't
touched him at all—when he keeled over! Went out like a
light. I guess maybe he must have had a bad ticker or
something, but anyway . . ."

Mitch nodded judiciously. The Pig had indicated that
Lonsdale was in bad health. "So okay. Keep singing."

"W-well, he didn't have hardly any dough in cash like
we thought he would. Just that mess of checks. But we'd
pumped him for a lot of info, and we figured if we could
find the right kind of chump—excuse me, Mister—I mean,
a guy that could pass for Lonsdale—"

"So you did a little riding up and down the highway

until you found him. And you just damned near got him
killed!"

He gave the guy an irritated shake. The man whim-
pered apologetically. "We didn't mean to, Mister. We really
figured we was doing you a favor. Giving you a chance to
make a piece of change."

"I'll bet. But skip it. Where's Babe?"

"At the hotel."

"Nuts!" Mitch slapped him. "You were going to hole up
here until the heat was off! Now, where the hell is she?"

The man began to babble again. Babe hadn't known how
soon she could scram. There'd been no set time for joining
him here. She had to be at the hotel. If she wasn't, he
didn't know where she was.

"Maybe run out on me," he added bitterly. "Never could
trust her around the corner. I don't see how she could get
away, but—"

Mitch jerked a fist swiftly upward.

When the guy came to, he was naked and the room had
been stripped of its food, water and other supplies. His
clothes and everything else were bundled into one of the
blankets, which Mitch was just lugging out the door.

"Wait!" The man looked at him, fearfully. "What are you
going to do?"

"The question," said Mitch, "is what are *you* going to
do."

He departed. A mile or so back up the road, he threw the
stuff into the ditch. He arrived at the hotel, parked, and
indulged in some very deep thinking.

Babe had to be inside the joint. This money-hungry out-
fit was hiding her for a price. But exactly where she might
be—in which of its numerous rooms, the countless nooks
and crannies, cellars and sub-cellars that a place like this
had—there was no way of telling. Or finding out. The employees would know nothing. They'd simply hide themselves if they saw him coming. And naturally he couldn't
search the place from top to bottom. It would take too long.
Delivery men—possibly other guests—would be showing

up. And then there was The Pig to contend with. Someone must have driven him out here, and he would not have planned to stay later than morning. So someone would be calling for him, and—

Well, never mind. He had to find Babe. He had to do it fast. And since he had no way of learning her hiding place, there was only one thing to do. Force her out of it.

Leaving the hotel, Mitch walked around to the rear and located a rubbish pile. With no great difficulty, he found a five-gallon lard can and a quantity of rags. He returned to the parking lot. He shoved the can under the car's gas tank, and opened the petcock. While it was filling, he knotted the rags into a rope. Then, having shut off the flow of gasoline, he went to the telephone booth and called the hotel's switchboard.

The clerk-manager answered. He advised Mitch to beat it before he called the cops. "I know you're not Lonsdale, understand? I know you're a crook. And if you're not gone from the premises in five minutes—"

"Look who's talking!" Mitch jeered. "Go ahead and call the cops! I'd like to see you do it, you liver-lipped, yellow-bellied—"

The manager hung up on him. Mitch called him back.

"Now, get this," he said harshly. "You said I was a crook. All right, I am one and I'm dangerous. I'm a crib man, an explosives expert. I've got plenty of stuff to work with. So send that dame out here and do it fast, or I'll blow your damned shack apart!"

"Really? My, my!" The man laughed sneeringly, but somewhat shakily. "Just think of that!"

"I'm telling you," Mitch said. "And this is the last time I'll tell you. Get that dame out of the woodwork, or there won't be any left."

"You wouldn't dare! If you think you can bluff—"

"In exactly five minutes," Mitch cut in, "the first charge will be set off, outside. If the dame doesn't come out, your building goes up."

He replaced the receiver, went back to the car. He

picked up the rags and gasoline, moved down the walk to the red-and-white mailbox. It stood in the deep shadows of the *port-cochere* and he was not observed. Also, the hotel employees apparently were keeping far back from the entrance.

Mitch soaked the rag rope in the gasoline and tucked a length of it down inside the mail box. Then he lifted the can and trickled its entire contents through the letter slot. It practically filled the box to the brim. The fluid oozed through its seams, and dripped down upon the ground.

Mitch carefully scrubbed his hands with his handkerchief. Then, he ignited a book of matches, dropped them on the end of the rope. And ran.

His flight was unnecessary, as it turned out. Virtually unnecessary. For the "bomb" was an almost embarrassing failure. There was a weak rumble, a kind of growl—a hungry man's stomach, Mitch thought bitterly, would make a louder one. A few blasts of smoke, and the box jiggled a bit on its moorings. But that was the size of it. That was the "explosion." It wouldn't have startled a nervous baby. As for scaring those rats inside the joint, hell, they were probably laughing themselves sick.

Oh, sure, the box burned; it practically melted. And that would give them some trouble. But that didn't help him Mitch Allison any.

From far down the lawn, he looked dejectedly at the dying flames, wondering what to do now; he gasped, his eyes widening suddenly as two women burst through the entrance of El Ciudad.

One—the one in front—was Babe, barelegged, barefooted; dressed only in her bra and panties. She screamed as she ran, slapping and clawing wildly at her posterior. And it was easy to see why. For the woman chasing her was Bette, and Bette was clutching a blazing blow-torch.

She was holding it in front of her, its long blue flame aimed straight at the brassy blonde's flanks. Babe increased her speed. But Bette stayed right with her.

They came racing down the lawn toward him. Then,

Bette tripped and stumbled, the torch flying from her hands. And at practically the same instant, Babe collided head-on with the steel flagpole. The impact knocked her senseless. Leaving her to listen to the birdies. Mitch sat down by Bette and drew her onto his lap. Bette threw her arms around him, hugging him frantically.

"You're all right, honey? I was so worried about you! You didn't really think I meant the way I acted, did you?"

"I wouldn't have blamed you if you had," Mitch said.

"Well, I didn't. Of course, I was awfully mad at you, but you *are* my husband. I feel like murdering you myself lots of times, but I'm certainly not going to let anyone else do it!"

"That's my girl." Mitch kissed her fondly. "But—"

"I thought it was the best thing to do, honey. Just play dumb, and then go get some help. Well—"

"Just a minute," Mitch interrupted. "Where's your car?"

"Over by the ocean." Bette pointed, continued. "Like I was saying, I found *her* listening out in the hall. I mean, she ducked away real fast, but I knew she had been listening. So I figured you'd probably be all right for a little while, and I'd better see about her."

"Right," Mitch nodded. "You did exactly right, honey."

"Well, she had a room just a few doors away, Mitch. I guess they had to move her nearby because they didn't have much time. Anyway, she went in and I went right in with her . . ."

She had asked Babe the score. Babe had told her to go jump, and Bette had gone to work on her, ripping off her clothes in the process. Babe had spilled, after a time. Bette had learned, consequently, that there would be no help for Mitch unless she provided it.

"So I locked her in, and went back to your room. But you were gone, and I guessed you must be all right from the looks of things. That guy in the bathtub, I mean." Bette burst into giggles, remembering. "He looked so funny, Mitch! How in the world do you ever think of those stunts?"

"Just comes natural, I guess," Mitch murmured modestly. "Go on, precious."

"Well, I went back to her room, and the clerk called and said you were threatening to blow up the place. But she wouldn't go for it. She said she was going to stay right there, no matter what, and anyway you were just bluffing. Well, I was pretty sure you were, too, but I knew you wanted to get her outside. So I went out in the hall again, and dug up that big cigar lighter—"

Mitch chuckled, and kissed her again. "You did fine, baby. I'm really proud of you. You gave her a good frisk, I suppose? Searched her baggage?"

Bette nodded, biting her lip. "Yes, Mitch. She doesn't have the money."

"Don't look so down about it—" he gave her a little pat. "I didn't figure she'd keep it with her. She's ditched it outside somewhere."

"But, Mitch, you don't understand. I talked to her, and—"

"I know. She's a very stubborn girl." Mitch got to his feet. "But I'll fix that."

"But, Mitch—she told me where she put the money. When I was chasing her with the torch."

"Told you! Why didn't you say so? Where is it, for Pete's sake?"

"It isn't," Bette said miserably. "But it was." She pointed toward the hotel. "It was up there."

"Huh? What are you talking about?"

"She . . . she mailed it to herself."

4.

Sick with self-disgust, Mitch climbed behind the wheel of Bette's car and turned it onto the highway. Bette studied his dark face. She patted him comfortingly on the knee.

"Now, don't take it so hard, honey. It wasn't your fault."

"Whose was it, then? How a guy can be so stupid and

live so long! Fifty grand, and I do myself out of it! I do it to myself, that's what kills me!"

"But you can't expect to be perfect, Mitch. No one can be smart all the time."

"Nuts!" Mitch grunted bitterly. "When was I ever smart?"

Bette declared stoutly that he had been smart lots of times. Lots and lots of times. "You know you have, honey! Just look at all the capers you've pulled! Just think of all the people who are trying to find you! I guess they wouldn't be, would they, if you hadn't outsmarted them."

"Well . . ." Mitch's shoulders straightened a little.

Bette increased her praise.

"Why, I'll bet you're the best hustler that ever was! I'll bet you could steal the socks off a guy with sore feet, without taking off his shoes!"

"You—uh—you really mean that, honey?"

"I most certainly do!" Bette nodded vigorously. "They just don't make 'em any sneakier than my Mitch. Why—why, I'll bet you're the biggest heel in the world!"

Mitch sighed on a note of contentment. Bette snuggled close to him. They rode on through the night, moving, inappropriately enough, toward the City of Angels.

PASSING FOR LOVE

by Bill Crenshaw

☐ "READ IT," SHE SNAPPED.

Scott looked at the letter drooping in his hand. It started the way they all had started. " 'Dear Lovebirds,' " he began.

Lucinda cut him off in a voice angry, weary. "How much? Another ten thousand each?"

Scott read on to himself a second before looking up slowly. He cleared his throat. "Fifty thousand. Midnight Friday."

She went white. "They're crazy. Four days. I can't . . ." Her fist went to her mouth. "My God, Scott, what will I do?"

Scott laid the letter on the back of the couch and wiped his hands on his pants. "Marry me," he said.

She turned away and crossed the room to the window, her shoulders hunched, head bowed as she stared down at the traffic below, at the long fall between her and the street. The window leapt from floor to ceiling, and she stood framed, the sun splitting and dancing on auburn hair sweeping down past her shoulders, falling by her face like curtains.

"Lucie," he began, but her right hand came up. It hung in the air above her shoulder, then drifted back to her mouth. He waited. She stood motionless, glowing in the afternoon light, her shadow stretching behind her nearly to his feet. She would stand like that for a long time. He tensed and relaxed and tensed his calves. He tried to watch her shadow move with the sun. Finally she shuddered and sighed and pulled a thick cascade of hair behind her ear.

"Divorce him," said Scott, "Marry me."

She did not move.

"I know we've been through this before," he said. "But isn't it the answer?" He snatched up the letter and held it out to her back. "Isn't it the only thing that will stop this?"

She said nothing.

He waited. She would stand a while longer, frozen, stone. Then her shoulders would start to quiver as she tried to squeeze the tears back in, and then he could cross the room and put his hands on those shoulders and turn her into him, and she would bury her face in his shirt and clutch at him and sob. "Oh, Scott," she'd sob, "I can't, I just can't." Then she'd take his face in her hands, slide her fingers into his hair, he'd feel the tapered nails along his scalp, then she would pull his lips to hers, crushing, insistent, always surprisingly urgent. "Love me, Scott," she'd say. "Just love me." Then they would go to the bedroom and make desperate love. It was the game they played. He waited.

She turned slowly, fist still at lips. She raised her face, back-lit, her hair burning around her, looking young. "All right," she said evenly. "I'll marry you."

Scott felt his insides freeze solid. What had he done?

"You went too far," Connie snapped, pacing, hands slicing the air. Her voice was a blade. "You pushed her too hard."

"*We* pushed her too hard," Scott said. Even to himself, it sounded like a whine. "You're the one who said go for fifty."

Connie stopped pacing and squared off, finger pointing like a pistol at his heart. "You're the one *there*. You're the one who's supposed to be in control. That was the whole point."

"The point," said Scott, bristling, "was to make sure she didn't call the police and that she did pay up and that we knew what she was going to do."

"Well, it worked. We know what she's going to do. She's going to marry us."

He felt blood rushing to his face. He hated that, and he hated the way she could get to him. "What was I supposed to say? 'You'll raise the cash somehow? Don't worry, darling, we'll see this through together?' "

Connie gave exaggerated, sarcastic nods, eyes wide. "Better. That's better than your little macho 'Marry me.' But you just love it. You love working her up and melting her down, love making love to a woman the age of your mother."

Scott stood up. "My mother—"

"Oh, shut up, Scott." She turned away, pacing again. "You had something to prove. It's months down the drain."

Sometimes he just wanted to hit her. Easy for her to criticize, she wasn't the one out front. But when they argued, and she had all the right words and all the right answers and there was nothing he could say, all he wanted to do was to hit her and make her listen to him for once, make her just shut up. He clenched his fists and slowed his breathing as she stormed back and forth in her sky-blue teddy, bitching, thigh muscles tightening as she moved about with casual, unthinking grace, strength taut beneath the dewy skin, but maybe right, goddammit, maybe she was right, because he *did* like it when Lucinda rose hot at his command, when his touch traced fire across her skin, when he molded her under his fingertips.

Maybe he'd really screwed things up. Lucinda wasn't like the others. The others were bored and rich and horny and didn't mind being scammed for a few thousand, thought the sex was worth it. But this one, this one was the right combination of money, desire, and fear, had gotten hooked, addicted to the attention, the sex, to the love, finally, or what passed for love, what she thought was love. And then Connie had gotten the idea for blackmail.

Scott had shaken his head. He wanted to stick with scams. With a scam, you had a mark too embarrassed or ashamed or afraid to bring in the cops when they got burned, and with a scam you could always walk away if it wasn't working out, and who'd ever know. But blackmail drew cops like flies and could go wrong in too many places. "Too dangerous," he'd said.

"Not if you're blackmailing yourself," Connie had answered. "Not if you're *both* victims. You'll both be threatened. You'll follow the instructions to the letter. You'll raise the cash and make the payoff and console each other all night."

"No," Scott had said, but he had given in as he always did, because Connie was clever and Connie, well, Connie . . .

So a letter arrived at Lucinda's condo, addressed to Lucinda, but demanding ten thousand dollars each from both her and her loverboy. *Dear Lovebirds,* it began. *Enclosed please find several photographs . . .*

And Lucinda had paid, had hocked jewels she hadn't worn in years or sold what little stock she claimed she had listed in her name alone. And Scott and Connie had paid too, scraping up almost six thousand on their own, borrowing the rest from a shark named Bennie who knew them and gave them a deal, ten percent per week, one week minimum. And Scott had sat at Lucinda's kitchen table and wrapped his ten grand and Lucinda's ten grand in newspaper exactly as instructed and bagged it exactly as instructed and made the drop exactly as instructed, and he and Connie had cleared nearly nine thousand after expenses, including Bennie, and not including all Scott's clothes and cigarette lighters and gold neck chains and such, presents from Lucinda, with love.

And they'd done it again, and again, three letters so far, and each one had worked fine, just as Connie planned.

But now . . .

Maybe Connie was right. Maybe he'd been stupid. Maybe he had gotten carried away with Lucinda, this woman whose face was in the newspaper with other wives of the important, who attended all the right functions with all the powerful people on the arm of her most right and powerful husband—this woman went limp over him, over *him,* for Christ's sake. When she drove herself at him, when she needed him so clearly, like a junkie needed a fix, his limbs felt hot and light with power. Good for the ego. Bad for business.

And now business was blown. So as Connie said, now what?

"We pull out," he offered. "We take what we've got and head for Miami."

Connie slowed her pacing, stopped, hand on hip, hand rubbing forehead.

"What else can we do?" he persisted. "We got, what, twenty-five, thirty grand? Let's get out of here."

"Maybe we can salvage this." She wasn't talking to him. She wasn't even thinking about him.

"We've got enough," he said, which was not what he wanted to say. He didn't know what he wanted to say exactly. He could say anything to Lucinda, he made beautiful speeches to Lucinda, but this was Connie, and he couldn't string together things he didn't mean and couldn't say what he did mean, and even when he wanted to hit Connie, it was so that she'd respect him more, or love him more, or something. Things would be different, maybe, if they got married. He wasn't sure exactly, but he thought that in Miami maybe he'd even ask her to marry him. She'd like that, he thought. They could go to Miami now, drop Lucinda and fly. "Bird in the hand, Connie. Let's take what we've got."

She was silent. She was mad. He'd really messed up this time, really made her mad. He hated it when she got mad at him.

He sank back onto the couch. "I'm sorry, Con," he said. She stared at him and finally she smiled, and she crossed to him and sat in his lap.

"Not your fault," she said, stroking his hair. "One of those things."

"Yeah, well," he said, "what now?"

Connie was silent again, staring off into middle distances.

She was beautiful, the smell, the warmth of her was beautiful. Scott felt himself shifting, making the transition from Lucinda to Connie. He was in a room with Connie now, his Connie, and with her he didn't care about Lucinda or any more of Lucinda's money or Lucinda's driving, electric sexuality. He was with Connie.

"Connie?"

She sat up, gave him a small pat as she refocused her attention. "How does she feel about it all?"

Scott shrugged. "She keeps saying she's happy, like a weight's gone, she says. Her fingers keep trembling."

"Has she told her husband?"

"Not when I left."

Connie shook her head. "Didn't think she had the guts to tell him. Maybe she still doesn't. Okay," she said softly, "okay. She's excited. The blushing bride. She's nervous. We can keep her nervous. Keep her from telling her husband."

"She was excited. She's probably already told him."

"I don't think so."

"You haven't seen her."

Connie chewed her lower lip. "So we go ahead on the big score. We call her bluff."

"What if she's told him?" he said.

"Then we've got no hold." She tousled his hair. He could see that she didn't think for one second that Lucinda would tell her husband.

He raised his face to her. She smiled again, and kissed him.

Connie decided to let Lucinda go it alone for a couple of days. "It's one thing," she said, sitting in bed, sheet-covered, knees to chin, arms crossed around legs in the faded light of the full moon, "it's one thing to say yes in the heat of the night. Let's give her a couple of cold mornings."

"But if she's told . . ."

Connie gave him a patient smile. "And you have to make sure," she said, "that you don't encourage her to tell him. Not yet. You need to go iffy on the marriage. Give her a reason to back out gracefully herself."

"What should I say?"

Connie shrugged and smiled, a gesture consciously showing faith—her way, he supposed, of apologizing. "You'll know what to say," she said.

Standing in front of the mirror on Friday afternoon, he wasn't sure. He hadn't seen Lucinda since she'd said yes on Monday, and on the phone today she'd been in one of her moods, panting and insistent, nervous and hungry. She didn't care what he had to tell his wife. He had to come tonight. He'd been away too long, and just when she really needed him. And anyway, she had a surprise. Lucinda's voice was strange to him after four days with Connie. He remembered her breasts in his hands.

He leaned toward the mirror and inspected minutely the lines at the corners of his eyes, the faint blue shadow of freshly shaved cheeks and chin. He leaned back for a broader view, then unknotted the tie Lucinda had given him and tried again. Lucinda liked him neat, precise, elegant. Decorative, Connie had said. An adornment. Something she wears on her arm.

The idea buzzed around him like a swarm of gnats. It was more than that. How could Connie know what he meant to Lucinda? She hadn't seen them together. Which was good, he thought suddenly, which was good, because if she had seen them together, then, well, then what hope would he have with Connie?

Maybe a lot, he thought. Maybe if she *could* see them together, could see Lucinda latch onto him like a vampire, gather him to her as if he held life itself, maybe Connie would have to look at him with new respect, jealous, seeing what she had in front of her for the first time. Maybe Connie needed some competition.

No. Whatever she needed, it wasn't competition. He didn't know what she needed.

He checked the tie and unknotted it again.

He found himself hoping that Lucinda *had* already told her husband, no matter how afraid of him she was. And the mood she was in, she might have, please God, might have decided to make a clean breast of it, she'd say, get it out in the open where it belonged. Her little surprise. It'd be just like her to spring it over one of her sweet dessert wines or a was-it-good-for-you-too cigarette. "Isn't that wonderful, Scott darling," she'd say. "We're free, now. Really free."

But what would he say to her then? That he hadn't been able to tell his wife yet? He had tried, he'd say, but it wasn't easy like he thought it would be? It wasn't like he hated her?

Yes, that was good. He practiced it in front of the mirror. "It's not like I hate her," he said to his reflection. "It's that I love you more, in ways I didn't know I could love. But it's so hard to tell them, isn't it? They'll think they've failed, but they haven't." Yes, that was very good. Then he could leave, he could say that he was going home to tell his wife right then, that minute, and then he could kiss Lucinda goodbye, and then he and Connie would just keep going. He'd have been right, and Connie would have been wrong, and she'd say, "Now what," and he'd say Miami. Maybe Connie needed to be wrong.

He made a final adjustment to the tie and stared into his reflected face.

Unless Connie decided something else. Unless she decided that planning a marriage would be an even better scam, that as the future Mr. Lucinda he wouldn't need to blackmail, he could just reach out and take, and they could keep taking right to the altar. He could milk her up to the wedding and then just not show.

Then Miami.

Maybe.

Because Connie might even decide that marriage itself was the best scam of all. Everything Lucinda had would be his, and he could share it all with Connie, and everything could chug along pretty much like it was now, except without the danger that always hovered around any scam. Married, there'd be no scam.

Scott was suddenly tired.

Connie was right after all. Lucinda hadn't told her husband. Instead, Lucinda's surprise was a deadline party, a celebration of freedom and burned bridges, a ritual to mark, she said, her new courage.

"You've got to tell him," Scott heard himself saying, surprised that he was saying it. What would Connie say if she could hear him say that? But Lucinda was all around him and Connie seemed so distant at the moment. His head swam.

"I will," said Lucinda. "After tonight, I'll have courage." She put her hand on his chest. "My new heart," she said. "Courage means heart in French, having heart. You give me heart. You are my heart." She kissed him gently then, tenderly, without passion but with great feeling. It startled him, frightened him. He pulled away. Her grip tightened. "Don't, Scott," she said.

"You've got to tell him," he said, his voice again sounding far away, as if from someone else. "I've told her. You've got to tell him."

He felt her fingernails digging into his arms.

"Help me tonight, just tonight. Help me past the deadline. I'm not good at defiance, Scott. I need you."

She was trembling. He folded her to him, her head on his chest, and he stared beyond her into the lights of the night and the city and smiled. It wasn't a party to celebrate the deadline, he realized; it was to get her past it. She was afraid of the blackmailer out there in the dark even while she held him in her arms.

He stroked her hair. "I'm here," he said. "We'll see this through together. They can't hurt us now."

She turned her face toward him and managed a smile. "At midnight," she said, "we'll be making love, and fuck them." From her the word sounded ugly. And she started unbuttoning his shirt.

But as midnight neared she lay brittle and knotted. She asked Scott for a cigarette. He lit two, like in the movies, and passed one to her. She held it between her fingers and ignored it.

Scott's watch gave two tiny beeps. The clock in the next room chimed twelve times. Her body stiffened.

He rolled onto his elbow, stroked her hair. "Will you relax?"

She twisted away and sat up, pulling the sheet to her neck and her knees to her chest. She jammed the cigarette to her lips and took a hard drag, illuminating nostrils and cheekbones in the brief orange flare. The long ash curled and fell on the sheet. "What will they do?"

"Nothing," he said. She looked at him as if he were crazy. "*Nothing.* We're not going to play any more. Game's over."

"Don't patronize me," she snapped. The cigarette shook, leaking zigzag columns of smoke. "What will they do?"

"What *can* they do?"

She stared blankly at the foot of the bed. "Will they hurt us?" The question sounded wrenched out of her, as if the act of naming were an act of invoking.

"That's the last thing they want," Scott said.

She was silent, staring beyond the room now, face locked in fear. Scott felt the deep electric jolt of power. She was still afraid. Better. She was scared to death.

"Look," he said, soothing, calming. "Why should they hurt us? Blackmail only works if everybody plays. If we quit paying, they'll go somewhere else. They won't take chances. They won't hurt us."

She said nothing. She was a statue again, like at the window, as she was when she went deep somewhere to hide or to think. She sat, eyes fixed. Scott wanted to pinch her, slap her, just to see if he could get a reaction, or to reach for her and watch his touch transform the marble into warm and eager flesh again. The cigarette slipped from her fingers and rolled down the sheet and under the spread at her feet.

"Jesus," Scott shouted, flinging back the spread and smacking at the cigarette with his bare hand. "Jesus, Lucinda, what the hell?" The orange coal exploded under his pounding and the sparks blasted away, fiery gnats that landed all over the sheets. "Jesus," he said over and over again, beating at the tiny orange sparks eating holes in the fabric. He smelled satin burning.

"I can't believe she told him," Connie said. She sat on the couch. Scott stood holding out a can of beer to her. He waited. Connie looked up finally, realized he'd been standing there. "Sorry," she said. "Thanks."

Scott crossed the room and stood as if in thought. It was working better than he had hoped, better than he imagined, not that he had really planned this out, he admitted, he couldn't claim that. It was just that he'd been tired when he stumbled back to the apartment after a long night with Lucinda, and Connie had been so cocky, so sure of herself, her scenarios all laid out. He hadn't planned to lie, but it sure changed the weather when he said that Lucinda had told her husband and that her husband hadn't objected to a quiet divorce. Connie, for the first time, was at a loss.

"I just can't believe it," she said again. "She'd *never* tell him."

Scott shrugged. "I tried to tell you she was serious. I mean, we hooked her good, Con. She's in love deep."

"I mean this wasn't just I-don't-want-a-scandal. She was afraid to tell him, *scared* to tell him." She took a swallow of beer. She shook her head. "Now what?"

He smiled.

But she didn't give him a chance to answer, making

plans already. "Miami, I guess," she said. "Sure wish I'd known this yesterday. Could've saved us another month's rent on this dump. I guess we need to . . ."

"Let's don't quit just yet," said Scott.

Connie gave him her tolerant smile. "Hon, it's over. She's not going to pay another dime."

"Well, just let me . . ."

"Thought you wanted to go to Miami."

"Just let me try something out here, all right? Is that okay?"

"There's nothing to try."

"There's more to be had."

"Anything you get now'll be chump change. 'Here, dar-lin', go buy yourself a suit, a new car, another . . .' "

She mimicked what she thought was Lucinda. It made Scott mad.

"Is a hundred grand chump change?" he snapped. That shut her up. "I think we still have a shot at a big score here, if you'll just give it a chance."

She pulled at her beer again, watching him over the top of the can.

"Okay," she said. "I'm listening."

Scott stood at Lucinda's window, the traffic stories beneath him. He imagined holding a brick over the street. How much damage would it do, he wondered, just from opening his fingers.

Far below a cab pulled to the curb. He wasn't surprised that he recognized Lucinda getting out, even from this height. All part of feeling in control.

He turned back to the room, waiting. She'd be glad to see him, of course. It had been two days, so she'd be more than glad. She'd be hungry. And for the last two days, Connie had been . . . well, more like Lucinda, more like she needed him, too. But still his Connie.

If he had a choice, he wondered, who would he pick? Just as Lucinda's key hit the lock, he realized he did have a choice. Both were his for the plucking. He had only to reach out and take.

He didn't need to paste on the smile for Lucinda. It was already there.

Lucinda swept into the room, kissed him violently, the plastic bag on her arm banging his ribs, as she spun away and swirled toward the kitchen. "I've got a surpri-ise," she sang.

"What?" he called.

"You just sit down," she called back. "I'll be out in a jif."

He heard the cork pop. Champagne. That's what had hit his ribs. Launching their freedom, maybe. "Champagne," he called.

"Oh, you," she said in mock exasperation. "And caviar. And news."

"What news?" he called, but she was there handing him the long-stemmed glass.

She clinked hers to his. "To us," she said, raising her glass.

"To us," he echoed, and drank. "What news?"

She turned and snuggled her back into his chest and wrapped his arms around her waist. "I can keep you."

He laughed and leaned to her ear. She tucked her head and laughed and lifted her face and kissed him. "I talked to my husband," she said, "and he didn't kill me. He said I could not have a divorce, but that I could keep you."

Late that night, sitting in bed next to Lucinda's sleeping shape, drinking bourbon neat and lighting one cigarette from another, Scott tried to think of the word floating just out of reach in his mind.

What the hell did it mean, I can keep you. Kept man . . . access to bank accounts maybe . . . living in style . . . but it also meant a stud farm role, it meant losing Connie, or worse, it meant that Connie would see the chance to extend the scam so that he drained Lucinda slowly. He'd be kept by both.

He watched the smoke rise in a solid column and disintegrate into chaos and cloud.

Or, he thought, Lucinda was lying. Which was worse. Or better. Better, because she was afraid to tell her husband after all. Worse because now she was running a scam, and he couldn't exactly call the old hubby up and ask if she'd told him about her hot affair.

He stared at the curve of her hip, remembering her lips fastening on him, and the word floated into view, as if forming out of the smoke. Succubus.

He decided on Connie. Things were better there, now, and they could run the last scam on Lucinda and collect the hundred grand and go go go. If he stayed with Lucinda, she'd smother him.

"I can't believe you mean this," said Connie.

"If it's going to work," said Scott, "she's got to believe the threat is real."

"We can slash her tires or something."

"Fine, that too."

She picked at her blouse. "I just don't want you hurt."

He smiled and shrugged. "I haven't been in a good barroom brawl since the army. Kind of looking forward to it, to tell you the truth. You go on. Give me fifteen minutes."

Connie kissed him, hand resting lightly on his chest, then walked down the street and turned into the bar. Scott walked in the opposite direction. Connie was worried. Worried and protective. Worried and deferential. Connie with the parts of Lucinda he liked best.

He smiled. He walked three blocks up, then turned and walked back.

He didn't look around until he had ordered a beer, and then he did most of his looking in the mirror behind the bartender.

It wasn't hard to pick a fight in a bar. The trick was to pick the right kind of fight. What he needed was a pair of buddies who'd had a little too much, just enough to make them cocky and to slow their reactions, just enough to make them sensitive to insults and eager to gang up on one guy.

There was a likely pair at a table just off the far end of the bar, telling jokes, putting their heads together, laughing a little too long and a little too loud. A pair of happy jacks.

In the mirror Scott caught Connie's eye and inclined his head a fraction towards the end of the bar. Connie followed his gaze, saw the pair, nodded. Scott drained his beer and ordered a new bottle. He stood and made his way toward them. He could look at their beefy faces and tell which whispered insult would start them swinging. He could even make it look as if they jumped him without provocation.

Connie was there to limit damage. When the fight started, she'd yell "Police!" to break it up. That way Scott could duck out the back and wouldn't get beaten up too bad.

He needed to get beaten up some, though. It had to be real enough to scare Lucinda, to build on the terror he had seen at the deadline party. Getting beaten up in the bar would be proof that she had been right, and the letter that Connie would mail would say, "Dear Lovebirds: What happened last night is just the beginning. The price just doubled. You're going to pay one way or another. Cash or flesh. Take your choice." Then he'd see how Lucinda reacted. And Connie. He'd see the effect on Connie, too.

He leaned toward the happy jacks and smiled. This was going to be fun.

"We could have them arrested," Lucinda said.

Scott shook his head, winced from real pain. "Wouldn't do any good," he said. "They'd claim I started it. They'd pay a fine. Then they'd kill me. Or worse, they'd hurt you. They want their money. They think we owe them." His words came thick through his bruised lips. The right side of his face was swollen and purple. His right eye was shut. A split above his left eye was closed with eight tiny black x's. He looked terrible. He looked a lot worse than he felt, but he didn't feel good.

"I'm going to pay," said Scott. "What else can I do?"

They were sitting at the kitchen table. Very domestic, he thought, except that across from him Lucinda sat silent and staring, tears filling her eyes and running down her cheeks and splashing onto the white ceramic tile of the table. She had started when she saw his face. She had continued through the story of the fight. She wasn't sobbing, wasn't breathing hard or funny; her voice, when she spoke, was almost normal. It was as if she didn't know she was crying. It was more like overflowing than crying. The tears just poured out. They were making Scott nervous.

"It will never stop," she said.

"I think they're skipping town. I think that's why they asked for so much. I think this will be the last time."

She smiled at him as if at a child who had said something almost clever. She reached out and touched his cheek. "They hurt you. Poor face. Poor face."

Scott pulled away as if her touch hurt. "I can have the money in a couple of days. But that's going to wipe me out."

She just stared, tears leaking from her unblinking eyes.

"Couple of days enough for you, Lucinda?" he asked.

"I'll have to make some phone calls," she said, as if talking to a third person.

Scott nodded and put his head down and hoped there was a way he could get out of there early that night.

Connie laid the money out in neat little stacks on the coffee table. A hundred thousand dollars. Twenty thousand of it theirs. Eighty thousand Bennie's, at the same terms. Borrow eighty, pay back eighty-eight. Scott thought it was high, since they'd been such good customers lately. Connie said that it took money to make money. "You're paying eight to get a hundred," she'd said. "You clear ninety-two." Looked at that way, it was a good deal.

Scott had a package of brown lunch bags with Mickey Mouse waving in sunglasses and flowery shirt. Miami.

Connie's hands danced over the stacks, counting. There were a lot of stacks.

"Okay," she said. "All here. Now remember, ten thousand a bag, ten bags in the grocery sack, grocery sack in the green leaf bag. Lucinda's ten bags in another grocery sack, that sack in the same leaf bag. Be sure you bag hers like you're really worried about following orders. Where's the drop?"

Scott squinted into the distance and ran through the directions to the green dumpster out in the pastureland.

Connie was smiling, shaking her head. "Poor face," she said. "No more of this. We've got to change the kind of operation we run. You've got to take better care of that poor face. I want it handsomed up again in Miami."

He tried to smile. It hurt a little.

"Well," she said. "That's it. Don't forget, Gate 7, at ten forty-three, Flight 398. Don't push her too far this time."

Scott smiled again. "Don't worry."

Connie touched his cheek. "Love you," she said. She'd never said that before.

Lucinda was late.

If she didn't hurry, they wouldn't make the drop. Maybe she was having trouble getting the cash.

Scott stared down at the long fall from the condo window, hoping that she hadn't done something stupid. God, she was so moody, she could do anything. The last thing he needed was to get linked up to a suicide.

It was scary, standing at the edge of the big payoff for all that work, for performing for Lucinda, for sometimes losing himself in the performance, for sneaking around to meet Connie. Final performance coming up. It would be worth it if it worked.

He sat down at the kitchen table and counted out ten Mickey Mouse lunch bags and waited. *Traffic,* he thought, *or trouble getting the cash. She'll be frantic. Be calm.*

And then Lucinda came breezing in, not frantic, but

happy, smiling. She gave him a hug. If she was carrying the money, he didn't see it. She laughed.

"Oh, darling," she said. "Oh, *darling.*"

Scott didn't even try to smile. "We've got to hurry if we want to make the drop. We . . ."

"I have a surprise," she said, fumbling through a drawer, pulling out a corkscrew. It was disorienting, like the other day being replayed. "Sit down."

"Lucinda," he began.

"Just sit down." There was an edge there that he couldn't ignore, an edge like Connie's voice could get.

She opened a bottle of wine, humming. She poured two glasses. She gave him one. "To us," she said. Scott raised his glass and sipped. She drained hers.

From her shoulder bag she removed a blank white envelope. "Surprise," she said, handing it to Scott. "Happy birthday, Merry Christmas, and many happy returns."

There were two pictures inside, pictures of two men. The happy jacks from the bar. They were quite obviously dead.

"Hurting you was where they made their mistake, of course," Lucinda went on, refilling the glasses, spilling the red wine across the tablecloth, across Scott's sleeve. "It wasn't hard to find them after that."

Scott looked from the pictures to Lucinda. "You . . . ?"

She laughed. "Not me, silly. Friends. Well, people my husband knows. We can't keep these pictures, so look while you can." She looked at the pictures. She looked at him. "Well? Isn't this wonderful?"

Oh God, Scott thought frantically. *Oh God.* He tried to say something, found himself stammering, got control by twisting his shock to fit her expectations. He was stunned, he said. It was incredible. It was great. He never expected it. She beamed.

He had to get out of there. She had served up the bodies on the kitchen table like a favorite dessert. *Calm, calm,* he told himself. *You've got the money. Get it, get out, get out of town.*

The doorbell rang. He jumped up, knocking over his glass. She laughed again, put her hands on his shoulders, sat him down. She took the pictures with her. He could hear her talking to someone, male, deep-voiced, but he couldn't make out the words, wasn't sure he'd understand them if he could. Wine ran to the edge of the table, hung there, building, building, then broke and ran, dripping into his lap. She came back into the kitchen and picked up the green leaf bag. Scott leaned forward, reaching, trying to say something, but she cut him off.

"It bought our freedom," she said. "And it cost us only half of what they wanted." And she was gone, with the money. His money and Connie's. And Bennie's.

He was numb.

But he could still leave.

Connie already had the tickets. That, and the money in her purse, was all they had. They'd had less. It would be hard in Miami, at first, anyway. But when his face healed they could work another scam. Or they could get into something safe, like drug running.

He heard Lucinda say thank you and goodbye, heard the door close. He took a deep breath and tried to gain some kind of control, to appear normal, whatever that was, so that he could leave, so that he could meet Connie, so that he could get the hell out.

Lucinda sat across from him, smiling. "It's almost over, darling." She shuddered. "They're a little scary," she said. "They said they'd call us later."

"Call us later?" he said.

"About the girl. They're going to take care of her, too. Then we really will be free, darling, once she's gone."

Scott was thinking about Bennie's money, about Bennie. He and Connie were through in this town. With Bennie, they might even have to watch their backs in Miami. He realized that Lucinda was talking to him. What was she saying? "Once who's gone?" he said. "Take care of who?" But part of him already knew.

She reached across the table and took his hand. "There

was a girl," she said. "At the bar. A lookout. One of the
blackmailers. She warned them that the police were coming."

Scott stood up, his ears roaring, room tilting. Lucinda
took a sip of wine. Scott turned toward where he thought
the door was.

"Maybe you saw her?" Lucinda said.

"Saw her?" he repeated.

"The girl. The one who warned them. Maybe you saw
her. They say she was already there when you came in.
Sitting at a table just inside the door. Blonde? Pretty?
Young?"

He shook his head slowly. He wanted to leave, just to
find the door and go through it. But Bennie was out there.
He turned and looked at Lucinda. "You didn't tell your
husband."

She stared at him. "If I told him, he'd make me watch
you die before he killed me."

Scott didn't know whether to believe her or not. His legs
felt wet. He looked down. There was wine all over his
pants. He didn't know what to do.

She wiped up the spilled wine at his place, righted his
glass, filled it. "Sit down, darling," she said.

He sat. He stared down at his empty hands.

"I hope," she said, a smile flickering across her face, "I
hope that I always love you as much as I do right now."
She reached out and stroked his cheek.

It took all of his willpower not to flinch away.

ONE OF THE OLDEST CON GAMES

by Robert L. Fish

❒ "ONE OF THE OLDEST GIMMICKS IN THE WORLD," SAM SAID, NOT because anyone needed to know but because he was a compulsive talker, "and easy as clubbing carp in a washtub. But they still go for it, you'd be amazed. First thing you do when you hit a new town, you go down to the library and get hold of a copy of a local newspaper, say, three, four months back. Pick out the name of some local character who died, no big-shot, nobody they have a special article about, just a guy from the list of the guys who died that day.

"Pick a foreign name, a Wojenowski, or a Bruno, or a Svenson—Danes are good, or Germans, or Poles, people who save their dough. You pick a guy in his late sixties, early seventies—a guy whose widow would be pretty close to his own age, maybe a little younger, but a guy who, if he has any children, they'd be long married and with their own place. Right?"

"I know," Ralph said resignedly, and sighed.

"Right," Sam said. "Then you get the address where the widow lives. If it isn't in the newspaper squib, and they usually aren't, then you call the undertaker, tell him you just heard about your old pal dying, and want to drop the widow a condolence card."

"You could also look it up in the phone book," Ralph said.

"Oh, you could do that too, but there could be two Michael Wojenowskis or whatever listed in the phone book and you have to be sure you've got the right one. Anyway, once you have the right address, then you go and scout the house. Best ones are maybe forty years old, in an older neighborhood, but still clean, one-family house, two-story, probably with the mortgage paid off twenty, thirty years back.

"Then if the house checks out, you check out the widow, make sure she isn't a nut, maybe follow her to the supermarket when she's shopping, see what she picks up for supper.

"Then if all that checks out, you go round the neighborhood until you find the nearest branch bank, probably in the same shopping center as the supermarket. Ten to one that's where the widow banks. Then you call her at home, any nutty excuse to find out if she really does bank there—"

"And if she doesn't bank there?" Ralph asked, not because he hadn't heard Sam give the answer many times before, but just to get a word in edgewise.

"Nine times out of ten these old ladies bank at the nearest place," Sam said confidentially, "but if she doesn't, then forget her and pick out another dead guy, is all. Right?"

"Right," Ralph said wearily.

Old Mrs. Kuhlmann paused in her labors and stared upward toward the basement ceiling. Had her telephone been ringing? She lowered the volume on the small radio that usually accompanied her on her chores around the house and listened carefully. She would have been the first to admit her hearing wasn't what it had been years before, but then what was? When Jake had been alive he often used to kid her about her hearing going downhill, but when Jake was alive they had joked about many things. She used to tell him her hearing was good enough to hear him when he came back from his weekly poker

game, tiptoeing up the stairs so he wouldn't have to tell
her how much he lost until she'd had breakfast and was in
a better mood. But even then it was hard to stay angry
with Jake, he was such a good husband—

She suddenly realized she had fallen into her newly acquired habit of daydreaming while the telephone continued to ring. I'm really getting old, she thought, and was
reminded of it again when the stairs took their toll as she
climbed up them, one wizened hand holding the railing
while the other wiped itself nervously against her apron.

"All right, all right, I'm coming," she told the telephone
and raised the receiver, silencing the shrill beast at last.
"Hello?" she said.

"Hello, Mrs. Kuhlmann?" It was a strange voice, but
pleasant enough.

"Yes, that's me."

"Mrs. Kuhlmann," the man said, "I hope you'll forgive
us for bothering you, but this is Mr. Romney at the Crestview National Bank, and I'd like to ask you a question. Did
you make a deposit here a short time ago? About thirty
minutes ago, to be exact?"

"A deposit?" Mrs. Kuhlmann said, surprised. "Why, no."

"That's strange," the man said, and sounded puzzled.
"You do bank here, Mrs. Kuhlmann, don't you?"

"Why, yes, but—"

"Ah, well," the man said. "It's probably just a bookkeeping error. Well, thank you, Mrs. Kuhlmann. Sorry to have
bothered you." The receiver was softly replaced at the
other end of the line.

Old Mrs. Kuhlmann hung up and stared at the telephone, perplexed. A deposit to her account? Who on earth
could have done that? It was undoubtedly a mistake. Like
the man said, a bookkeeping error. Jake would have been
able to make something of it, possibly, if he had answered
the phone. In the old days Jake always answered the
phone when it rang—when he was home, that is, which
had been more and more after he quit the printing shop
and started to work at home, but there was no sense

thinking about Jake because there wasn't any Jake any
more, and there was never, never going to be any Jake any
more on this earth, and sitting here feeling sorry for herself wasn't going to solve anything, or feed anybody, either.

She sighed and came to her feet, automatically wiping
the little table where the telephone sat, using a corner of
her apron, and then jumped a little as the telephone rang,
more sharply this time it seemed to her. She picked it up,
frowning. "Hello?"

"Mrs. Kuhlmann?"

"Yes, this is me." My Lord! Two telephone calls in one
day! And she had been about to have the thing taken out,
because she never used it. She became aware that the
man was speaking and concentrated on listening.

"Mrs. Kuhlmann, this is Lieutenant Garrett of the police department. Precinct number—" The deep voice was
suddenly lowered while still remaining quite audible, even
to old Mrs. Kuhlmann's failing ears. "What is it, Mike?
Can't you handle it? Then tell the Captain. What? Oh, all
right. I suppose so." The voice returned to Mrs. Kuhlmann. "I'm sorry, Mrs. Kuhlmann, but something just
came up. It'll only take a moment. Don't hang up."

The authority in those final words made the thought of
hanging up impossible. There was the sharp sound of the
receiver being placed down on something hard, like a bare
desk top, and then the background noises Mrs. Kuhlmann
had been vaguely aware of while the lieutenant had been
speaking became noticeably louder. There was the sound
of several automobile horns blaring, and one of the constantly intermingling voices said, "Hey, somebody shut
that window, will you?" There was a slam and the street
noises abated. "That's better," said the voice, while another one was saying, "Sergeant, can I see you over here
for a minute?" and a third voice overrode them both, saying, "Now, there's nothing to worry about, Miss. I'm sure
we'll locate your father in a matter of days."

Through it all the urgent and frequent ringing of a telephone punctuated the ebb and flow of muffled conversation while the incessant rattle of a typewriter furnished an almost hypnotic backdrop to the entire acoustic tapestry.

Old Mrs. Kuhlmann fell back into daydreaming. She had met Jake when he had come to work at the printing shop where she was a typist. Fifty-three years ago, that had been. Fifty-three years—how the time flew! She'd been a good typist too, but Jake made her quit when they got married, saying that no wife of his would ever work in an office or a factory, and she never had.

She had helped Jake at home when he started out on his own, of course, but that was only natural and not at all the same thing as working on the outside. And it had been fun working with Jake. He'd been a good man, and a good provider while he was alive, and while he hadn't left her a whole lot of cash, he'd left her everything else, including some fine memories. She really couldn't complain—

"Mrs. Kuhlmann?" The deep voice brought Mrs. Kuhlmann from her thoughts. "Sorry about the interruption, but that's how it goes in a busy police precinct. Now, where were we? Oh, yes. You see, Mrs. Kuhlmann, one of the officers of the Crestview National Bank is under suspicion of embezzling, and we wonder if we could use your help in our investigation."

"Me? My help?" Mrs. Kuhlmann stared at the telephone. "So that's what the man from the bank was calling about, was it?"

"That's right. You're pretty sharp, Mrs. Kuhlmann." There was admiration in the lieutenant's tone.

"Thank you." Well, she told herself defensively, I'm not in my dotage yet! "Of course I'd like to help, but I don't quite see what I can do."

"Don't worry about that, Mrs. Kuhlmann," the lieutenant said. "We wouldn't have called you if we weren't sure you were the right person for us." His voice became more official. "What we'd like you to do is to withdraw some funds from your account, temporarily. A day at the most.

We guarantee you'll lose no interest, and we'll see that detectives are assigned to make sure you won't be robbed for the short time the money will be out of the bank. You won't even see these men, so don't be disturbed by the thought of your neighbors seeing policemen around you. And you'll be doing your duty as a citizen, Mrs. Kuhlmann, and that's something you can always be proud of."

"Oh!" Well, old Mrs. Kuhlmann didn't know many things, but she knew what Jake would have said in the circumstances. Jake was very proud of being a citizen, because he came over as a youngster, apprenticed to— There she went again, daydreaming! "Of course," she said. "Tell me what to do."

"Thank you," the lieutenant said. "It's really quite simple. All you have to do is withdraw money from the bank, temporarily. After that we'll have further instructions for you, but both you and your money will be protected at all times, and it will only be for a day at the most. And by the way," he added, "under no circumstances are you to mention at the bank the reason for the withdrawal." His voice dropped conspiratorially. "I'm sure a smart woman like you can understand the reason for that. Until we have the necessary evidence in hand to convict, any leak in our plans could ruin our case."

"Oh, I can understand that," old Mrs. Kuhlmann said, and knew that Jake would have been proud of her. He always said she had to be sharper than she acted. Of course, he used to kid her, too, when she did something silly, like the time she forgot the potatoes when they had the Millikens over for supper—she brought her mind back to the business at hand. "How much do you think I should withdraw, Lieutenant? Would—uh—forty-five dollars be enough?"

The lieutenant chuckled and then instantly wiped the chuckle away as not being proper to a case of such serious dimensions. "I'm afraid we could scarcely convict a man for embezzlement on the basis of a mere forty-five dollars, Mrs. Kuhlmann. We're not after him for pilfering, or petty larceny. We want him for the big one." His tone chided old Mrs. Kuhlmann for having failed him in his newly acquired expectations of her. "How much do you have in the bank?"

Mrs. Kuhlmann wet her lips and looked about the room.

"Come, come, Mrs. Kuhlmann," the lieutenant said in a kindly tone. "We are the police. We're here to protect you, don't forget that. How much do you have in the bank?"

"Um—ah—six thousand dollars," Mrs. Kuhlmann said at last.

"Well, take out forty-nine hundred and leave the rest," the lieutenant said. It was almost an order. "I'm sure that will be enough to tempt the scoundrel." He added soothingly, "It's really quite all right, Mrs. Kuhlmann. You'll be under constant surveillance until the money is returned to the bank. And I wouldn't be surprised," he added, "if the bank didn't offer a reward when the matter is cleared up. So don't worry."

"I wasn't worried about *that*," old Mrs. Kuhlmann said a bit untruthfully, and then asked a question that had occurred to her. "Do you think they would be suspicious if I took the money out in"—the old lady's voice dropped as she mentioned the sacred figures—"in hundred-dollar bills?"

"The bank? Not at all." The lieutenant's tone moved on to more important things. "And I'd get over to the bank as soon as possible, Mrs. Kuhlmann. They close in less than an hour, you know."

"Oh, yes, oh, yes!" old Mrs. Kuhlmann said hastily, and hung up instantly, hurrying to put on her hat and coat.

Sam swung around from the telephone in the cheap hotel room and then reached over to switch off the small cassette tape recorder that had provided such an authentic audio portrayal of a busy police station. It had taken a lot of over-taping and dubbed sound effects to produce that particular tape, as Sam had told Ralph often enough, and

Sam was rightly proud of it. He winked at Ralph and came to his feet.

"Easy?"

"They often are," Ralph said dryly, and bit back a yawn.

"And you get the drift of only asking for forty-nine hundred?"

"You always only ask for forty-nine hundred no matter how much they've got," Ralph said wearily.

"Right. Because banks get real fussy whenever anyone withdraws more than five thousand at a time in cash," Sam said, as if Ralph had not spoken. "Don't ask me why, but you come in with a check for over five thousand and you have to get about sixteen bank officials to countersign it. But under five thousand and there's no question, if they know you. Don't ask me why."

"I won't," Ralph promised.

"And now we go over to the bank and make sure the little old lady really goes there," Sam said, "because when we make the pickup we don't want to find out she was stringing us along all the time and just waited for me to hang up to call the cops. We don't want that, do we?"

"No," Ralph said in a tired voice. "We don't want that."

They drove the few blocks to the bank, parked in a space that provided proper surveillance, and watched as a few minutes later little old Mrs. Kuhlmann came bustling down the street in her dowdy hat and coat, her purse under her arm, and hurried into the bank. Five minutes later and the old lady was out again, her purse now clutched desperately between the skinny but strong fingers of both hands. The corner of a stiff brown envelope peeked out of the stuffed purse. Sam grinned and put the car in gear.

"Now," he said, "when we get back to the hotel, we synchronize our watches, because exactly one hour from now I make the call, and exactly one minute after I start dialing I want you knocking on her door. It's the old one-two punch that gets them! We wait that one hour because the longer she has that much cold cash in that big house all alone, the quicker she's going to be relieved to hand it over

to Detective Brownell, which is you. Right? And less than
an hour and she might not be nervous enough, and any
more than an hour and she might get so nervous she'd be
calling the station house for protection." He winked at
Ralph. "It's all in the timing. Psychology. Right?"

"Sam," Ralph said in desperation, "you talk too much,
you know that? You go on and on like a damn phonograph!
I've done this caper with you a dozen times or more, so will
you please quit going through that damn monologue of
yours, for God's sake?"

"Right!" Sam said happily, not having heard a single
word, and turned the car toward the hotel.

This time when the telephone rang, old Mrs. Kuhlmann
had been awaiting the noisy summons. She hurried from
the basement, one hand clutching an envelope, and raised
the receiver quickly. "Yes?"

"Mrs. Kuhlmann." She was relieved to hear the voice of
Lieutenant Whatever-his-name-was. "Do you have the
money?"

"Oh, yes!"

"Good! And has Detective Brownell shown up?"

"Who? Nobody's been here—" She paused. Somebody
was knocking on the front door and she suddenly remembered that the doorbell was out of order. Jake would have
fixed it long ago, he was so clever with his hands, but she
wasn't handy with tools and she'd meant to ask the man at
the hardware store, but she'd forgotten. And actually, not
many people ever came to the door, except the mailman,
and all he brought were the utility bills—

She suddenly became aware that the rapping had increased in volume and tempo. There she went again! Daydreaming when things had to be done! "Just a second," she
said to the telephone a bit breathlessly. "Somebody's at
the door. Maybe it's him."

She put the instrument down and hurried to the door,
opening it to face a tall thin man with a bored look on his
face and a set of handcuffs dangling from his belt. She
smiled at him a bit timidly. "Is your name Brownell?" He

nodded. "Lieutenant What's-his-name," old Mrs. Kuhlmann said. "I think he wants to talk to you."

"Right. I mean, thank you," said Detective Brownell. He
marched to the instrument and picked it up. "Brownell,"
he said succinctly, and listened. There was a faint buzz
from the phone as Brownell received his instructions. He
nodded from time to time as old Mrs. Kuhlmann waited.
"Right," he said into the telephone, listened some more,
and then could not help but add, trying desperately not to
sound savage, "I know, I know!"

He hung up and turned to face the little old lady,
straightening his face.

"Mrs. Kuhlmann," he said in as detective-like a manner
as he could, "it will be necessary for me to take the money
down to headquarters and have it marked, after which it
will be returned to the bank. Then when the embezzler
tries to get his hands on it"—he suddenly clenched one
fist, wishing it was Sam's tongue between his fingers—
"we'll have him!" He regained his official mien. "May I
have the money, please?"

Mrs. Kuhlmann handed over the envelope she had been
clutching so tightly. Detective Brownell riffled the bills,
counting them quickly. "On the button," he muttered to
himself, and stuffed the envelope in his pocket. He looked
up sternly. "And we must repeat—please tell no one at the
bank about this. Or anybody else, for that matter. It could
seriously hamper our investigation."

"Well, of course I won't tell anyone!" old Mrs. Kuhlmann
said indignantly. My Lord, everyone thought she was stupid!

It was the following evening, and Sam and Ralph were
hundreds of miles from Crestview and little old Mrs. Kuhlmann, and the only time Sam had stopped talking in all
that time, Ralph thought, verging on despondency, was
when he dropped by the local library for a few minutes in
the afternoon. Now, with an excellent meal at one of the
plushier clubs in the city inside him, and the bill paid,

Sam sipped at his brandy, tucked his dollar cigar into one corner of his mouth, and fished a small bit of newsprint from his vest pocket. He referred to it, a satisfied smile on his face.

"Tenza, Emil. Age seventy-two years. Passed away April seventh, four months ago. Beloved husband of Helen, devoted father of Isabel Probst of Chicago and Evelyn Kellerman of Detroit, not to mention devoted grandfather of Thomas, Joseph, and Sally Probst, as well as Billy Kellerman, Junior." He looked up, his eyes twinkling. "And I'm sure both dutiful daughters showed up at the funeral and then went home, leaving poor old Mama all alone in the big empty house."

He tucked the clipping back into his pocket, rolled the cigar in his mouth, and leaned back, puffing luxuriously. "Like I keep trying to tell you, Ralph, one of the oldest gimmicks in the world and as easy as clubbing carp in a washtub. But they still go for it, you'd be amazed."

Ralph stared hopelessly at the ceiling. The thought of hearing that tireless voice go on and on, repeating the endless litany for the thousandth time, was enough to ruin even the fine meal they had just finished. Eight courses, which weren't too many for a peaceful dinner, since when Sam was chewing at least he wasn't talking. Heaven help me! Ralph thought piously, but was suddenly saved by a more earthly entity. Before Sam could continue, there was a touch on his arm and he looked up to find a huge man in a tuxedo standing beside him.

"Yes?" Sam said politely, thinking it might be his change.

"This hundred dollar bill," the big man said, and pushed it under Sam's nose. "With *Lincoln* on the face of it?" His tone indicated total incredulity. "Passing slush in *my* club? You guys must be suicidal."

Ralph stared at Sam in startled shock. *That little old lady?* For once Sam was silent, stunned into speechlessness, but for once Ralph was not relieved.

"Let's go into the office," the huge man said grimly, "and

see if you guys can smoke my buck cigars when you each got two broken elbows!"

And old Mrs. Kuhlmann, as she put the newspaper-wrapped package back into the bank's safety-deposit box, smiled a little nervously when she thought what Jake's reaction would have been to her using the one-hundred-dollar plates. He had just been experimenting when he made them, perfecting his art, and he only put Lincoln's picture on them to please her, because she insisted he engraved Abraham Lincoln much better than he did Benjamin Franklin. Well, the truth of the matter was—whether Jake admitted it or not—he did do Lincoln better than he did Franklin. In fact, the only plates he ever let her print were the ones that had Lincoln's picture on them; and heaven only knows what she would have done if she didn't have those, because when Jake died all he left her were the plates, a safety-deposit box paid up for years to keep them in, and $45 in their joint account.

"I know you told me never to print those big plates," she told the ceiling of the small room off the main vault, her quavering voice apologetic, "but I couldn't admit to that nice Lieutenant What's-his-name that you didn't even leave me six thousand dollars, could I? It would have made you look bad, Jake, and you weren't bad at all," she said. "Only sometimes not too bright . . ."

HOW TO TRAP A CROOK

by Julian Symons

☐ A PRETTY LITTLE SWINDLE, FRANCIS QUARLES SAID AFTERWARD, one that showed how the most intelligent of detectives can be made to look like a fool. But in telling the story, which involved at one point his own distinct discomfiture, Quarles retained the air of imperturbable self-esteem that infuriated so many of his acquaintances.

The affair began, as Quarles told it, when Charles Henderson was brought by Molly Player into Quarles's office with the big window overlooking Trafalgar Square. Henderson was a big, ruddy, conservatively dressed American.

"Mr. Quarles, you may not know who I am—"

Quarles held up a hand. "I should think it very remiss not to have *Who's Who in America* on my shelves, and after your telephone call not to consult it. You are the president of the Porkette Manufacturing and Canning Company, you have a wife and three children, an apartment in New York, and a house on Long Island. You are known colloquially as Porkette Henderson. The financial section of the *Times* tells me that you are here to find new retail outlets for Porkette. Correct so far?"

"Correct but irrelevant," Henderson said. It is unusual for a detective to be disliked by a client, but as Quarles realized, Henderson obviously disliked him from the start. Was it the rather extravagantly Edwardian cut of the detective's jacket, the large diamond ring he wore, or simply his air of knowing beforehand what you were about to say? Whatever the reason, Quarles sensed the antagonism and responded to it. As Henderson's manner became more brisk and businesslike, Quarles's appeared more esthetically languid.

"I suspect I may be about to be conned, and my friend Willard Monteith—"

"The Chicago attorney."

"Yes. Willard told me you'd helped him in a matter relating to a dispute about a picture."

"An attempt to provide a provenance for a fake Matisse, yes. A flight to Paris, a chat with a couple of colleagues there, and the matter was settled."

"Willard reckoned you knew your way about the art world." Henderson's gaze shifted to the picture above Quarles's desk. "That's a nice Utrillo."

"Yves Poirier of the Galerie Poirier gave it to me after I had recovered his wife's three kidnaped cats."

"I like to think I've got the finest private collection of Nineteenth Century paintings in New York," Henderson said. "And every time I come over I try to add to it. Have you heard of a man named Charles Scrutton?"

"The Scrutton Gallery, just off New Bond Street. I know him slightly, only slightly."

"He's offered me a Corot landscape. It's done in that typical silvery Corot style. And the price is reasonable, very reasonable."

"And you are asking for my advice. Simple, Mr. Henderson. I said I knew Scrutton only slightly, but I know his reputation well enough. Don't buy from him. Or if you must buy, get the provenance of the picture established beyond doubt—speak to its former owner yourself if possible—"

"Mr. Quarles." Beneath his silver crew cut Henderson's face was red with annoyance. "I am not totally stupid about buying pictures, and I know Scrutton's reputation. At the same time I'm not convinced that I shouldn't buy from him."

"He has never been convicted, or even charged with anything, that's true."

"More than that, I know a couple of people who have bought pictures from him with which they're perfectly happy. They swear Scrutton's absolutely honest."

Quarles's bulky shoulders shrugged under the Edwardian jacket. "If you are not interested in my advice I don't see how I can help you."

"Willard said you were friendly with Max van Galen. I suppose he's just about the greatest expert on Corot and Manet outside France. If it was possible to get van Galen to take a look at this Corot of Scrutton's, I'd be grateful."

"Why not ask him yourself?"

"I've tried." Henderson's face grew redder. "I never even got to talk to him. His secretary said Professor van Galen was too busy to deal with personal requests. You know he's Professor of Fine Art at London University."

"So you want me to arrange something for you that you can't do yourself? Just to make it clear."

Henderson glared. "I'll pay you for your services."

Quarles held up the hand on which the diamond ring glinted. "That doesn't arise. This will be for amusement only." He spoke to Molly in the outer office. "Molly, see if you can get me Max van Galen. In person. Thank you."

He smiled blandly at Henderson, who got up and looked out of the window at Nelson on his column and the lions below. The telephone rang, and Quarles spoke.

"Max? Francis Quarles. I'm very well, and how are you? No, nothing like that, just what may be an entertaining little problem concerning a Corot. An American acquaintance of mine has been offered one. By Charles Scrutton." A pause, and then Quarles laughed. "I've told him that, but he is not deterred. Is there any chance you might be able to look at it yourself? Of course you're busy, Max, but the walk to New Bond Street will do you good." He put his hand over the receiver. "When are you seeing Scrutton, to decide about the picture?"

"Eleven o'clock tomorrow."

"Could you be there at eleven fifteen tomorrow morning, Max? Marvelous. Yes, I'll promise that." He put down the telephone. "Max is a great man for fish. I promised him lunch at Prunier's after we'd looked at the picture. That will be at your expense."

Henderson grunted. "Why did you say eleven fifteen to him instead of eleven?"

"Because it will give Scrutton time to make his sales pitch for the picture and to guarantee its genuineness. Our objects are not identical, Mr. Henderson. You want to make sure that you are not conned. For me, this should be a simple demonstration of how to trap a crook."

"You're convinced Scrutton will try to put something over on me?"

"Of course. From his point of view that's the object of the exercise."

Henderson and Quarles got out of the taxi. The façade said *Charles Scrutton, Fine Art* in elegant lettering. In the window was a single small painting of a mill and trees, labeled *17th Century Dutch School.*

Inside the gallery a sleek assistant advanced and then retreated as Henderson identified himself. Charles Scrutton came forward with hand outstretched. He was a tall florid man with thick muttonchop whiskers, and he wore a suit of powerful checks. His manner was bluffly rural. He looked as little like an art dealer as it was possible to imagine.

"Mr. Henderson." He paused fractionally before giving Quarles a firm handshake. "And Francis Quarles, isn't it? I think we last met at that party for the Whistler exhibition."

"Mr. Quarles is interested," Henderson said. "He has a fine Utrillo on his office wall. He wanted to see this Corot."

"There it is." Scrutton switched on a light, illuminating a picture which showed rocks, trees, and a stream. The two men stood looking at it. Quarles could not have told whether it was by Corot or by one of a dozen other French artists.

"It's Corot's style, all right," Henderson said.

Scrutton pulled at his muttonchop whiskers. "Mr. Henderson, I'm not going to sell you this picture."

"You mean you've got another buyer?" Henderson flushed angrily. "I call that—"

"I won't sell it to you because it is not a genuine Corot. I'm very much afraid it's from Dr. Jousseaume's collection. You've heard of Jousseaume? He made a tremendous collection of Corot paintings and drawings. When he died in 1923 they were let loose on the market and three-quarters of them turned out to be fakes, done especially for the doctor's benefit. Like other dealers I watch out for things from the Jousseaume collection and try to avoid them, but every so often you get caught. I've checked this one thoroughly, and I'm afraid there's no doubt about it." He gave them a ruefully comical glance. "It doesn't often happen, but this time Charles Scrutton's been had."

Quarles asked, "As a matter of interest, what will you do with the painting now?"

"Put it in a sale as 'attributed to Corot' or 'in the manner of Corot,' for whatever it will fetch. That won't be much." The telephone rang. The assistant murmured something to Scrutton, who excused himself and left them.

Henderson turned to Quarles. "A simple demonstration of how to trap a crook, eh? How about that, Quarles? Admit you were wrong."

Before the detective could reply the door opened and Max van Galen came into the gallery.

The art expert was a short squat man with a hurried, jerky walk, and the wide mouth and popping eyes of a frog. His voice was a frog's croak.

"Quarles, how are you, nice to see you again." He gave a perfunctory handshake and a popeyed stare at Henderson, and said, "Now, where's this picture you want me to look at?"

Scrutton came back and said, "Professor, this is a plea-

sure. And an honor. You don't know me, but I recognize
you. I'm Charles Scrutton."

Van Galen allowed his hand to be pumped. "The picture."

Henderson spoke in some confusion. "Mr. Scrutton, I
may as well admit I asked the Professor to come along
here and check on the picture. I'm not feeling too proud of
myself at the moment."

"*You* asked?" van Galen snapped at him. "I don't know
you. I spoke to Francis Quarles here."

Quarles said, "The point is that Mr. Scrutton has discovered that the painting is not genuine and has very properly withdrawn it."

"It's one of the Jousseaume lot, I'm afraid. See for yourself." Scrutton switched on the light above the painting
again. Van Galen took a magnifying glass from his pocket,
glanced at the painting, and immediately put the glass
back.

"A close inspection is not necessary. This is a very poor
piece of work. I am surprised you should have bought it."

"We all make mistakes," Scrutton said cheerfully. His
glance moved quickly from one to the other of them. "Professor van Galen, since you're here I should like to ask you
a favor. A couple of days ago I acquired another picture,
which I do believe to be a genuine Corot. Would you care to
give your opinion of it?"

"I am always ready to look at a picture."

"I'm grateful. Jordan, will you get that little Corot landscape." Scrutton said to Henderson, "I couldn't offer you
this picture because at the time you got in touch with me I
didn't possess it."

Jordan returned with a picture which he stood on a
small table. It showed a snowy landscape, with a small
house in the background and a man standing beside it.
The four of them looked at it.

"Full of charm, don't you think?" Scrutton said. "It's
called 'Winter Landscape.' Rather like the Lincolnshire
fen country, where I was brought up."

"This is a different matter from that other—affair." Van Galen bent over, examining the picture closely under his magnifying glass. He put away the glass and went on looking, then straightened up with a sigh of pleasure, and said simply, "Yes."

"It's a genuine Corot?" the American asked.

"It is a very good Corot, a lovely picture. It is a pleasure to see it."

"Mr. Scrutton, would you like to put a price on that picture?"

"If you'll just come into my office, we can talk about it."

Henderson paused at the office door and said with heavy irony, "You don't have any doubts, Quarles?"

"As far as I'm concerned, Max van Galen's word is law."

"And of course you're not an art expert yourself."

"I'm not an art expert," Quarles agreed.

Van Galen rubbed his hands. "I am looking forward to lunch. Are plovers' eggs in season?"

Quarles was standing beside the picture, with his back to van Galen. "I doubt it. You may have to settle for caviar as an opening course." He turned. "There's no doubt about the authenticity of this Corot?"

Van Galen laughed. "You know the definition of being positive? To be mistaken at the top of your voice. An expert learns to be careful. But I should be prepared to offer a sporting bet of twenty to one that this is a genuine Corot. You didn't expect this to happen?"

Before Quarles could reply, Henderson and Scrutton returned. "Can I take it with me?" the American asked. "I want to do a little gloating in my suite at the Savoy."

"I'd sooner send it along—there are customs forms to complete, and so on."

"I should like to take it now, Mr. Scrutton. You have my check."

Scrutton hesitated, then said, "Yes, of course. Jordan, will you pack up this picture for Mr. Henderson." The sleek assistant came forward and took the Corot. "It's a pleasure to sell something to a man who's going to enjoy it."

"I'm very very happy." A smile spread over Henderson's face. "Are you happy, Quarles?"

"I'm glad you've got what you wanted." Quarles strolled about the gallery, looking at the other pictures. He turned as Jordan came back with the picture wrapped in heavy paper. "I thought it was charming, as Scrutton said."

"Pleased you approve of my choice."

"So charming that I should like to see it again." Scrutton stared at him. "Would you unwrap it, please?"

"What the hell d'you mean, what are you talking about? Jordan, stop him."

Quarles was already at the wrapping paper, tearing it away. There was an undignified scuffle, and then the picture was revealed. It showed a snowy landscape, with a small house in the background and a man standing beside it.

"Are you off your head, Quarles?" Henderson asked. "That's my picture."

"It is not your picture." Quarles moved quickly across to the room where Jordan had taken the Corot, went in, and came out with another picture in his hands showing the same scene. *"This* is your Corot. If you'll just lift that telephone and ring for the police, Max, I'll make sure that Mr. Scrutton stays here."

"It was a neat variation on an old trick," Quarles said. "He gained your confidence by denouncing an obvious fake, then showed the genuine Corot, and then substituted the copy. Max being there was a stroke of luck for him, because his authentication left you without the shadow of a doubt. You wouldn't have bothered about any further examination, would you?"

A chastened Henderson shook his head. Van Galen said through a mouthful of caviar, "It was a very good copy. Carefully done. I should have needed a close examination to be sure about it."

"That's what I don't understand," Henderson said hesitantly. "You knew it was a copy immediately, Quarles. That seems like magic to me. How did you do it?"

"A genuine, a perfect lobster bisque." Quarles looked at his empty plate with regret. "I knew there must be some trick involved, you see."

"So?"

"So I marked the frame of the genuine Corot on the back with a cross, while you were making your deal with Scrutton. There was no cross on the frame of the other one."

Henderson looked disappointed. "I see. Really very simple."

"But of course. Didn't I tell you it would be a simple demonstration of how to trap a crook?"

THE MAN WHO FLIM-FLAMMED
HIWASSEE COUNTY

by William M. Stephens

☐ WE DON'T GET MANY PROFESSIONAL SWINDLERS IN BALSAM Gap, and it was just my luck to get involved with a real humdinger. Kent "Parrot" Barrone was a rogue and scoundrel of the first water. He not only conned the sheriff and the judge; he conned his own lawyer—who happened to be me.

It was in 1951, not long after I'd passed the bar and hung my shingle out, when Parrot Barrone came into my office above the drugstore. As far as I know, he picked me entirely by chance. It had nothing to do with my being female. In fact, I doubt if he knew. The sign on the outside of the building gave no hint. It just read: LEE MURPHY—ATTORNEY AT LAW—UPSTAIRS.

Parrot Barrone would attract attention anywhere in rural East Tennessee because of his slick look and high-heeled cowboy boots. In Nashville, of course, you'd take him for just another musician, but Balsam Gap is a far cry from Nashville. He was slender and catlike and wore tight pants and a fancy jacket. I'm not sure where he came from. He claimed to be a Texan, and he had a Latin air, but with his talent for dialects and mimicry he could have been from anywhere. My first impression of him was that he was as phony as a three-dollar bill.

That afternoon I was typing up a will. He came up the stairs so quietly I didn't hear him coming and had no time to get into my lawyer's chair before he came through the door. Consequently, we had to go through the routine of my explaining that I was not the secretary; I was the lawyer.

We went into my tiny private office. He said, "This is all very embarrassing, Miss Murphy—I don't know where to begin." He examined his long, delicate fingers. "We were just passing through—Kathy and I—and, due to an unfortunate chain of errors, Kathy was arrested on suspicion of passing bad checks."

I nodded sagely. "How big were the checks, and who cashed them?"

"One was for seventy-five dollars and one was for fifty. We stopped last night at the Limestone Bluff Court. Kathy cashed a check at the gift shop, and another this morning at the office. After we left we had car trouble and had to get a wrecker to tow us to a garage. The sheriff arrested Kathy there and impounded our new Packard convertible."

I made little sounds of sympathy. "You picked the wrong place to pass bad checks, Mr. Barrone. The Limestone Bluff is owned by Clem Ricketts, who happens to be the sheriff's brother."

"My God!"

"Did you gas up there too?"

He nodded. "A burly man with close-cropped hair filled the tank and checked the oil."

"That was Clem. I imagine he pulled a distributor wire or something to put you out of commission while he had his brother check you out."

He shook his head ruefully. "Welcome to Tennessee, huh? So that's the way you treat tourists around here."

"That's the way *some* folks treat you when they think you're trying to take them to the cleaners. These backwoods rubes are not as dumb as they look, Mr. Barrone."

"My mistake." He looked at me speculatively. "You're not a native of this region, are you?"

"Oh, yes, indeed. I'm strictly a local yokel—born and raised in Happy Valley, way back in the sticks about ten miles from here."

"But you went to Harvard Law School?" he said, glancing at the diploma on the wall.

I nodded. "I'm still a hick, though." Pushing my chin forward, I went on, "Suppose you level with me, Mr. Barrone. How many worthless checks is the sheriff apt to come up with if he keeps your car in hock and your wife in jail for a few days while he investigates?"

"Oh, you misjudge me," he said with a pained expression. "What do you take me for?"

I smiled. "You look like a client to me. But if you want me to represent you, I need to know all the facts."

"Of course," he said earnestly. "Let me explain how this preposterous situation came about."

"That would be nice."

"Kathy and I are on our honeymoon."

"Congratulations. I hope you'll be very happy."

He looked at me quickly, then went on. "Before we were married, Kathy had her checking account at the Bank of Houston. But since I was a director of the Oilman's National, she closed out her account. This week, however, due to the excitement of our honeymoon trip and the news that Kathy's mother has been critically injured in an accident so that we had to change plans suddenly and head for the hospital she's in in Birmingham—" He paused to take a deep breath. "Kathy's a very delicate girl. She tends to lose her equilibrium under strain. In her anxiety, she completely forgot she had closed out her checking account. So—" he shrugged "—in all innocence, she wrote those checks."

"Sounds reasonable," I said charitably. "However, writing a check on a nonexistent account is a felony in this state."

He slumped in his chair.

"This is more serious than I thought. I assumed we could simply make restitution."

"Well, restitution would help," I said. "If the checks were paid off, the attorney general might agree to reduce the charge to a misdemeanor. Your wife might get off with a fine."

He bit his lip. "How much money are we talking about?"

"It's hard to say. The fine could be hundreds of dollars. The checks come to a hundred and twenty-five. Getting her out on bond will be expensive too. How much is the bond?"

"They haven't set one."

I shook my head. "I figured as much—but we can force them to. Since you're a transient, however, no bondsman in this county will touch you. You may have to post a cash bond."

He sighed. "In addition to the towing charge on the car, a repair bill, and a hotel bill at the Daniel Boone, where I just checked in."

"Also," I said, "if you'll forgive my mentioning it, your attorney's fee."

"Yes, of course." He shrugged helplessly. "At the moment my fluid resources are severely limited."

"What about this bank you're director of? Can't you get some help there?"

Frowning, he said, "Unfortunately, we had a shakeup at the bank. I resigned and withdrew my funds. Most of my assets are now in gold and oil stocks. It will take a day or two to come up with cash."

"I'll need a hundred dollars as a retainer," I said. "Cash. If you want me to get a bond set and start negotiations with the attorney general—"

"My dear lady," he said, "I will definitely pay your fee. My father is quite wealthy."

"Would you like to telephone him and reverse the charges?"

"I've already tried. He's off hunting tigers in Nepal. I have other possibilities, but it will take a little while."

"Well, I've got to have a retainer, and I don't take checks." I was sick and tired of working for nothing and was damned if I'd let this smoothie talk me out of my fee.

He smiled. "I understand. How about a twenty-dollar gold piece? Hey, there's one!" Opening his eyes wide and reaching out to a point near my left ear, he produced a gold coin out of the air. Or so it seemed.

"How did you do that?"

He took my hand and pressed the coin gently into the palm. His hands were remarkably soft. "I created it," he said, "out of the rich energy lodes in your lovely aura."

I examined the coin. "It looks real."

"It *is* real. Whoops, there's another one coming out of the other ear." Reaching, he plucked another gold piece out of the air.

"Don't stop now," I said. "Between your magic fingers and my rich aura, we can make a fortune. First my fee; then the bad checks; then—Acapulco."

He laughed. "I wish it were that simple. Unfortunately, it takes a lot of energy to make gold. About two coins a day is my limit." He took my hand and pressed the second coin into my palm. "Take my advice," he said, "and keep these in a safe place—after the government takes the ceiling off gold prices they may be worth a hundred dollars each."

"But it's against the law to keep gold."

"Technically." He shrugged. "You're the lawyer. Would you rather wait until I have currency?"

"No. I'll hold onto these until you redeem them with long green."

"Fine. But don't leave them lying around. Put them in a safe place."

I nodded and pulled out the bottom drawer in my desk. Placing the coins in my cash box, I wrote him a receipt while he watched with a funny kind of smile.

"Now," he said, "what I want you to do first is get a writ of habeas corpus. Kathy is being held for investigation with no formal charges. Let's force them either to release her or to set a reasonable bond."

I looked at him in surprise. "That's exactly what I planned to do. How do you know so much about habeas corpus?"

Waving a hand carelessly, he said, "I went to law school for a while, before Dad talked me into studying geology. He thought geology would be more valuable in our business. He heads Barrone Oil Wells, Limited."

"Good for him. O.K., Mr. Barrone. I'll draw up a petition this afternoon and see if the judge will schedule a hearing for tomorrow morning. Then we'll find out what kind of case the prosecutor has."

He nodded. "Time is of the essence."

"Absolutely." Giving him a sideways glance I said, "Just in case there *might* be some other checks floating around, we'd better get Kathy out on bond before the attorney general's office is deluged by bad paper."

"My sentiments exactly, ma'am." He smiled. "You're very perceptive, Miss Murphy. I knew in a flash today that you should be our lawyer. I have certain psychic abilities, as you may have suspected."

"Do you really?" I said innocently. "How *did* you happen to come to me? I'm curious."

"Elementary, my dear. I simply looked in the yellow pages under Attorneys, then closed my eyes and moved my hand slowly across the page. A special vibration told me you were the one."

"I don't know whether to believe you or not."

He held up his right hand. "God's truth. Already my intuition has been confirmed. I can tell from your deep blue eyes that you are intelligent, warm, and compassionate." He placed the tips of his fingers lightly on my arm and stared intently at me. "I can sense," he said slowly, his voice vibrant, "that you have great empathy for people. You *will* help me . . . you *want* to help me . . . and you will be richly rewarded for doing so."

His eyes were hypnotic and his voice made me feel strange. With an effort I turned my head away.

"Perhaps you'll have dinner with me tonight," he said softly.

I was tempted—he had a certain charm, even if he was a crook and a bounder. I don't meet many interesting men in Balsam Gap. But there was something in his eyes that disturbed me. Besides, he was a paying client—and a married man.

"No," I said. "I have to start earning my fee and get your wife out of jail. But since you don't have transportation, I'll give you a ride to the Daniel Boone. Telephone me in a few hours and I'll tell you when the hearing is scheduled."

We went down the steps and through the alley to the back of the building where I parked my 1941 Studebaker. "Since you're accustomed to touring in a Packard convertible," I said, "I hope you won't mind slumming for a few blocks."

"Not at all," he said. "Actually, this is quite nice."

"I use it only for driving back and forth to court," I said facetiously, glancing at the courthouse directly across the street from my office.

But Parrot Barrone was absorbed in his thoughts and failed to catch my little joke.

The writ of habeas corpus, Blackstone said, is the greatest protection the common man has under the common law. In America today, just as in England five hundred years ago, it safeguards the individual against flagrant abuse of police power. And also, of course, it sometimes allows a scoundrel to beat the system.

Habeas corpus gives a confined person an absolute right to have a judicial inquiry into the legality of his imprisonment. This means that no one can be held under an "open" charge or "for investigation." Not for long, anyway, if he can get word to a lawyer or even smuggle a note to a judge, who has a sworn duty to honor the application and order a prompt hearing.

Besides these advantages, the writ is the criminal lawyer's best friend. At a habeas corpus hearing, the accused has everything to gain and nothing to lose. He can find out everything about the prosecutor's case without tipping his own hand.

The hearing was held in Judge Lively's courtroom. Sheriff Rex Ricketts brought Kathy Barrone over from the jail and she took a seat beside her husband and me. The sheriff and the attorney general sat at the other counsel table. Kathy had long black hair and flashing eyes. She didn't look delicate or frail to me. In fact, I'd bet she could pin Parrot two falls out of three. I didn't sense as much affection between them as I'd expect to find between honeymooners who had been forced to spend the night in separate beds. But maybe they had other things on their minds.

Judge Lively rapped his gavel. "All right, let's get started. This is a hearing in the matter of Kent Barrone and wife Kathy Fernandez Barrone versus Rex Ricketts, sheriff of Hiwassee County. Let's hear from the petitioners." He nodded to me.

"If the court please," I said, "I represent the petitioners. Your honor, these young people, while passing through Hiwassee County, were seized and deprived of their liberty and their property without due process of law. Mrs. Barrone has been locked up without a charge being filed and without being taken before a magistrate. This is an outrage, your honor, inflicted on two citizens who have a compelling need to be on their way."

The judge nodded, then looked at Rufus Haggle. "All right, Mr. Attorney General."

Haggle stood up and arched his back to look down his long nose at Parrot and Kathy. "Yes, they *do* have compelling reasons to get out of this county as quickly as possible." With a dry chuckle, he turned back to the bench. "Your honor, we've had a plague of bad checks these past few months. All up and down the John Sevier Highway, people in big touring cars have been stopping at roadside stands and tourist courts to pass bum checks. It's getting so the local folks are losing their faith in the Golden Rule.

They help the tourists out and get slapped in the face for their trouble."

"If the court please, your honor," I interrupted, "we're not here for a morality lecture. My clients have been deprived of—"

"You made your little speech and I'm making mine," snapped Rufus Haggle.

"All right, all right," said the judge, "but get on with it. What kind of charges are you making against these petitioners?"

With a brief smile, the attorney general opened his file and withdrew two oblong slips of paper. "Here are two checks, your honor, dated November seventeenth, written on the Bank of Houston, in Texas, in the amounts of seventy-five and fifty dollars. They are signed by K. Fernandez, which we understand is an alias of Kathy Barrone."

"We object, your honor. It's not an alias. It's her maiden name."

The judge nodded. "She did write these checks, then? You admit that?"

"With all due respect, your honor," I said, "it's not incumbent on Mrs. Barrone to admit *or* deny anything at this point. No legal charge has been made. No prima facie case has been established. If the attorney general intends to use those checks as evidence of some kind of wrongdoing, he must first establish that a crime has been committed, and secondly that there is reason to believe Mrs. Barrone is the person who committed it."

"What about that, Mr. Attorney General?" the judge said. "Let's hear your proof."

Haggle hesitated, then nodded brusquely. "Take the stand, Sheriff."

After being sworn, Sheriff Ricketts testified he had received a call from his brother at the Limestone Bluff Court. "He said a couple of suspicious characters had passed some—"

"We object," I said. "Hearsay."

"Sustained."

"Let me ask you this, Sheriff," said Haggle. "Please state whether or not you acted upon information received from your brother, and subsequently apprehended these suspects?"

"Yes, I did. It seems they had a slight problem in the distributor of their Packard—" he hid a grin behind his hand "—and they got towed in. I found them at Watkins' garage and showed them the checks. The lady admitted—"

"Objection! Also hearsay," I said.

"Overruled. An admission against interest is an exception to the hearsay rule, as you well know, counselor." Turning to the sheriff, he asked, "Did she admit she'd signed and passed the checks?"

"She sure did, Judge."

Judge Lively compressed his lips. "Anything else from this witness, General?"

Rufus Haggle, glancing through his file, looked up. "I think that's all, your honor."

"Cross-examine," said the judge.

"Sheriff," I said, walking toward the witness stand, "let me see those checks." He handed them over and I examined them, front and back. "What's wrong with them, Sheriff? Why do you call them bad checks?"

He darted a glance at the attorney general, then said, "They're no good. They're not worth the paper they're written on. That's what's wrong with them."

"How can you tell?" I asked innocently. "They look perfectly good to me." With a perplexed expression, I handed them to the judge, who frowned as he turned them over in his hands.

"They've never even been presented for payment," he said. "How can you make an arrest for passing worthless checks when the checks haven't yet been refused by the bank?"

The sheriff glanced again at Haggle. "Well, I telephoned Houston, Judge, and they told me at the bank that—"

"I object!" I said. "You can't tell what they told you, Sheriff. That's *clearly* hearsay, your honor."

"I'm well aware of that, counselor." Turning to the witness, the judge said, "You can't relate the telephone conversation."

Glaring at me, the sheriff said, "But that's how I know the checks are bad."

"You *don't* know they're bad," I said. "That's your problem. You don't know, of your own knowledge, anything about Kathy Barrone's dealings with the Bank of Houston, do you?"

"No, but—"

"That's all. Step down," I said.

"Any other witnesses for the respondent?"

Rufus Haggle stood. "Not at this time, your honor."

The judge rubbed his chin and frowned. Beckoning with both hands, he said, "Approach the bench, General. You too, counselor."

We went up to the bench and the judge said, in a low voice, "Rufus, is that all you've got to hold the lady on?"

"That's all I've got at this moment, Judge, but in a day or two we'll have more. They fit the description of a couple who've passed beaucoup checks in Boone and Watauga Counties. Also, the woman is believed to have bilked a bank in Kingsport of five hundred dollars."

"She passed a bad check at a *bank?*"

"A male confederate made a phone call impersonating the president of the bank. It fooled the cashier and he gave her the money. They're real flim-flam artists, Judge. That's why we're trying to tie them up while we get all our ducks in a row."

"Well," I said, "while you're getting your ducks in a row, General, you're violating the constitutional rights of my clients. Your honor, you heard the so-called evidence against these people. The State's case is a travesty. They've got absolutely nothing on Mr. and Mrs. Barrone. They have already had their honeymoon interrupted by this farce, and they need to get to Birmingham to see Mrs. Barrone's mother, who is critically ill."

"Well, she *is* entitled to bond," said the judge. "Rufus,

have you personally contacted the bank in Houston to see if they're holding a bale of bad checks written by these two?"

"No, I haven't, your honor. As you know, that information wouldn't be admissible unless we got a bank official up here and—"

"Who's talking about admissibility? Damn it, Rufus, at least we'd *know*. Right now we don't know pea turkey, and I'm gonna have to release that woman unless you make a charge. You got to fish or cut bait, buddy."

"All right." Haggle spoke through tight lips. "We'll charge her on two counts of passing worthless checks and see what else crops up. Two thousand dollars bond."

"One thousand," I said. "Those two checks only come to a hundred and twenty-five dollars."

The judge nodded. "I think a thousand is enough. Can they make it?"

"I don't know," I said. "Possibly. Also, I want their car released."

The attorney general shook his head. "Judge, we think that car is stolen. There are papers in the glove compartment in the name of one William D. Walker. We think—"

"Wait a minute!" I said. "Did you have a search warrant when you went rummaging through the car?"

He glared at me without answering.

"Damn it," I said, "you know you needed a warrant to search that car. Anything you found will be inadmissible."

"What the hell's the difference?" he said. "As soon as we get the F.B.I. report, we'll have plenty of corroborating evidence." Flushing angrily, he said, "I'm not going to release that car, Judge. Not unless you order me to."

The judge nodded. "You've got till noon tomorrow to make a case on the car. Otherwise, you'll have to release it."

Haggle smiled. "That's fine. By tomorrow a federal lien is liable to be slapped on that car for a charge of transporting a stolen automobile across a state line."

"*If* the car is stolen," I said.

* * *

So that was the way the judge left it, and I was satisfied with the outcome. The sheriff took Kathy back to jail and Parrot Barrone walked back to my office with me. He was jubilant and had a strange, wild look in his eyes.

"I can get a thousand dollars easy," he said, "by telephoning my dad's office. Also—" he raised his eyebrows "—I'll get an extra hundred for you, for doing such a great job."

"That would be nice," I said.

"If you'll let me use the telephone in your office, I'll make a collect call and get the money wired to me right away."

"Be my guest," I said, ushering him into the office. Then, while he closed the door and made his call, I caught up on my filing.

He came out with a grin a yard wide. "Success!" he said. "They're sending enough to cover everything. I'll pick up the money at Western Union late this afternoon."

"Wonderful!"

"As soon as it arrives I'll settle up with you and post Kathy's bond. Then perhaps you'll join us for dinner tonight?"

"I'd love to."

He gave my hand a warm squeeze and said, "See you later, Lee. Will you be here in the office all afternoon?"

"Till five, at least," I said. "Call me when you know something."

"Of course." He winked. *"Adios, señorita."*

I worked all afternoon, typing up a couple of title abstracts, pausing occasionally to gloat over the way the hearing had gone. I was delighted to have earned a nice fee on a walk-in case. If I could get one like it every week or so, I'd soon be in clover.

Thinking back over it, I decided my initial impression of Parrot had been harsh and judgmental. Maybe he *was* a crook, but he operated with verve and charm. And quite possibly he *wasn't* a crook. Who was I to say? In any event, he was entitled to legal counsel. I was a lawyer, not a moralist.

About five-thirty, I decided to lock up. Parrot still hadn't called, so I assumed it had taken longer than he'd anticipated for the people at the other end to get the cash together. The money would surely arrive by morning.

I opened my purse to get my keys. They weren't there. I stood there, puzzled. I'd had the keys when we got back from court. I'd unlocked the outer door and then dropped the keys into my purse, which had been on my desk all afternoon.

A chill went through my heart. Parrot! He'd been in my office with the door closed. Quickly I yanked the bottom drawer open and looked in the cash box. Empty. Cleaned out. The two gold pieces were gone, plus forty dollars and some change. Another twelve dollars had been taken from my purse.

Furious with myself for being so trusting, I ran down the steps and around the building. My car was gone. In a black, seething rage, I stalked into Sheriff Rex Ricketts' office next door.

Rex was reading the Balsam Gap *Bugle,* his feet propped on the desk. He glanced up at me, then put his feet down. "What in the world is wrong, Lee?" he said with concern.

"That carpetbagging reprobate!" I sputtered. "That depraved scalawag! That oily-tongued hustler! Rex, I want to swear out a warrant against Parrot Barrone."

"Parrot Barrone?" he said, astonished. "But he's your client."

"*Was* my client. That no-account swindler took my car and all the cash I had. I want him, Rex—" I pounded the desk "—I *want* him!" Then came a sudden thought. "And you'd better make sure his wife is still in her cell. I wouldn't put anything past those two flim-flammers."

The sheriff had a funny look on his face. "Why, she's been gone since noon, Lee. Didn't you know?"

"Are you serious? Since *noon?* How in the—? You mean Parrot posted bond?"

"Why, no. The judge said he didn't need to. After the hearing this morning—right after I brought Kathy back to the jail—Judge Lively called me on the telephone and said he'd reconsidered. Said he'd decided to release Kathy on her own recognizance."

"Her own *recognizance?*" Bewildered, I shook my head. That didn't sound like Judge Lively. He'd have told me first, wouldn't he? Then I thought about the phone call Parrot had made from my private office and I felt the blood drain from my face. "Oh, my God," I said, sitting down. "Rex, what time did the judge call you?"

"Lemme check the log. Here it is. Eleven-forty-two, only a few minutes after we got back from the courthouse. Right after I hung up from talking with the judge, Parrot Barrone walked in and said the judge had sent him over to get Kathy. So I signed her out, naturally."

"Naturally," I said in a tiny voice. "We've been had, Rex. You and the judge and me and everybody." I released my breath in a long, hoarse sigh. "We'd better get the judge on the phone."

Sitting down to dial, I closed my eyes for a long moment and wondered why I hadn't gone into teaching like my mother wanted me to.

Well, Parrot had indeed conned us all. He'd imitated the judge's voice so well that the sheriff had been completely fooled. Later, after rehashing the whole mess, I concluded that Parrot had planned from the beginning to spring Kathy with a phone call, but he needed an opportunity to listen to Judge Lively's voice. That was why he wanted the hearing. He was a master of voice mimicry. And he'd had to work fast, before the sheriff got an F.B.I. report on him. If he couldn't get the Packard out of hock, he'd take my car, which I'd very conveniently pointed out to him. The Packard wasn't his anyway, we learned. He was wanted in California, Arizona, and Nevada for larceny, embezzlement, bank fraud, larceny by trick, impersonating a bank officer, forgery, and even practicing medicine without a license. As far as the record showed he'd never been to Texas.

The Boone county police found my Studebaker, none the worse for wear, at the Booneville Airport. Parrot and Kathy had caught a plane for Charlotte, and there the trail turned cold.

The next day I received a postcard from Charlotte.

"Dear Miss Murphy, Thanks for letting me borrow your car, and for all your help. We really are grateful, and I'll pay your fee in full the next time I strike oil. Kathy sends her best. Don't take any wooden nickels. Love, Parrot."

Strange as it seems, he did eventually pay my fee, and in a totally unexpected way. But that's another story.

THE PARTNERSHIP

by David Morrell

☐ SURE, IT WAS COLD-BLOODED, BUT THERE DIDN'T SEEM ANOTHER way. MacKenzie had spent months considering alternatives. He'd tried to buy his partner out but Dolan had refused.

Well, not exactly. Dolan's first response had simply been to laugh and say, "I wouldn't let you have the satisfaction." When MacKenzie kept insisting, Dolan's next response was, "Sure I'll let you buy me out. It only takes a million dollars."

Dolan might as well have wanted ten. MacKenzie couldn't raise a million, even half a million or a quarter— and he knew Dolan knew that.

It was typical. MacKenzie couldn't say "Good morning" without Dolan's disagreeing. If MacKenzie bought a car, Dolan bought a bigger, more expensive one and, just to rub it in, bragged about the deal he got. If MacKenzie took his wife and children on vacation to Bermuda, Dolan told him that Bermuda wasn't anything compared to Mazatlan, where Dolan had taken his wife and kids.

The two men argued constantly. They favored different football teams. Their taste in food was wildly different— mutton versus corned beef. When MacKenzie took up golf, Dolan suddenly was playing tennis, pointing out that golf was just a game while tennis was good exercise. But Dolan, even with his so-called exercise, was overweight. Mac-

Kenzie, on the other hand, was trim, but Dolan always made remarks about the hairpiece MacKenzie wore.

It was impossible—a Scotsman trying to maintain a business with an Irishman. MacKenzie should have known their relationship would never work. At the start, they had been rival builders, each attempting to outbid the other for construction jobs and losing money in the process. So they'd formed a partnership. Together they were more successful than they had been independently. Trying to outdo each other, one would think of ways to turn a greater profit and the other would feel challenged to be twice as clever. They cut costs by mixing too much gravel with the concrete, by installing low-grade pipes and sub-spec insulation. They kept special books for Uncle Sam.

MacKenzie-Dolan Enterprises. The two of them were enterprising, all right, but they couldn't bear to talk to one another. They had tried to solve that problem by dividing the work so that MacKenzie ran the office and let Dolan go out troubleshooting.

For a time that did the trick. But they still had to meet to make decisions and though they were seeing each other less, they seemed to save their tension up and aggravate each other more when they met.

To make things worse, their wives became good friends. The women were constantly organizing barbecues and swimming parties. The men tried not to argue at these get-togethers. When they did, they heard about it from their wives.

"I hate the guy," MacKenzie would tell his wife after a party. "He bugs me at the office and he made me sick tonight."

"You just listen to me, Bob—Vickie Dolan is my friend and I won't have your childish antics breaking up our friendship. I'll sleep on the couch tonight."

So both men braced themselves while their wives exchanged recipes.

What finally caused the big trouble was when Dolan started making threats.

"I wonder what the government would do if they knew about your special way of keeping books."

"What about the sub-spec plumbing and the extra gravel in the concrete?" MacKenzie had replied. "You're responsible for that, Dolan."

"But that's not a criminal offense—the judge would simply fine me," Dolan answered. "The IRS is quite a different kettle. If they knew you were keeping separate books, they'd lock you in a dungeon where I'd never have to see your ugly puss again."

MacKenzie stared at Dolan and decided there was no other choice. He'd tried to do the right thing, but his partner wouldn't sell. There wasn't any way around it. This was self-defense.

The man was waiting at the monkey cage, a tall, thin, friendly-looking fellow, young and blond. He wore a tailored light-blue jogging suit and he was eating peanuts.

At the water fountain, bending down to drink, MacKenzie glanced around. The zoo was crowded. It was noon on a sunny weekday, and people on their lunch breaks sat on benches munching sandwiches or strolled among the cages. There were children, mothers, old folks playing checkers. He heard tinny music from an organ grinder, muffled conversations, strident chattering and chirping. He was satisfied that no one was paying any attention to him, so he wiped water from his mouth and walked over.

"Mr. Smith?" he said.

The young man didn't turn—he just chewed another peanut—and MacKenzie was afraid he'd spoken to the wrong man. After all, the zoo was crowded and there were other men in jogging suits. Besides, no matter what the papers said, it wasn't easy finding someone who would do this kind of work. MacKenzie had spent several evenings haunting low-life bars before getting a lead. Once someone thought he was a cop and threatened to break both his legs. But hundred-dollar bills had eventually paid off and at last he'd arranged this meeting on a pay phone. But the man, apparently afraid of a trap, either had not arrived for the appointment or was playing possum.

As MacKenzie moved to leave, the young blond fellow turned to him. "Just a second, Bob," he said.

MacKenzie blinked. "Your name is Smith?"

"Just call me John." The young man's smile was brilliant. He was holding out the bag. "You want a peanut?"

"No, I don't think so—"

"Go on and have a peanut, Bob." The young man gestured with the bag.

MacKenzie took a peanut. He ate it, but he didn't taste it.

"That's right, relax, live a little. You don't mind if I call you Bob?"

"I don't care what you call me as long as we get this matter settled. You're not quite what I expected."

The young man nodded. "You were counting on George Raft and instead you got Troy Donohue. I know it's disappointing." He was frowning sympathetically. "But nothing's what it seems today. Would you believe I was a business major? But with the recession I couldn't get a job in management, so I'm doing this."

"You mean you're not experienced?"

"Take it easy, Bob. I didn't say that. I can handle my end. Don't you fret about a thing. You see these monkeys? Just watch this." He threw some peanuts. All the monkeys scrambled, fighting for them.

"See—they're just like us, Bob. We're all scrambling for the peanuts."

"Well, I'm sure that's very symbolic—"

"All right, you're impatient. I'm just trying to be sociable." He sighed. "No one takes the time any more. So what's your problem, Bob?"

"My business partner."

"Is he stealing from the kitty?"

"No."

"He's fooling with your wife then?"

"No."

The young man nodded. "I understand."

"You do?"

"Of course. It's very simple. What I call the marriage syndrome."

"What?"

"It's like you're married to your partner, but you hate him and he won't agree to get divorced."

"Why, that's incredible!"

"Excuse me?"

"You're right. That's it."

The young man shrugged and threw a peanut. "Bob, I've seen it all. My specialty is human nature. So you don't care how I do it?"

"Just as long as it's—"

"An accident. Precisely. You recall my price when we discussed this on the phone?"

"Two thousand dollars."

"Half now, half later. Did you bring the money?"

"It's in my pocket."

"Don't give it to me yet. Go over and put the envelope inside that waste container. In a moment I'll walk over and stuff this empty bag in. When I leave I'll take the envelope."

"His name is Patrick Dolan."

"The particulars are with the money?"

"As you asked."

"Then don't worry. I'll be in touch."

"Hey, wait a minute. Afterward, I don't have any guarantee that—"

"Blackmail? You're afraid I'll extort you? Bob, I'm surprised at you! That wouldn't be good business!"

Dolan walked out of the hardware store. The afternoon was glaring hot. He wiped his brow and squinted. There was someone in his pickup truck, a young guy eating corn chips. Blond, good-looking, in a jogging suit.

He stalked across the parking lot, reached the truck, and yanked open the door. "Hey, buddy, this is my truck you're—"

The young man turned. His smile was disarming. "Hi there, Pat. You want some corn chips?"

Dolan's mouth hung open. Sweat was trickling from his forehead. "What?"

"The way you're sweating, you need salt. Have some corn chips."

Dolan's jaw went rigid. "Out!"

"Excuse me?"

"Get out before I throw you out."

The young man sighed. Tugging down the zipper on his sweatshirt, he revealed the big revolver bulging from a shoulder holster.

Dolan's stomach lurched. He blanched and stumbled backward, gaping.

"What the—?"

"Just relax," the young man said.

"Look, buddy, all I've got is twenty dollars."

"You don't understand. Climb on up here and we'll talk a little."

Dolan glanced around in panic. No one seemed to notice him. He wondered if he ought to run.

"Don't try to run, Pat."

Relieved of that decision, Dolan quickly climbed inside the truck. He ate the corn chips the blond offered a second time but he couldn't taste the salt. His shirt was sticking to the back of the seat. All he could think of was the bulging object underneath the jogging suit.

"Here's the thing," the young man told him. "I'm supposed to kill you."

Dolan sat up so hard he bumped his head against the ceiling. "What?"

"Your partner hired me. For two thousand dollars."

"If this is a joke—"

"It's business, Pat. He paid a thousand down. You want to see it?"

"But that's crazy!"

"I wish you hadn't said that." The young man reached inside his sweatshirt.

"No, wait a minute! I didn't mean that!"

"I only want to show the note your partner gave me. Here. You'll recognize his handwriting."

Dolan glared down at the note. "It's my name and address."

"And your physical description and your habits. See, he wants your death to seem like an accident."

Dolan finally accepted this wasn't any joke. His stomach burned with sudden rage. "That dirty—"

"Temper, Pat."

"He wants to buy me out—but I won't let him have the satisfaction!"

"I understand. It's like the two of you are married and you want to make him suffer."

"You're damn right I want to make him suffer! I've put up with him for twenty years! So now he figures he can have me killed and take the business for himself? That sneaky, rotten—"

"Bob, I've got bad news for you."

MacKenzie almost spilled his Scotch. He turned. The young man had come up beside him without warning and was eating popcorn at the bar.

"Don't tell me you botched the job!" MacKenzie's eyes went wide with horror. He glanced quickly around as if expecting to be arrested.

"Bob, I never even got the chance to start." The young man picked at something in his teeth.

"My God, what happened?"

"Nearly broke a tooth. These kernels aren't all popped."

"I meant with Dolan!"

"Keep your voice down, Bob. I know you meant with him. No one cares if someone else breaks a tooth. They only care about themselves. Do you believe in competition?"

"What?"

"Do you support free enterprise, the thing that made this country great?"

MacKenzie felt his knees go weak. He clutched the bar and nodded weakly.

"Then you'll understand. When I went to see your partner—"

"Oh, my God, you *told* him!"

"Bob, I couldn't simply kill him and not let him have a chance to make a bid. That wouldn't be fair."

MacKenzie started trembling. "Bid? What kind of bid?"

"Don't get excited, Bob. We figured he could pay me not to kill him. But you'd just send someone else. So what we finally decided was that he'd pay me to come back and kill you. He offered double—two grand now and two when you were shoveled under."

"He can't do that!"

"But he did, Bob. Don't go simple on me now. You should have seen his face. I mean to tell you, he was angry."

"You accepted what *I* offered! You agreed to take *my* contract!"

"A verbal contract isn't binding. Anyhow, you're in a seller's market. What I'm selling is worth more now."

"You're a crook!"

The young man's face looked pained. "I'm sorry you feel that way."

"No, wait. Don't leave. I didn't mean it."

"Bob, you hurt my feelings."

"I apologize. I don't know what I'm saying. Every time I think about that guy—"

"I understand, Bob. You're forgiven."

"Pat, you'll never guess what Bob did."

At the railing, Dolan shuddered. He was watching as the horses thundered toward the finish line. He turned. The young man stood beside him, chewing on a hot dog.

"You don't mean you told him?"

"Pat, I had to. Fair is fair. He offered double our agreement. Four grand now, four later."

"And you've come to me to raise the price?"

"They're at the stretch!" the track announcer shouted.

"It's inflation, Pat. It's killing us." The young man wiped some mustard from his lips.

"You think I'm stupid?" Dolan asked.

The young man frowned.

"That I'm a moron?" Dolan said.

"Excuse me, Pat?"

"If I pay more, you'll go to him and *he'll* pay more. Then you'll come back to me and *I'll* pay more. Forget it! I'm not paying!"

"Fine with me, Pat. Nice to see you."

"Wait a minute!"

"Is something wrong?"

"Of course there's something wrong! You're going to kill me!"

"Well, the choice is up to you."

"The winner is number three, Big Trouble—" the track announcer shouted.

Horses rumbled by, their jockeys standing up to slow them. Dust was drifting.

"Damn it, yes. I'll pay you," Dolan muttered. "But do it this time! I can't sleep. I'm losing weight. I've got an ulcer."

"Pat, the race is over. Did you have a bet?"

"On number six to win."

"A nag, Pat. She came in last. If you had asked me, I'd have told you number three."

"You'll never guess what Pat did, Bob."

MacKenzie stiffened. Dolan stopped beside him, looked around and sighed, then sat down on the park bench. "So you figured you'd have me killed," Dolan said.

MacKenzie's face was gaunt. "You weren't above the same temptation yourself."

Dolan shrugged. "Self-defense."

"I should sit back while you sic the IRS on me?"

"That was just a joke."

"Some joke. It's costing me a fortune."

"It's costing me too."

"We've got a problem."

"I've been thinking," Dolan said. "The only answer I can see—"

"—is for both of us to kill him."

"Only way."

"He'll bleed us dry."

"But if we pay someone else to kill him, the new guy might try something cute too."

"We'll do it together. That way you can't point the blame at me."

"Or vice versa."

"What's the matter? Don't you trust me?"

They were glaring at each other.

"Hi there, Bob. How are you, Pat?"

The young man smiled from behind their files. He was munching a taco as he went through their records.

"What the hell is this now?" MacKenzie said.

"He claimed you expected him," the secretary said.

"Just shut the door," Dolan told her.

"Hey, fellas, your records really are a mess. This skimping on the concrete. And this sub-spec insulation. I don't know, guys—we've got lots of work ahead of us."

A drop of taco sauce fell on a file folder.

"*Us?*"

"Well, sure—we're partners now."

"We're *what?*"

"I took the money you gave me and invested it."

"In what?"

"Insurance. You remember how I said I was a business major? Well, I decided this sideline doesn't suit me, so I went to see a specialist. The things a graduate is forced to do to get a job these days!"

"A specialist?"

"A hit man. If the two of you decide to have me killed, you'll be killed as well."

MacKenzie's chest began to stab. Dolan's ulcer started burning.

"So we're partners. Here, I even had some cards made up."

He handed one across to each of them. MACKENZIE-DOLAN-SMITH, it read. And at the bottom: CONTRACTORS.

BREAD UPON THE WATERS

by Robert Edward Eckels

◻ THE FIRST TIME I MET THE MAJOR I WAS IN JAIL, SERVING OUT a $100 fine for disturbing the peace at the time-honored rate of $1 a day. I understand inflation has played havoc with that as it has with all things these days, and the judges now trade the time you have for the money you haven't at the rate of $3 or even $4 a day. But be that as it may, it was $1 a day then. And by my reckoning I still had 72 days to go when the turnkey lumbered down the corridor, unlocked my cell, and jerked his thumb up to motion me to my feet.

"Vacation's over," he said. "It's back to the cold cruel world for you."

"Now?" I said. "Just when the chef is learning to make hash the way I like it?"

The turnkey gave me a sour look. "You want to lay there and crack wise," he said, "or do you want to get out?"

I really didn't have to give that much thought. "I want to get out," I said.

I was curious, though, and at the entrance to the cell block I asked the bored clerk who passed over the envelope containing my meager personal possessions, "How come I'm being sprung?"

"Ask the man at the front desk," he said without looking up.

Which I did. "Your fine's been paid," he said. "By your

friend over there," he added, nodding his head to indicate a short barrel-chested man with a square ruddy face, full gray mustache, and close-cropped hair of the same gray color. The man was standing near the door.

His face lit up as soon as he caught me looking at him curiously, and he advanced with his hand outstretched to grasp mine. "Ah, James," he said. "Thought I recognized you from your picture. Sorry not to have got here sooner, but I only just learned your whereabouts this morning. Still, better late than never, eh?"

"If you say so," I said, "although—"

"I have the advantage of you, eh? Of course. But let me rectify that." He drew himself to his full five-foot-five and thrust out his chest even farther. "Major Henry T. McDonlevy, late U.S. Army. And the world's greatest adjutant until some bureaucratic mixup got me passed over for promotion and forced my retirement. Still," he added cheerfully, "the Army's loss is your gain. Because if I hadn't retired I wouldn't have been your fellow lodger at Mrs. Peters' and therefore wouldn't have heard about your plight."

"Yes," I said, "that's all very interesting. But—"

"But you don't want to hang around a jailhouse discussing it. Of course not." He took my arm and guided me out through the double doors. "On a beautiful day like this," he went on, "a young man—and even an old one—can find better things to do."

I let him take me a couple of steps down the street. Then I carefully disengaged my arm. "I don't want to appear ungrateful," I said, "but I can't help wondering just why you'd plunk down $100 for a total stranger, fellow lodger or not."

The Major's face sobered and he nodded thoughtfully. "Yes," he said, "I suppose it does seem a little odd. But," he continued, taking my arm again and pulling me with him down the street, "you see, my boy, I try to guide my life by the Good Book."

"You mean 'Do unto others' and that sort of thing?" I asked.

"No," the Major said, dragging the word out. "As a matter of fact, I had a different text in mind. Ecclesiastes ten, twenty: 'Cast thy bread upon the waters.' "

"Now," I said, "I do see. But if you're looking for a thousandfold return from me, I'm afraid you're in for a disappointment. If I had any money, Major, or any prospects of getting any, I'd have paid that fine myself."

"I think you'll find the exact text is 'for thou shalt find it after many days,' " the Major said unperturbed. "Although I must admit most people would have it your way and I myself have found that my investments generally result in a tidy profit.

"As for your prospects. Well"—he coughed delicately into his cupped hand—"I'm afraid I overstated the case somewhat when I said we were fellow lodgers. Actually, I rented your room after you—ah—vacated it. Apparently, however, the postman wasn't aware of the change and this morning he delivered this."

He took an envelope from his breast pocket and handed it to me. "I'm afraid I opened it—inadvertently, of course, before I noticed the name of the addressee."

"Of course," I said drily, opening the letter. It was three months old, having kicked around a bit before catching up with me, and it was clearly addressed to Thomas James.

"Dear Mr. James (it read), I regret to inform you that your great-uncle Arthur Wallace passed away on the 15th of last month, naming you his sole heir. If you will call at my office with proper proof of identity I will arrange transfer to you of his estate, said estate consisting of 750 acres in the heart of Michigan's vacationland."

It was signed Byron Swope, Administrator of the Estate of Arthur Wallace, Appleby, Michigan.

I glanced up from reading and as my eyes met the Major's he smiled brightly. "I took the liberty of doing a little research on your behalf," he said. "And the area *is* booming, summer cottages being a big thing right at the moment."

I refolded the letter and stuck it in my pocket. "All right, Major," I said. "Fair's fair. I'll see you get your money back plus a reasonable profit."

"Fine," the Major said. He puffed out his chest and strutted along beside me. "We can discuss what constitutes 'reasonable' later, after the extent of my services has been determined. For now, though, let's concentrate on getting you to Michigan. And since one should never undertake a journey of that magnitude alone, I'll just trot along—if you don't mind."

Actually, whether I minded was something of a moot question. If I was going to get to Michigan at all, somebody was going to have to pay for the trip. And the Major was as good a prospect as any.

I'd never been to Appleby, Michigan, but I had a pretty good idea of what the town was like from my mother's description of her childhood—a wide spot on the road somewhere between Tawas and Traverse City. As far as I could tell from my admittedly limited knowledge, about the only thing that had been added since her day was a sign at the edge of town proclaiming it "The Heart of Michigan's Vacationland."

I remarked as much to the Major as we drove past in the car we'd rented when we'd found that the only public transportation north from Saginaw was a bus.

"Tush, tush, my boy," he said. "Nobody's asking you to live here. We simply realize our profit and move on to greener pastures, as agreed."

"And the sooner the better," I said, surveying the weathering storefronts that made up Main Street. The area might be booming as the Major had said, but the town certainly wasn't being ostentatious about it.

Swope's office turned out to be a narrow book-and-paper-cluttered cubicle on the second floor above the town's only restaurant. And Swope himself was a tall spare individual in his mid to late sixties with small glittering eyes in a long narrow face and a tight, almost lipless mouth.

"Well," he said, as the Major and I presented ourselves, "this *is* something of a surprise. After all these months I'd just about decided you didn't intend to claim your inheritance."

That should have alerted me. What I mean is, people just don't *not* claim inheritances. Unless, of course, there's some reason not to. But to tell the truth, in the last several days I'd sort of got used to letting the Major make the decisions. So I just stood there and let him take charge now.

"No mystery," he said bluffly. "The lad had simply moved and I didn't manage to track him down with the news until just recently."

Swope favored the Major with a long cool glance, then turned back to me. "I suppose you've brought your birth certificate," he said.

"I did," I said and passed it over.

Swope examined it briefly, then nodded. "Seems to be in order," he said. "Now, all we have to do is transfer the land formally to you. Let's see now. I've got one of those forms around here somewhere." He rummaged through his desk and the cabinets surrounding it, finally coming up with a legal-sized document which he began to fill in with a ballpoint pen, the only modern touch as far as I could see in the entire office.

"I should warn you, though," Swope said, "that this is going to cost you some money."

"I knew it," I said. I took hold of the Major's arm. "Come on, Major, Let's go."

But McDonlevy held back. "Not so fast," he said. "First let's find out how much."

"Well," Swope said, scratching behind his ear with the click button end of the ballpoint, "as I recollect, the taxes are paid through the end of this year, and there was enough in Arthur's bank account to cover my fee as administrator." His face brightened. "So all you have to pay is the standard recorder's fee of $20."

"Well," the Major said heartily, "I think we can afford that." He took two $10 bills from his wallet. "I assume we pay this to you," he said to Swope.

"That's right," Swope said, deftly lifting the bills from the Major's hand and stuffing them into his own pocket. "Among other things I'm deputy clerk of the court here and the recorder."

Swope set about finishing filling in the form, stamped it with an official-looking seal, and handed it to the Major who passed it on to me. I looked at it briefly, then folded it and put it in my coat pocket.

"Now that that's out of the way," the Major said, "my young friend and I would like to see the property. You can tell us how to find it, I assume."

"Sure," Swope said. "It's about five miles northeast of town. You can't miss it. It's the only slue land anywhere close by."

The Major looked blank. "I don't think I'm familiar with the term," he said. "Slue land?"

"I am," I said. I looked hard at Swope. "Do you mean to tell me that what I've traveled so far to inherit is nothing but a swamp?"

"Well," Swope said, " 'swamp' is probably too strong a word. But it is wet. Except in the winter, of course, when it freezes."

"Sure, though, man," the Major said, "it must be worth something?"

"It would be," Swope admitted, "if you could find a buyer. Which isn't too likely, I'm afraid, unless you can figure out how to drain it. About eight, ten years ago Arthur had some engineers up from Bay City. They said it wasn't 'feasible.' That means you can do it, but it'd cost more than the land's worth."

"I know what it means," I said. "Tell me, though, if the land's so worthless why did you bother to write me in the first place?"

"Had to," Swope said. "The law says the heir has to be notified." He smiled tightly. "I suppose I could have told you before you paid the transfer fee. But to tell the truth it never occurred to me."

"I'll bet," I said and left, followed by the Major.

"Sorry," I said to him outside, "but it looks as if you cast your bread on the wrong waters this time."

"Perhaps," he said. "But if I may mix metaphors—no battle's lost until the last shot's been fired."

"And just what shots do you plan to fire in this particular battle?"

"Who knows?" he said cheerfully. "But surely it wouldn't hurt to spend one night in the hostelry here, would it?"

I agreed it probably wouldn't. But I wasn't so sure when I saw the room they gave me. Still, I'd learned in jail that you can sleep anywhere and on anything when you're tired enough. And that's just what I was preparing to do—sleep—when the Major popped in. "Come, come, my boy," he said, "moping alone is no good. Let's be out where the action is."

"Action?" I said. "In Appleby, Michigan?"

"There's action everywhere, my boy," the Major said. "All it requires is a nose to ferret it out."

The particular action the Major's nose had ferreted out this time was a poker game at—of all places—Swope's bachelor quarters. Besides Swope there were two others present—a frail-looking, much younger man named Forbus who taught English at the local high school and a stolid hulk of a man named Mitchell whom I took to be a farmer.

"Good of you to help us out, Major," Swope said. "The man who usually fills in the fourth chair had to go out of town and we don't like to play three-handed."

"My pleasure," the Major said, settling into the fourth chair.

Swope picked up the deck and began to shuffle. "Seven-card stud all right with everybody?" he said.

Forbus and Mitchell nodded, and so did the Major after a moment. "I'm more partial to draw," he said. "But when in Rome, you know."

Swope gave the Major another of his long cool looks. "Yes, of course," he said, finished shuffling and began to deal.

Everybody seemed to take it for granted that I was just there to kibbitz. Which was fine with me, because seven-card stud is a game I try to avoid even when I'm flush. On the surface, it's a deceptively simple game. You're dealt two cards face down, then four more face up and another face down in rotation. Best poker hand based on any five cards wins. The kicker is that you bet after *every* card except the first two. In other words, there are five bets (six if there's a raise along the way) to be met on each hand. Compared with regular draw poker, stud is a real plunger's game where you can lose a lot of money in a very short time if you're not careful. Sometimes even if you are.

Partial to the game or not, the Major knew his way around a card table, and it soon became apparent—at least to me—that he and Swope were the only real poker players present. Forbus was the eternal optimist, always hoping for a miracle and consequently always staying with a hand too long. Mitchell, on the other hand, was an out-and-out bluffer who hadn't learned that bluffing works only when it's the exception to the rule.

Poker isn't entirely a game of skill, though. Luck enters into it as it does in everything else, and the other two couldn't help but win a pot now and then. And since both the Major and Swope played especially tight games, drop-ping out unless the third or fourth card showed strength, that wasn't as infrequent as you might expect.

So it began to look like the Major's "action" was just what it appeared to be on the surface—a friendly, not too exciting game in which not enough money was going to change hands to make or break anybody. Until 11:30, that is.

At 11:30 Forbus glanced nervously up at the clock on the mantlepiece as he passed his cards back to the dealer —Swope again—at the end of a hand. "Half an hour to go," he said.

"So it is," Swope said mildly. "We always make it a rule," he explained to the Major as he shuffled and reshuffled the cards, "to quit exactly at twelve. Saves argument and embarrassment. But," he added, "for the last half hour we pull out all the stops and play no limit. We find it makes a more interesting evening."

"I'm sure it does," the Major murmured. He straightened in his chair and put his hands flat on the table before him.

Something flickered momentarily behind Swope's eyes. Then he finished shuffling and began to deal the cards. The Major's first face-up card was an ace. Swope showed a king, Forbus a three, and Mitchell an eight. "Your bet, Major," Swope said.

The Major sat quietly for a moment, his fingers toying with a stack of white chips. "When a man says 'no limit'," he said at last, "I have to assume he means just that." He pushed the stack of chips forward into the pot. "Fifty dollars," he said.

That was exactly twenty-five times the highest bet made up to that moment, and it effectively served to separate the men from the boys. Forbus and Mitchell pushed their hands in and for all practical purposes joined the kibbitzers' circle, leaving the game to the Major and Swope.

With only two hands to deal, the game went faster than before. And by the time the large and small hands on the clock met at twelve, the Major owed Swope slightly over $900.

"I assume you'll accept my check," the Major said, reaching inside his jacket for his check book.

Swope's eyes went bleaker than usual.

"And," the Major added, "give me a chance to win it back before I leave town."

Swope's eyes brightened. "Planning on staying around for a while, are you, Major?" he said. "In that case, I'll be glad to take your check *and* honor your request."

He accepted the check the Major dashed off and, holding it loosely in his hand, walked with us to the door. "Same time tomorrow night then?" he said.

"Looking forward to it," the Major said.

I waited until we were about half a block away from the house. Then I said, "Operating on the assumption that that check is going to bounce back faster than a tennis ball, I suggest we just keep on going and not even bother stopping at the hotel. That Swope looks like a mean enemy and this is his town, not ours."

"Nonsense, my boy," the Major said. "All I did tonight was cast a little more bread on the waters and it would be foolish to leave before we found it again. But if it bothers you, reflect on this: it will be Monday morning—two days from now—before friend Swope can present that check at any bank and several days more before it clears to the bank it's drawn on. Surely that should give us ample grace period to do what we have to do and leave—even if, as you assume, the check is no good."

"Well, maybe," I admitted.

The Major slapped my shoulder heartily. "Of course it does," he said.

"Now have a good sleep. Things will look better in the morning."

Actually, they looked worse. Because when I stopped by the Major's room on my way to breakfast, he was gone and his bed hadn't been slept in.

It took about a minute for the realization to sink in. Then I spent another minute swearing silently at him before settling down to figure out what to do. Instinct told me to cut out, too. Because even if technically only the Major stood to fall on the bad-check charge, small town justice has the regrettable tendency to overlook technicalities and settle for the bird in hand. And if they wanted a peg to hang a case on, there was the small matter of a hotel bill I couldn't pay.

Unfortunately, getting out of town wasn't going to be that easy. The Major had taken the car and hitchhiking meant at least a ten-mile walk down to the main highway since rural drivers are understandably skittish about picking up strangers in city clothes.

Of course, there are worse things than walking ten miles, and going to jail is one of them. But I felt I still had some grace period left. And when some unobtrusive checking around revealed that there was a bus at four that afternoon I opted for it, figuring I could slip on board just before it pulled out and be on my way before anybody realized what had happened.

What I failed to take into account, though, was just how fast and efficiently news spreads in small towns. Swope and Mitchell cornered me a half hour before the bus was due to leave. Mitchell had changed into his working clothes. And despite his farmerish appearance and willingness to break the laws against gambling, it turned out he was a deputy sheriff.

"Haven't seen much of your friend, the Major, today," Swope said conversationally.

"As a matter of fact," Mitchell put in more bluntly, "we haven't seen him at all."

"I'm not surprised," I said, "he said he was tired and was going to stick pretty close to his room."

"Now that's strange," Swope said, "because he isn't there now. And the chambermaid told the desk clerk the room looked as if not a thing had been touched."

"Well," I said, searching for something to say, "you know how it is with these military types. They spend so much time getting ready for inspection they forget how not to be neat."

"Perhaps," Swope said. "But his—shall we say, unavailability—does raise some questions. Particularly since I

had our local banker call a banker friend of his in Detroit
and neither one of them had ever heard of the bank your
friend's check is drawn on."

"Now, look," I said. "That check is a matter strictly between you and the Major."

"It certainly is," a familiar clipped voice said, bringing
all heads swiveling around.

The Major glowered from the doorway, hands locked
behind his back and his barrel chest thrust out. "What's
this all about, Swope?" he said.

"Just a little misunderstanding, Major," Swope said
coolly.

"Hmph," the Major sniffed. "It seems to me that gentlemen don't misunderstand each other this way."

"Perhaps not," Swope agreed. "But then how would either of us know?" He moved to the door, followed by Mitchell. "Same time tonight?"

"Of course," the Major said stiffly, stepping aside to let
them pass. "Cheeky buzzards," he added in a mild, almost
disinterested voice after they had disappeared down the
hall.

"Maybe I'm one, too," I said. "Because I sure would like
to know where you disappeared to today."

The Major's face brightened into a smile. "Just following
the Good Book again, my boy," he said. "And now if you'll
excuse me I'd better get some rest if I'm to be at my best
tonight."

The same players as before were waiting for us at Swope's
house that evening. No one made any reference to the
events of that afternoon. But, whether for effect or not,
Mitchell had left on his deputy sheriff's uniform. The only
thing lacking was for him to place his gun meaningfully on
the table beside his cards.

"Seven-card stud still all right, Major?" Swope said as
the Major took his seat.

"It's your game," the Major said. "I do have one sugges-
tion, though. Since I'm the big loser, how about giving me

a chance to catch up by extending the no-limit period to—oh—an hour or two? Or even," he added a shade too casually, "to the whole game?"

Forbus and Mitchell both looked at Swope, who let the moment drag out before shaking his head. "No," he said. "A rule's a rule. And as you said yourself, 'When in Rome—' "

"Do as the Romans," the Major finished. "Of course."

But it was apparent from the way he fidgeted in his seat and slapped his cards down that he was straining at the leash, impatient for the real game to begin. It wasn't long before Forbus began to fidget, too, and even Mitchell began to show signs of nervousness. Only Swope appeared unaffected, accepting his cards and playing them as unperturbedly as ever.

As for myself—well, I'd thought time had passed slowly in jail. But those days were sprints compared with tonight. And it was with a real sense of relief that I heard Swope announce: "Well, Major, half an hour to go. Now's your chance to get even—if you can."

As before, the game narrowed down immediately to Swope and the Major, and the cards and chips passed back and forth between them with such rapidity that it was impossible to keep track of who was winning. Still, when the dust settled at midnight, the Major was ahead.

"$800, I make it," he said, tallying his chips.

"So do I," Swope said equably, "and since you said you wanted a chance to win your check back, I saved it for you." He reached in his pocket and threw the now folded and crumpled check on the table between them. "I'll take my change in cash if you don't mind," he said. "$125, *I* make that."

He permitted himself a sly smile, and Forbus and Mitchell both grinned openly. The Major looked at them blankly for a moment. Then he smiled, although a bit wryly. "I have to hand it to you, Swope," he said. "You're a hard man to get the better of."

"I try to be," Swope said drily. He flicked his thumb rapidly over his fingers. "Now I'll take my money, please."

"Of course," the Major said. He counted $125 out of his wallet, passed it over to Swope, then picked up the deck of cards and regarded it with the wry expression still on his face. "Perhaps from now on I should stick to parlor tricks." He grinned suddenly, fanned the deck, and offered it to Swope. "Go ahead," he said. "Pick a card."

Swope hesitated, then selected a card, showed it to Forbus, Mitchell and me, and put it back in the deck for the Major. The Major cut and recut swiftly, then began dealing cards, laying them out in neat rows. When he'd got about halfway through the deck, he stopped, his thumb just flicking up the edge of the top remaining card. "One last fling, Swope," he said. "My next half-year's income against your next half-year's fees of office that the next card I turn over is yours."

I started to open my mouth, because Swope's card—the four of Spades—lay about a third of the way back in the rows of cards already face up! But a heavy look from Mitchell killed whatever I had planned to say.

Swope's face was as impassive as ever. "You have a bet," he said.

Smiling faintly, the Major reached out and turned the four of Spades face down!

There was a moment of silence. Then Mitchell guffawed and slapped Swope hard across the shoulders. "By God, Byron, he took you that time," he said.

"So he did," Swope said mildly. His eyes came up to the Major's. "That was clever," he said. "Deliberately going past the card you knew was mine. It lured me into overlooking the first rule of gambling—never bet on another man's game.

"Still, maybe you haven't won as much as you thought. I make my living from law and real estate. I only took that job as deputy clerk and recorder for the political weight it carries. That $20 I got from you was the first fee I've collected in six months and the last I'm likely to collect in as

many—unless, of course, you manage to find someone foolish enough to buy that worthless land your friend James
inherited, in which case you'll be more than welcome to
the $20 that sale will bring." And with that he laughed
nastily. So did Forbus and Mitchell. They were still laughing when the Major and I let ourselves out.

"Satisfied now, Major?" I said after the door had closed
behind us.

"Very much so," he said.

"Then let's get out of this town while we still have
money to buy gas."

"Nonsense, my boy," the Major said. "It would be foolish
to leave now when we're just about to find again the bread
we've cast upon the waters." He took my arm and marched
me along beside him. "Old Swope was right about one
thing," he said. "You *can't* sell that land of yours. But you
can give it away. Which, as your agent, is just what I
proceeded to arrange for this afternoon.

"First thing Monday morning a reliable direct-mail firm
in Detroit will begin releasing letters notifying the lucky
3000—selected at random from the telephone directories
maintained at the excellent public library there—that
they have each won a quarter of acre of land 'in the heart
of Michigan's vacationland.' All that's required to confirm
the prize is that the lucky winner record the deed and pay
the standard $20 fee before the end of the month.

"Naturally, I wouldn't expect too many to be able to
come up and do that in person. So a convenient return
envelope will be enclosed. And all we have to do as the
letters come in is simply extract the money and pass the
work on to Swope." He smiled benignly. "If experience is
any guide, we can expect about fifty percent to respond,
giving us a gross of $20 times 1500, or $30,000. Which
isn't a bad return at all."

THE BIG BUNCO

by William Bankier

❒ I HAVE A CRAZY PARTNER. WHICH IS NOT SO BAD MOST OF THE
time because our job is writing scripts for a television situ-
ation-comedy series called "Rooms Without Doors" and
when you're sweating to come up with a funny premise for
episode number 46 and the deadline is yesterday afternoon, a little crazy can be a good thing.

"Stan, we are dead," I will say from my place at the
typewriter, little strands of spiderweb stretching from my
cramped fingers to the dusty keys. "That rumbling sound
you hear above us is clods of earth hitting the lid of our
coffin."

And then Stan Percival will heave up his 260 pounds
from the folding canvas deck chair, which is the only other
piece of furniture in our cubbyhole office, and he will say,
"No, Joe. No. We are not dead. We are on the verge of a
great idea. All I have to do is say it."

He is looming over me, six feet four inches, his hands
working the air like clay, and I know he doesn't have an
idea, not in his conscious mind anyway. But there is a look
on his face like a man who has a chicken bone in his throat
and is trying to work it back up and spit it out. Stan's eyes
are bulging, his lips are pursing, and there are beads of
sweat on his big round face.

"And this is the idea," he says. "Cousin Mary is locked in
a church overnight." It is insane; there is no reason for a

church to be mentioned, but I keep listening. "She doesn't know how to get out but she has a bottle of brandy with her because she'd been to the liquor store to get supplies for their anniversary party. Back home Uncle Walt misinterprets a phone call because he's lost his hearing aid, so he thinks she's been kidnaped. The police are called in which gets Larry uptight because he's expecting a delivery of forged lottery tickets. And at the end Mary will be up in the bell tower playing 'I'll Be with You in Apple Blossom Time' with her feet, which tips Larry off because this is *their song.*"

The whole thing is sheer madness, but I start laughing and I start typing and pretty soon we have a script. Which is why I say a little crazy can be a good thing. Sometimes but not always. Because the time Stan got it into his head that we should sell somebody the Jacques Cartier Bridge was something else. And that is the time I propose to tell you about.

It all began one morning in August when Stan arrived late. We had quit work at nine o'clock the night before, solidly blocked and frustrated at page ten of a difficult, no, an impossible script. I had always feared this day.

When Stan came into the office he didn't go to his deck chair. Instead he went to the window which was open a few inches and flung it up all the way so that the glass rattled. Then he thrust the top of his body through the aperture and screamed across Ste. Catherine Street, "Freedom now!"

There must have been some response from the street because he hung out there for a few minutes and I heard one end of an abusive conversation before he drew himself back in and said to me, "Bore, bore, bore! I can't do this any more, Joe Huck. I am dying of boredom." Then he prostrated himself, not in the chair but on the floor.

"Ready when you are, Stanley," I said.

But he went on, "I couldn't sleep last night. I lay awake asking myself where's the excitement? Where's the adventure? Man was not created to lurch round and round on a treadmill. You know who has it all figured out? That former playwright what's-his-name, who wrote *African Genitals.* Robert Aardvark."

"Robert Ardrey. *African Genesis.*"

"That's the guy. He has a new book in which he theorizes that man's Number One need is not security, it's excitement. Freedom from boredom. I think he's right."

"Okay. How do we work that into episode number 52?"

Stan Percival reared up on one elbow, his large head appearing over the edge of my desk like the Kraken's. "Damn it, that's the point. I am not going to write episode number 52. I am off the treadmill as of now. I seek a new adventure."

"Fine. And what will you do for money?"

Our weekly situation comedy on CBC Television was an imitation of similar American series and we never kidded ourselves. Its existence was predicated on a political demand for Canadian content on the taxpayers' network. But the pay was good and there were no other jobs like it for writers in Montreal.

"Money," said Stan, "will have to be one of the essential ingredients of our new adventure."

"You've got me in it too?"

"Of course. You're just as bored as I am. You're just too security-bound to show it."

It was clear he needed humoring. "Okay, partner, tell me about *our* adventure."

Stan sat up on his blue-denimed haunches. "It has to be some sort of crime."

"Crime?"

"Right. That's where the adventure is. I figured it all out last night. I'm convinced half the people involved in criminal acts do it because the straight-and-narrow bores them stiff."

"But we can't kill anybody. I doubt we could even rob a bank. No experience."

"Pay attention, oh, Lucky Huck. There is crime and there is crime. The category I have in mind is the kind that involves no violence. It demands ingenuity on the part of the criminal, and usually a degree of crookedness in the victim who wants something for nothing. I speak, noble Huck, of the big con, the big bunco."

I shook my head. "These things are not easy."

"Of course not. That's precisely the challenge. But aren't we in the con game already? Don't we spend our days making up preposterous stories that involve the manipulation of a lot of characters to achieve a desired end?" He was on his knees now, sprawled halfway across the desk. "All we have to do is apply our skills to inventing a con. Some sort of plot that feeds on human greed and ends up milking some sucker who deserves it because he goes along."

I sensed the momentum in Stan's persuasion, but it was too late to get off the track. "And I suppose you have something in mind."

"It hit me in the wee hours," he said. "We are going to sell the Jacques Cartier Bridge."

I raised my eyes to the window and saw in the distance the massive steel structure vaulting the St. Lawrence River to the South Shore. "Stanley," I said, "this is another fine mess you're getting us into."

"It's an idea. We've had crazier ones. Now all we have to do is work out the details."

I must admit it was an interesting exercise. I went along because there was no way Stan Percival would get back to the script until he had played out his game. By late afternoon we had hacked out a scenario which, given a bit of luck, might just work.

It involved our actor-friend Yves Paquette doing his uncanny impersonation of the Mayor of Montreal and it included an important role for Stan's girlfriend, Portia Fleming. If all went well, the plan ended with a payoff to us of $50,000.

When I raised my eyebrows at that, Stan said, "I won't kid you, I need the money. My alimony payments are killing me." He stood up, displaying his denims and faded

T-shirt. "You think I enjoy dressing like a middle-aged hippie?"

My $200 sports jacket hung majestically on the back of the chair. "I've tried to tell you—" I began.

"I know. I waste money. But I'm trying to change." He went to the door. "Come on, I'll buy us both dinner."

That evening we prowled hotel lobbies looking for a setting. We were lucky. We had covered the Mount Royal and the Laurentian. Then, in the Queen Elizabeth, we saw listed on the bulletin board: CANADIAN CONSTRUCTION INDUSTRY CONVENTION.

"These are the guys we want," Stan said.

"But it's today, Thursday, Friday, and Saturday. That's too sudden."

"Nonsense. 'Mission Impossible' converts a warehouse into the Freedonian Museum overnight. The faster we have to work, the better. Verve, Brother Huck, panache, élan."

I drifted past a table where ticketed conventioneers were registering and I picked up a membership roster. Then Stan and I went into the bar, ordered a beer, and perused the list for a potential bridge buyer. We were halfway through when I spotted a familiar name and a jolt of adrenalin made my hand tremble.

"Lewicki," I said. "E. J. Lewicki from Baytown, Ontario."

Stan's grinning face was clenched like a fist. "It's working, isn't it? The pieces are falling into place."

"Back home in Baytown everybody's heard of E. J. Lewicki. Made his fortune building airfields for the Commonwealth Training Plan during the war. Always in the papers. A hint of scandal one year about kickbacks."

"Our man," Stan said. "Our pigeon."

"Keeps getting hassled by the Provincials for driving fast under the influence. Usually has a pretty chick beside him."

"Oh, my goodness." Stan was cracking his huge knuckles like walnuts. "We couldn't have written a better character ourselves. You say he likes pretty girls? I'll go and get Portia. You pick up Yves Paquette and we'll meet back at the office in half an hour."

We did. Yves and I had possession of the two chairs when Stan arrived with Portia and a paper bag containing six quarts of beer and a roll of paper cups. Drinking beer out of a paper cup is an abomination, but it is just one of the things I hate and yet keep doing when working with Stan Percival. Another is embarking on a venture like selling the Jacques Cartier Bridge to a rich unscrupulous Ontario construction magnate. But I knew there would be no getting my partner back to episode number 52 until he got this quirk out of his system. If it were done, it were best done quickly.

I offered Portia my chair, but she preferred to recline on the desk which caused Stan's huge face to assume a thoughtful expression. I was afraid he might cancel the meeting and order me and Yves out of the office, but the caper held too firm a grip on his mind.

A word about Portia. She is 23 years old and features miles of cascading blonde hair at one end and miles of devastating leg at the other. Her torso is generous too, and stretched out as she was now on one elbow with one knee up, a backless sandal dangling from the other foot and her blouse losing the battle to stay closed three buttons to two, you had to admit nothing more was required of Portia Fleming. Which was just as well because she is a terrible actress.

"Stanley," she said now, "how is my part coming in the series? Are you writing me more lines?"

This was Stan's current trap. Only by using extreme persuasion had he wangled her a bit part in "Rooms Without Doors." The director, a good judge of talent, abhorred any script in which she appeared and was urging Stan to write her out. Meanwhile, from Portia's side the pressure was maintained for a fatter part. And when Portia applied pressure, it was warm and fragrant and sweet. Stan was caught in the vise of life; some day soon he would have to find a way to escape its squeeze.

"This is not a script conference," Stan said. "We are here on a more important matter." And he proceeded to outline our plan. At this point you may be wondering why these two newcomers did not reject the scheme which was, of course, strictly illegal. You must remember Stan was talking to actors. As long as he is playing a part, an actor will do anything from undressing in a department-store window to selling a shoddy product on TV. An actor must act.

"Portia, you will make contact with E. J. Lewicki—Joe will point him out to you. Remember, you are playing the part of a confidential secretary to Mayor Martel of Montreal. All you have to do is drop a hint about the plans to build a new University on Ste. Helen's Island. Just let him know that it will be a big project. A lot of steel will be used."

Yves Paquette said, "I guess you want me to play the part of the Mayor." He put on a tiny twisted smile and let his eyes slip into the famous glazed, maniacal stare and we had to laugh. Even without makeup he was almost His Worship.

"Remember," I said to Yves, "Lewicki will have seen the real Mayor addressing the dinner a few hours earlier, so you'll have to be good."

Yves opened his private door just enough to let me catch a glimpse of the giant ego lurking inside. "I am good," he said.

We confirmed our times, rehearsed our lines, finished the beer, then went home to bed—I to mine, Yves to his, and Stan, presumably, to Portia's.

Next afternoon I telephoned the hotel and reserved a room in the name of Finn, a clever alias since my name is Huck. I checked in at 5:00, telephoned Stan, and he showed up an hour later carrying the inevitable paper bag. This time it contained a bottle of rye. Stan phoned for ice. Then he called Yves and gave him the room number.

At eight o'clock we met Portia in the doorway of the

main salon where the Construction Conventioneers had just finished dinner. The real mayor was beginning his speech. Portia had trouble spotting us because we were both wearing glasses we didn't need and Stan had pasted on a false mustache. I tipped the headwaiter and he let us lurk along the wall until I spotted E. J. Lewicki and pointed him out to Portia.

It was years since I had seen the affable millionaire cruising the streets of Baytown, but he had not changed much. His hair was whiter, but it still covered his head like Good King Wenceslas's snow—deep and crisp and even. And the symbolic unlighted cigar still projected from between his teeth untouched by his fastidious lips which were drawn away from the tobacco in a rigid grin.

We left Portia Fleming thus loaded and pointed in the right direction and went back to the room to wait for Yves. Professional to the core, he showed up on the stroke of 9:00, hatted and cloaked to conceal his uncannily Mayorish appearance. At 9:30 we left him and went down to the bar where, according to plan, Portia was supposed to be drinking with Lewicki. And she was, seated at a table in the far corner, their heads so close that she could have bitten the other end of his cigar.

Portia greeted us with surprise as we passed by. "Carl, Peter," she called, using our assumed names, "did you hear the boss's speech?"

"Hello, Jenn. No. We just got here. His Worship wants to see us upstairs to ask how we're making out on the project."

Portia, as Jenny, introduced us in our roles as executive assistants to the Mayor of Montreal. We sat down, accepted a drink, and soon had our plot rolling along in high gear. Lewicki, unscrupulous and avaricious, was everything a con man could ask.

"You guys," he soon said, "must be right in there where the action is."

"Oh, we hear a thing or two."

"The young lady mentioned something about building a

new University down on the island. I'd sure like to get in on that."

"Well, sir," Stan said, "there's no reason why you shouldn't. You've certainly made a good friend in Jenny."

"I wonder," I said, "if Mr. Lewicki might not be the man for the Mayor's special project?"

I had let the cat out of the bag and Stan almost over-played his horror. I sensed that we were flirting with a Laurel and Hardy interpretation. But Lewicki seemed in-terested. Thank goodness for booze and bar lighting.

"Peter, the Mayor's special project is not for public con-sumption."

"You can talk freely at this table, boys. E. J. Lewicki can keep a secret."

Stan apologized, changed the subject, and for the time it took to finish our drinks and order another round he made empty conversation. But I could tell where Lewicki's thoughts were. Finally he said, "Your Mayor is famous for his big ideas. I guess this new one is a beaut."

My partner appeared to reconsider. He glanced at me. I nodded. "Very well," he said. "Part of our assignment is to find an entrepreneur who is big enough and fast enough to help put this deal over."

Lewicki said, "I just got up and ran twice around the room and you didn't even miss me."

"The deal is this. Now that the subway is running under the River to the South Shore, and the new Champlain Bridge is operating, the Mayor plans to close the old Jacques Cartier Bridge and dismantle it. The city will ac-cept an offer of five million dollars for the steel in the bridge."

"But if I do that, I end up with a lot of steel on my hands and nowhere to go with it."

"That's where the new University fits in. The proposed site is Ste. Helen's Island, right beneath the bridge. You won't have to go anywhere with the steel. You will sell it to the city for use in the new construction. In effect, you will be a broker, buying the bridge and selling it back almost

on the same day. At a nice profit. And the company that
dismantles the bridge will be working on a very nice mu-
nicipal contract too."

E. J. Lewicki turned his glittering eyes first on me, then
on Stan. The cold cigar pierced our hearts, one after the
other. "That's a handsome project. I expect the bidding
will be fierce."

"Mayor Martel doesn't work that way," Stan said. "He
is, as you may have heard, somewhat of an autocrat. He
works fast and he has the power to initiate projects as he
sees fit. No, this contract will go to the company the Mayor
chooses."

"And you boys are expected to make a recommendation."

"We are."

The elderly millionaire turned to Portia. "What do you
say, Jenny?"

She put her hand on his. "I know the Mayor would like
you."

"Done," Lewicki said. "Tell His Worship I'm interested."

"We can do better. We can take you to him right now."

So there we all were twenty minutes later in my room
on the fifteenth floor, raising our glasses of rye and tap
water while the Mayor of Montreal, played to the hilt by
Yves Paquette, proposed a toast.

"Félicitations á Monsieur Lewicki," he said, "and success
to all of us. May this project be brought to a very speedy
and profitable conclusion."

We drank and Yves drew Stan into a corner for a few
words. Then Yves put down his glass, shook hands with
everyone, took his coat and hat, and made his departure.

The room seemed empty after Yves's large performance.
Stan said to Lewicki, "The Mayor just reminded me of a
detail I neglected to mention. There are certain require-
ments he has to fulfill in order to expedite these projects
as quickly as he does. It is normal, in these cases, for the
successful contractor to pay a deposit—"

"What you're saying is there's a payoff."

"That's a harsh word. I would never use it to describe—"

He was interrupted again, this time by Lewicki's hearty laughter. "Don't be embarrassed, my boy. I've been in this game a long time. I was wondering when you were going to ask for it. How much do you want?"

"Fifty thousand dollars."

"Cash, I suppose?"

"Yes, sir. Used bills, small denominations."

When Lewicki and Portia left ten minutes later, Stan and I fell on the floor. Literally. "He went for it!" Stan said. "We have sold that man the Jacques Cartier Bridge!"

"I can't believe it!"

"Believe it, my son. Tomorrow morning, right after the banks open, Mr. Lewicki will be here with the money."

And it was so. We slept fitfully, woke at eight, shaved and dressed and had a large room-service breakfast. At 10:30 Lewicki and Portia arrived together with a satchel which, when opened, revealed the sum of $50,000 in used, low-denomination banknotes.

"Jenny," Stan said, still playing everything according to our beautiful script, "you'd better deliver this cash to the Mayor's office and tell His Worship that the deal has been consummated."

She took the satchel and left.

"Meanwhile," Stan said, "Peter and I will work fast drawing up the necessary papers to get this project underway. You'll be hearing from us very soon."

Lewicki was standing at the window looking downriver at his newest possession. "Fine," he said. "And now I wonder if you boys have any of that good Canadian whiskey left."

I am not a morning drinker, but for $50,000 I figured I could go along. We sipped and chatted while my impatience grew. The show was over. I wished to be gone.

Finally Lewicki set down his empty glass. Then he patted his pockets. "Oh, boys," he said. "I have just given the young lady all the cash I have. I'm checking out now and I have a lot of people to tip. How much money can you spare me?"

Stan said, "How much do you need?"

Lewicki pondered and mumbled. "Bellboys, maid, garage, waiters—they've all been real good to me. Can you let me have a couple of hundred?"

Stan and I pooled our funds. We just made $200 with cab fare left over. Back in the office, waiting for Portia to show up, I said, "Imagine that old bird hitting us up like that."

Stan said, "Relax, he said he'd mail it back. Besides, we pay out $200, we get back $50,000 less expenses. If you don't speculate, you can't accumulate."

By now we were hungry. By two o'clock we were tired and surly. By 3:30 we were suspicious. At 4:00, when Portia's telegram was delivered, we were angry and sick. I gave my last quarter to the boy while Stan took a long yellow sheet from the envelope. He read it aloud.

HI BOYS. I ALWAYS WANTED TO BE ABLE TO AFFORD TO SEND A LONG WIRE. NOW I'M RICH SO HERE GOES. STAN, I ALWAYS THOUGHT MY FAILURE IN TV WAS NOT BECAUSE I'M A BAD ACTRESS BUT BECAUSE YOU ARE A BAD WRITER. THIS PROVES IT. THE MOTIVATION YOU PROVIDED ME IN THIS CON GAME WAS VERY FLIMSY. WHY SHOULD I CHEAT THAT SWEET MR. LEWICKI JUST SO YOU AND YOUR DUMB PARTNER CAN MAKE A KILLING? ANYWAY E.J. TELLS ME YOUR PLAN WOULDN'T HAVE FOOLED ANYBODY. THE STEEL FROM A BRIDGE WOULD NEVER BE USED IN CONSTRUCTING UNIVERSITY BUILDINGS. JUST ANOTHER EXAMPLE OF YOUR CARELESS PLOTTING. YOU DO IT ALL THE TIME. GOOD ENOUGH FOR YOUR TACKY TELEVISION PLAYS BUT NOT FOR REAL LIFE. SO I AM HERE NOW IN BAYTOWN WITH SOMEBODY WHO REALLY KNOWS HOW TO BE NICE TO ME. TELL JOE I LIKE HIS HOMETOWN. HE SHOULD NEVER HAVE LEFT. LOVE. PORTIA.

After Stan had torn up the telegram and kicked the deck chair to pieces, nobody said anything for a while. Then I went over and tried to cheer him up.

"Well, at least you're rid of Portia Fleming. She was a problem in the series and now she's gone forever."

I said it, but I took no comfort from it, and I don't think

Stan did either. We wanted her gone because she was supposed to be dumb. But the way things worked out, it looks
like the smart cookies flew away to Baytown and left the
dumb guys in Montreal, out $200 plus expenses.

PLAYING IT COOL

by Simon Brett

☐ THERE WAS ONLY ONE GIRL WORTH LOOKING AT IN THAT PLANE-load. I'd been doing the job for two months, since May, and I'd got quicker at spotting them.

She was tall, but then I'm tall, so no problem there. Thin, but round in the right places. Dress: expensive casual. Good jeans, white cotton shirt, artless but pricey. Brown eyes, biscuit-colored hair pulled back into a rubber-band knot, skin which had already seen a bit of sun and just needed Corfu to polish up the color. (Have to watch that. With a lot of the girls—particularly from England—they're so pale you daren't go near them for the first week. Physical approaches get nothing but a little scream and a nasty smell of Nivea on your hands.)

The girl's presence moved me forward more keenly than usual with my little spiel. "Hello, Corforamic Tours, Corforamic Tours. I am your Corforamic representative, Rick Lawton. Could you gather up your baggage, please, and proceed outside the arrivals hall to your transport."

I ignored the puffing English matrons and homed in on the girl's luggage.

It was then that I saw the other one. She looked younger, shorter, dumpier; paler brown hair, paler eyes, a sort of diluted version, as if someone had got the proportions wrong when trying to clone from the dishy one.

They were obviously together, so I had to take one bag

for each. They thanked me in American accents. That in itself was unusual. Most of the girls who come on these package tours are spotty typists from Liverpool.

But then their destination was unusual, too. The majority of the Corforamic properties are tiny, twin-bedded apartments in Paleokastritsa and Ipsos. But there's one Rolls-Royce job near Aghios Spiridion—a converted windmill, sleeps eight, swimming pool, private beach, live-in maid, telephone. And that was where they were going. They'd booked for a month.

I read it on their labels. *Miss S. Stratton* (the dishy one). *Miss C. Stratton* (the other one). And underneath each name, the destination—Villa Costas.

By six I'd seen all the ordinary ones installed, answered the questions about whether it was safe to drink the water, given assurances that the plumbing worked, given the names of doctors to those with small children, told them which supermarkets sold Rice Krispies, quoted the minimal statistics for death by scorpion sting, and tried to convince them that the mere fact of their having paid for a fortnight's holiday was not automatically going to rid the island of mosquitoes.

Villa Costas was a long way to the north side of the island. I'd pay a call there the next day.

I drove to Niko's on the assumption that none of my charges would venture as far as his disco on their first evening. You get to value your privacy in this job. I sat under the vine-laden shelter of the bar and had an ouzo.

As I clouded the drink with water and looked out over the glittering sea, I felt low. Seeing a really beautiful woman always has that effect on me. Seems to accentuate the divide between the sort of man who gets that sort of girl and me. I always seem to end up with the ugly ones.

It wasn't just that. There was money, too, always money. Sure I got paid as the Corforamic rep, but not much. Winter in England loomed, winter doing some other demeaning selling job, earning peanuts. Not the sort of money that could coolly rent the Villa Costas for a month. Again there was the big divide. Rich and poor. And I knew to which side I really belonged. Poor, I was cramped and frustrated. Rich, I could really be myself.

Niko's voice cut into my gloom. "Telephone, Rick."

She identified herself as Samantha Stratton. The dishy one. Her sister had seen a rat in the kitchen at Villa Costas. Could I do something about it?

I said I'd be right out there. Rats may not be dragons, but they can still make you feel knight-errantish. And as any self-respecting knight errant knows, there is no damsel so susceptible as one in distress.

Old Manthos keeps a kind of general store just outside Kassiope. It's an unbelievable mess—slabs of soap mixed up with dried fish, oil lamps, saucepans, tins of powdered milk, brooms, faded postcards, coils of rope, tubes of liniment, deflated beach balls, dusty Turkish Delight, and novelty brandy bottles shaped like Ionic columns. Most of the stock appears to have been there since the days of his long-dead father, whose garlanded photograph earnestly surveys the chaos around him.

But, in spite of the mess, Manthos usually has what you want. May take a bit of time and considerable disturbance of dust, but he'll find it.

So it proved on this occasion. With my limping Greek it took a few minutes for him to understand the problem, but once he did, he knew exactly where to go. A crate of disinfectant was upturned, a bunch of children's fishing nets knocked over, a pile of scouring pads scattered, and the old man triumphantly produced a rusty tin, whose label was stained into illegibility.

"Very good," he said, "very good. Kills rats, kill anything." He drew his hand across his throat evocatively.

I paid him, and as I walked out of the shop he called out, "And if that doesn't work—"

"Yes?"

"Ask the priest. The Papas is sure to have a prayer for getting rid of rats."

It was nearly eight o'clock when I got to Villa Costas, but that's still hot in Corfu in July. Hot enough for Samantha to be on the balcony in a white bikini. The body fulfilled, or possibly exceeded, the promise I had noted at the airport.

"Candy's in bed," she said. "Shock of seeing the rat on top of all that traveling brought on a migraine."

"Ah. Well, let's see if we can put paid to this rat's little exploits," I said, in a businesslike and, to my mind, rather masculine manner.

"Sure."

I filled some little paper dishes with poison and laid them round the kitchen floor. Then I closed the tin and washed my hands. "Shall I leave the poison with you, so you can put down more if you want to?"

She was standing in the kitchen doorway. The glow of the dying sun burned away her bikini. Among other things I saw her head shake. "No, thanks. Dangerous stuff to have around. You take it."

"Okay."

"Like a drink?"

She was nice. Seemed very forthcoming with me, too. But I didn't want to queer anything up by moving too fast.

Still, when she asked where one went for fun on the island, I mentioned Niko's disco. And by the time I left—discreetly, playing it cool—we'd agreed to meet there the next evening.

And as I drove back to my flat in Corfu Town, I was beginning to wonder whether maybe after all I was about to become the sort of man who gets that sort of girl.

When I arrived at nine, there were quite a lot of people at the disco. But no tall beautiful American girl. Come to that, no less tall, less beautiful American girl.

I could wait. Niko signaled me over to where he was sitting, and I ordered an ouzo.

The group drinking at the table was predictable. Niko's two brothers (the one who drove a beer lorry and the one who rented out motor-scooters) were there, along with his cousin the electrician, and Police Inspector Kantalakis, whose relaxed interpretation of government regulations about overcrowding, noise, and hygiene always insured him a generous welcome at the bar.

There was also a new face. Wiry black hair thinning on top, thick black mustache draped over the mouth, healthy growth of chest hair escaping from carefully faded denims. Solid, mid-thirties maybe, ten years older than me. "Rick, this is Brad," said Niko.

He stretched out a hairy hand. "Hi." Another American. "We were just talking about Niko's wife," he said with a grin.

They all laughed, Niko slightly ruefully. Whereas some people have bad backs or business worries to be tenderly asked after, Niko always had a wife problem. It was a running joke, and from the way Brad raised it he seemed to know the group well. "How are things at home, Niko?" Brad continued.

The proprietor of the bar shrugged that round-shouldered gesture that encompasses the whole world of marital misery.

Brad chuckled. "Sure beats me why people get married at all."

Inspector Kantalakis and the others gave man-of-the-world laughs, siding with him and conveniently forgetting their own tenacious little wives. The American turned to me. "You married?"

I shook my head. "Never felt the necessity."

"Too right. There is no necessity."

The married men laughed again, slightly less easily. Brad called their bluff. "Now come on, all you lot got wives. Give me one good reason *why*, one argument in favor of marriage."

Inspector Kantalakis guffawed. "Well, there's the bedroom—"

"You don't have to get married for that," I said.

The Inspector looked at me with distaste. For some reason he never seemed to like me much.

"Come on, just one argument for marriage," insisted Brad.

They looked sheepish. Faced by this transatlantic sophisticate, none of them was going to show himself up by mentioning love, children, or religion. They wanted to appear modern, and were silent.

"You think of any reason, Rick?"

"Money," I said, partly for the laugh I knew the word would get, but also because the idea had been going through my mind for some years. Marriage remains one of the few legal ways that someone without exceptional talents can make a quick and significant change in his material circumstances. I reinforced the point, playing for another laugh. "Yes, I reckon that's the only thing that would get me to the altar. I'm prepared to marry for money."

As the laugh died, Brad looked at me shrewdly. "If that's so, then you ought to set your cap for what's just arriving."

I turned to see the girls from Villa Costas getting out of a rented car. "Those two," Brad continued, "are the daughters of L. K. Stratton of Stratton Oil & Gas. When the old man goes, the older one gets the lot."

I was feeling my usual frustration. The two girls had joined us at the table and had a couple of drinks. Seeing them together again had only reinforced my previous impression. Miss S. (Samantha) Stratton was not only beautiful she was also poised and entertaining. Miss C. (Candice, to give her full name) Stratton was not only drab in appearance she was mouselike and tentative in conversation. I waited for a lull in the chat so that I could ask Samantha to dance. If she had needed any recommendation other than that body, Brad's words had just supplied it.

But the minute I was about to suggest a dance, damn me if Brad, who seemed to know the girls quite well, didn't say, "C'mon, Sam, let's bop," and lead her off into the flashing interior of the disco. The way they started dancing suggested that they knew each other very well.

Within minutes Niko and his relations and Inspector Kantalakis had melted away, leaving me in a role I had suffered too often in double dates from schooltime onward —stuck with the ugly one.

And what made it worse was that I gathered in this case she was also the poor one.

I stole a look across at her. The sun had already started its work on her pale flesh. The nose glowed; in a couple of days the skin would be coming off like old wallpaper.

She caught my eye and gave a gauche little smile, then looked wistfully to the thundering interior.

No, no, I wasn't going to be caught that way. That terrible old feeling that you *ought* to ask a girl to dance. Hell, I was twenty-six, not some creepy little adolescent.

Still, I had to say something, or just leave. "Your big sister seems to be enjoying herself," I commented sourly.

"Half-sister, actually. And only big in the sense that she's taller than I am."

"You mean you're older than she is?"

"Two years and four months older."

"Would you like to dance?"

Candice was very shy and I treated her with exemplary tact. Met her every evening for most of the next week. Picked her up at the Villa Costas and took her down to Niko's. She was too shy to go there on her own, and Sam and Brad (who turned out to be engaged, for God's sake!) seemed anxious to be off on their own most of the time.

So I courted Candice like a dutiful boy-next-door. Looked at her soulfully, danced close, kissed her sedately goodbye. I was the kind of young man every mother would like her daughter to meet—serious, respectful, with intentions honorable even to the point of matrimony.

And once I'd written off any chance with Samantha, Candice really didn't seem too bad. Not unattractive at all.

Any personal lustre she lacked I could readily supply by
thinking of her father's millions.

The fourth night, as I kissed her goodbye with a kind of
boyish eagerness, I explained that a new planeload of
tourists was arriving the next day and I wouldn't have
time to pick her up. She looked disappointed, which
showed me I was getting somewhere. Rather than not see
me, she agreed to go under her own steam to Niko's and
meet me there at nine. That was a big step for her. I
promised I wouldn't be late.

By the middle of the following afternoon it was clear I was
going to be. The flight from London was delayed by an
hour and a half.

Never mind. Still the dutiful, solicitous boy-next-door, I
rang the Villa Costas. Brad answered. Sorry, would he
mind telling Candice I couldn't get to Niko's till half-past
ten? Either I'd see her there or pick her up usual time the
next evening.

Sure, Brad would see she got the message.

When I saw her face, at 10:20 that night at Niko's, it was
clear she hadn't got the message. She was sitting at the
same table as, but somehow not with, Niko's relations and
Inspector Kantalakis. And she looked furious.

It didn't surprise me. Greek men don't really approve of
women, even tourists, going to bars alone, and that lot
wouldn't have made any secret of their feelings. I moved
forward with smiling apologies on my lips.

But I didn't get a chance to make them. Candice rose to
her feet. "I only stayed," she spat out, "to tell you that I
think you're contemptible, and that we will not meet
again."

"Look, I left a message with Brad. I said I'd be late
and—"

"It is not just your lateness I'm talking about. Goodbye."
And she swept off to the rented car.

I sat down, shaken. Inspector Kantalakis was looking at

me with a rather unpleasant smile. "What the hell did you say to her?" I asked.

He shrugged. "I may have mentioned your views on marriage."

"What? Oh, damn—you mean about marrying for money?"

"I may have mentioned that, yes."

"But when I said it, it was only a joke."

"You sounded pretty serious to me," said the Inspector, confirming my impression that he didn't like me one bit.

But that evening wasn't over. I started hitting the local paint-stripper brandy. I was fit to be tied. The Inspector and the others sauntered off, as if satisfied by their evening's destruction. I gazed bitterly across the black sea to the few mysterious lights of Albania.

"Rick." I don't know how long a time had passed before the sound broke into my gloom. I looked up.

It was Samantha. And she was crying.

"What's the matter?"

"It's that swine, Brad."

"Oh. I've got a bone to pick with him, too. What's he done?"

"Oh, he's just—it's always the same. He treats me badly and he goes off with some other girl and always reckons he can just pick up again as if nothing has happened and—well, this is the last time, the last time." She was crying now.

"Can I get you a drink or—?"

"No. I just want to go back to the villa. I was looking for Candy. I wanted a lift. Brad's driven off in his car and—"

"Candy's gone, I'm afraid."

"Oh."

"I'll give you a lift."

When we were in the car park, she was seized by another burst of crying and turned toward me. Instinctively my arms were round her slender, soft body and I held her tight as the spasms subsided.

"Doesn't take you long," said a voice in Greek.

I saw Inspector Kantalakis' sardonic face in the gloom.

"Mind your own business," I said. At least, that would be a paraphrase. The expression on the Inspector's face showed that I was making great strides with my colloquial Greek.

"She's upset," I continued virtuously. "I'm just comforting her, as a friend."

But I wasn't, I wasn't.

Amazing how quickly things can change. Actually, since by "things" I mean women, I suppose it's not so amazing.

I got to know a lot more about Samantha on that drive back, and I discovered that appearances can be distinctly deceptive. For a start, the engagement with Brad was not, as it had appeared, the marriage of true minds, but a kind of professional blackmail exerted on an unwilling girl by a selfish and violent man. She had been trying to break it off for years.

Also—and this was the bit I enjoyed hearing—the reason for the quarrel of that night had been her admitting she fancied someone else. Me.

"But if you're so keen to get rid of him, why did you mind his going off with another girl?"

"Only because I know he'll be back. He never stays away for long. And then he thinks he can just pick up where he left off."

"Hmm. But he couldn't do that if he found you'd got someone else."

"That's true."

The car stopped outside Villa Costas. We were suddenly in each other's arms. Her body spoke its clear message to mine, while our tongues mumbled meaningless nothings. Yes, I was the only man who she'd ever felt like that about.

But no, I'd better not come into the villa now. Because of Candy. And she didn't really fancy the beach. Tomorrow. Tomorrow afternoon at three. She'd see that Candy was out. And then . . .

* * *

I arrived sharp at three the following afternoon in a state of—well, let's say in a predictable state of excitement.

But things weren't initially as private as I had hoped. Theodosia, the live-in maid, was sitting on the veranda under the shade of an olive tree. (Corfiots, unlike the tourists, regard sun as a necessary evil, and avoid it when possible.) She grinned at me in a way that I found presumptuous.

And then as if that wasn't enough, Candice Stratton appeared from the villa and stood for a moment blinded by the sun. She wore a bikini in multi-colored stripes that accentuated her dumpiness; she carried a box of Turkish Delight that would no doubt, in time, accentuate it further. The other hand held a striped towel and a thriller.

When her eyes were accommodated to the brightness, they saw me, and an expression of loathing took over her face. "You creep! I said I never wanted to see you again. So don't think you can come crawling back."

Any intentions I might have had to be nice to her vanished. "I didn't come to see *you,*" I said, and walked past her into the villa. I felt Theodosia's inquisitive eyes follow me.

Samantha was on the balcony in the white bikini. Momentarily I played the aggrieved lover. "I thought you were going to see Candy was out."

"Sorry, we got delayed. Brad came round."

I hadn't reckoned on that.

"Don't worry, Rick. I sent him off with a flea in his ear." She looked at me levelly. "I haven't changed my mind."

I relaxed. "How'd he take it?"

"Usual arrogance. Said he'd be back. Even tried his old trick of making up to Candy to make me jealous. Brought her a big box of Turkish Delight and all that. He ought to know by now it doesn't work."

"On you or on her?"

"On me, you fool." She rose and put an arm round my

waist. Together we watched Candy across the little private
bay, settling on her towel for further ritual peeling.

I looked into Samantha's brown eyes, squinting against
the glare of the sun. I was aware of the tracery of fine lines
around them as her body touched mine.

"Candy be out there for some time?" I murmured.

"You betcha. She'll eat her way right through that box of
Turkish Delight. Always eats when she's unhappy."

My hand glided up the curve of her back. "Shall we go
inside?"

There was a double bed (a rarity in the world of
Corforamic, another luxury feature of the Villa Costas). I
reached more purposefully for Samantha.

"Oh, damn," she said.

"What?"

"Candy didn't take her drink."

"So?"

"There's a large Coca-Cola in the fridge. She was going
to take it with her."

"So?" I shrugged.

"So . . . if she hasn't got it she'll be back here as soon
as she's thirsty. And the Turkish Delight's going to make
her very thirsty."

"Ah."

"You take it over to her."

"But she doesn't want to see me."

"Then we won't be disturbed." There was a kind of logic
in that. "Go on, Rick. And while you're away I'll get more
comfortable."

When I got back, Samantha was waiting with a bottle of
Remy Martin and two glasses.

Candy had been predictably annoyed to see me, but had
accepted the bottle of Coke wordlessly. And Theodosia's
beady little eyes had followed me all the way across the
beach and back.

But I soon forgot both of them. Samantha's charms
would have cleaned out the memory bank of a computer.

Time telescoped and distorted . . . Darkness came and

we didn't notice it. I didn't hear whether Candice came in or not, and eventually sleep claimed us . . .

It was therefore an unpleasant shock to be awakened by the sight of Inspector Kantalakis at the foot of the bed, and by the sound of his voice saying, in English, "Still furthering your marriage plans, Mr. Lawton?"

We both sat up. Samantha was still half asleep. "Marriage?" she echoed. "You did mean it, Rick, what you said last night, about wanting to marry me?"

"Uh?" I was still half asleep myself.

"I have bad news," said Inspector Kantalakis.

We looked at him blearily.

"Miss Stratton, your sister was found this morning on the beach. Dead."

"What?"

"She appears to have been poisoned."

I don't know if you've ever been involved in a murder inquiry in Greece, but let me tell you, it is something to be avoided. Questions, questions, questions, endlessly repeated in a hot concrete police cell. And expressions on the cops' faces that show they don't subscribe to the old British tradition of people being innocent until proved guilty.

I was with them for about twenty-four hours, I suppose, and the first thing I did when I got out was to go up to the Villa Costas. Samantha looked shaken. She'd had quite a grilling too, though some connection of her father's had pulled strings through the American Embassy in Athens and it hadn't taken as long as mine.

"And now the swine has disappeared," were her first words.

"Who?" My mind wasn't working very well.

"Brad."

"What do you mean?"

"Brad must have poisoned her."

"Why?" I couldn't catch up with all this.

"Because of the money."

"Uh?"

"He wanted me *and* Daddy's money. With Candy dead, I inherit."

"Good lord, that never occurred to me."

"Well, it's true."

"But how did he do it?"

"Obvious. The Turkish Delight."

"Are you sure?"

"The Inspector says he hasn't received the forensic analysis yet—everything takes that much longer on an island —but I'd put money on the results."

"Brad'll never get away with it."

"Oh, he'll have managed some sort of alibi. He's devious. He *will* get away with it, unless we can find some proof of his guilt."

"But it will all have been for nothing if he doesn't get you."

"Yes." She sounded listless.

"And he hasn't got you, has he?"

She pulled herself together and looked at me with a little smile. "No, he hasn't. You have."

"So that's all right."

She nodded, but still seemed troubled. "The only thing that worries me—"

"Yes?"

"—is that he still has power over me when I see him."

"Then we must make sure you don't see him. If he's disappeared, that doesn't sound too difficult. Anyway, as soon as the analysis of the Turkish Delight comes through, the police'll be after him."

"But suppose they're not. Suppose he's arranged some kind of alibi—"

"Don't worry." Suddenly I was full of crusading spirit. "If the police won't do it, I'll prove myself that he poisoned Candy."

"Oh, thank you, Rick. Thank God I've got you."

I tried all the contacts I had on the island, but none of them had seen Brad. I didn't give up, though. I wanted to do it for Samantha, to prove Brad's crime and see to it that he was put behind bars where he belonged.

It was the next day she told me she was going to have to fly back to the States. Her father, L. K. Stratton, had had a mild stroke when he heard the news of his older daughter's death, and the younger one had to fly back to be by his side. Inspector Kantalakis had cleared her from his inquiries, and she was free to go. Apparently, he was near an arrest—just needed the results of the forensic analysis to clinch it.

Though I was depressed about her going, the news on the investigation front was promising. The police were obviously close to nailing Brad, merely needing proof of the poison in the Turkish Delight.

All they had to do then was find him.

Unless I could find him first.

I promised to see Samantha off at the airport.

It was less than two weeks since I'd first seen her when I kissed her goodbye. A lot had happened in less than two weeks. When I first saw that splendid body I hadn't dared hope that it would ever be pressed to mine with such trust and hope.

"I'll come back as soon as I can, Rick. Really."

"I know. Let's hope you're back to give evidence at a murder trial."

"I will be. Don't worry."

Her baggage was checked through to Kennedy via London. There didn't seem much more to say. Our togetherness didn't need words.

Not many, anyway. "And then, Sam, we'll get married, huh?"

She nodded gently and gave me another kiss. Then she turned and went off toward the Departure Lounge. Tall, beautiful—and mine.

Not only mine, it occurred to me, but also very rich. Suddenly I had got it all, suddenly I was the sort of man who got that sort of girl.

I watched her into the Departure Lounge. She didn't turn round. We didn't need that sort of clinging farewell.

Suddenly I got a shock. A dark, denim-clad figure had appeared beside her in the Lounge. Brad.

I couldn't go through the ticket control to save her. I had to find the police. And fast.

I was in luck. As I rushed into the dazzle of sunlight, I saw Inspector Kantalakis leaning against my car.

"The man who murdered Candy—I know who it is," I panted.

"So do I," said the Inspector.

"He intended to marry Samantha, but he wanted the money, too, so he poisoned Candy."

"Exactly."

"Well, why don't you arrest him?"

"I've been waiting for a forensic report for final proof. Now I have it. Now there will be an arrest."

"Good. He's in the airport building. The plane leaves in half an hour."

"Yes." The Inspector made no move.

Fine, he must have the place staked out. We could relax; there was plenty of time. I grinned. "So the poison *was* in the Turkish Delight."

He shook his head. "No."

"No?"

"It is really a very straightforward case. Our murderer, who made no secret of his intention to marry for money, tried first with the older sister, the heiress. Unfortunately, they quarreled, so he took up with the younger one. But she would only inherit if her older sister died. So . . ." He shrugged.

"I didn't realize Brad had ever made a play for Candy."

"He hadn't. Nor did he kill her. After he saw the girls in the Villa Costas, he spent the rest of the day of the murder with me."

"Then who are we talking about?" I asked blankly.

Inspector Kantalakis drew one hand from behind his

back. It held a rusty tin, a tin which had been bought from Manthos' shop. "I found this in the trunk of your car."

"Yes, I bought it to deal with the rats at the Villa Costas."

"Really? It was this poison that killed Candice Stratton. It was put in the bottle of Coca-Cola."

"The Coca-Cola!"

"Yes. The Coca-Cola you gave to the murder victim. Do you deny you gave it to her? The maid Theodosia saw you."

"No, I gave it all right. I see! Brad must have dosed it, knowing Candy would drink it sooner or later. He must have fixed it when he came round that morning with the Turkish Delight. Samantha may have seen him go to the fridge. Ask her."

"I have asked her, Mr. Lawton. According to Miss Samantha Stratton, there never was any Coca-Cola in the Villa Costas. Nor, incidentally, were there any rats," Inspector Kantalakis added portentously.

Then he arrested me.

And I realized that, after all, I wasn't the sort of man who got that sort of girl.

THIEVES' BAZAAR

by W. L. Heath

I AM NOT AN ABNORMALLY SUSPICIOUS MAN, BUT THERE ARE some people I mistrust almost on sight. In my work I travel around considerably, and without paying myself any excessive compliments I think I can say that I have developed a pretty good eye for a "shady."

There are lots of them in the Middle East and the Orient, where I have had to do most of my traveling. Shadies come in all colors, shapes, and sizes, of course, but they are birds of a feather and easy enough to recognize, once you have seen them go into their act. They all peddle the same commodity—namely a deal, a skin game of one kind or another. In less time than it takes to buy them four scotch and sodas they will tell you, in confidential undertones, how to make a killing overnight—provided, of course, you have the sporting blood to lay a couple of American Express checks on the line. They flourish in second-rate bars all the way from Casablanca to Hong Kong, and while most of them are nothing more than small time confidence men, some are dangerous. If you think I'm talking melodramatic nonsense you simply haven't traveled in that part of the world.

Thompson was a shady, and I was sure of it from the start. He was one of those derelict white men you run across out there from time to time. They are always alone, these men, and shabbily dressed, and if you ask about

their business they tell you they are in "export-import."
That is the standard reply. Thompson's appearance alone
was enough to make me suspicious, but the circumstances
of our meeting him and his over-eager courtesy to Jan
were what really put me on guard.

We met Thompson in a bar across the street from the
Paradise Theater, in Karachi. Jan and I had been shopping since noon in the bazaar and had stopped there to
cool off before going back to the hotel. It was a fairly typical bar of the Great Eastern variety, more like an old fash-
ioned American drugstore than a cocktail parlor.

We took a seat under a fan, ordered a drink, and Jan
spread out her purchases to admire them.

"I'm still not satisfied," she said.

"Why not? You've got all the standard items—the ivory
comb, the *sari,* the brass elephant bell. What more could
the folks back in Philadelphia expect?"

She looked at me with a twinkle in her brown eyes. "A
star sapphire, Dave. I simply can't leave India without a
star sapphire."

I was tired. "Well, maybe tomorrow," I said.

"We won't have time tomorrow. Go with me this afternoon—please?" She put her hand on mine and gave me the
little pleading look I'd seen her use on her father. Jan was
a handsome girl with long dark eyelashes and the sort of
figure you expected of a wealthy American debutante.

"The ship won't sail till four," I said.

"I know, but there's so much to do—packing and all
that. I'm just positive we won't have time for any more
shopping tomorrow."

"But, honey, my feet are dead. They've quit. They've
surrendered."

She smiled at me and I thought she was about to give in,
but just then this man who called himself Thompson made
his gambit. He materialized suddenly at Jan's elbow,
cleared his throat and bowed. He was a big, pallid, puffy-
eyed man wearing a bush jacket and holding a soiled topee
in his hands.

"If you'll pardon the intrusion. I couldn't help overhearing what madam said."

The rest happened very fast, too fast for me to stop it. The next thing I knew, Thompson had introduced himself and pulled up a chair, and I was paying for another gin and lime.

"The important thing in buying gems is recognizing a valuable one when you see it," he said. "I presume you do know gems?"

"No, I don't," Jan said. "That's just the trouble."

Thompson frowned slightly and drummed his fingers on the crown of his sun helmet. "Then I'm afraid you do have a problem," he said. "Of course, I'm not suggesting that you'd be in any great danger of getting swindled—many of the merchants are scrupulously honest—but on the other hand we are in a foreign country and these Orientals . . ." He let his voice trail off on a note of regret, then looked up at me and smiled. "What we'd like to do is eliminate the element of doubt, wouldn't we?"

"What I'd like to do is go soak my feet," I said.

He evaded me with a laugh. "Shopping in this heat does tire one." He turned back to Jan and sipped his drink thoughtfully. I was trying to place his nationality. British, I thought, but possibly an American with a British accent.

"Maybe you could recommend a place where we'd be sure we were safe," Jan said.

"As a matter of fact, I was just about to suggest that," Thompson said. Things were going nicely. "There's a little shop down on—but no, you'd never find it alone." His face lit up suddenly and he looked at his watch. "Tell you what. I'm going that way and I'd be delighted to drop you off."

"Swell," Jan said.

"No," I said.

"Why not?"

"We couldn't impose on the gentleman that way."

"That's nonsense," Thompson exclaimed. "It's no imposition. I'd consider it a privilege. I say, we Anglos have to stick together out here, you know. We have to look out for one another."

"No," I said, "we appreciate your courtesy, but . . ."

"Oh, let's do go, Dave. It may be the last chance I'll have."

Thompson pressed his advantage carefully, and I argued, but it was no use. Jan had swallowed the bait, and though I didn't know her very well, I knew she was the sort of girl who's accustomed to having her way. Finally, out of fear that she might try it alone, I consented to go. The worst that could happen wasn't likely to be very bad, I thought, and if she wanted to throw away a hundred bucks or so on a back alley bargain that was her business, not mine. Her father could probably foot the bill without any discomfort and maybe the lesson would be good for her.

As we were about to leave the bar, Thompson excused himself and went to the rear of the room to make a phone call. I had expected that, too. We waited at the door. And when he joined us again, I asked him what his business was in Karachi.

"I'm in export-import," he said.

We hailed a cab—a horse-drawn victoria—and Thompson gave the driver instructions in Urdu, which he seemed to speak quite well. As we rode across town and through the bazaar, he sat facing us on the little jump seat behind the driver, chatting pleasantly and inquiring politely into our reasons for being in Pakistan. I explained that I was a photographer for *Geographics Illustrated,* now on my way home from an assignment in Ceylon.

"Then you two aren't married?"

"Oh no," Jan said. "We've only known each other for two weeks. We met on board ship after leaving Calcutta."

"Are you traveling alone?"

"No, my father is with me," she said. "He stayed at the hotel this afternoon to take a nap." She explained that her father was a steel manufacturer from Philadelphia, and that they were making a trip around the world. Her mother had died in February the year before, and she had pressed her father into making the trip, hoping it would take his mind off her death.

Thompson, apparently satisfied, was silent after that, and we clopped across Elephant Stone Street and down a wide avenue bordered on both sides by tall thirsty looking trees. I had never seen that section of the city before, and it still isn't clear to me exactly where we went. We passed through a park at one place, and then turned into a narrow, crowded street where half-naked children trotted beside the carriage crying for *baksheesh*—a handout.

Finally, we stopped in front of a shop with a corrugated tin awning, and I got out with considerable misgivings. It was a bad part of town, and I was beginning to be uneasy about letting Jan come here. The facade of the building was very ornate and above the street floor there was a sort of turret, a crown-shaped hexagonal chamber with shuttered windows on each side and several small minarets carved like the posts of a spool bed. In front of the shop a blind beggar sat on a filthy pallet.

We went up a flight of stone steps and into the arched doorway, where we were greeted by a little man wearing a black alpaca suit and a fez.

"Good afternoon," he said, indicating that we would be able to speak in English. He bowed and smiled and ushered us into a sort of anteroom to the right of the entrance. It appeared to be clean enough in there, but the odors of the street had followed us in. Thompson introduced us, explaining to the proprietor that we were interested in gems. We were given chairs then, and when we were seated the man in the fez began to bring out the stones. Thompson sat quietly at one side.

I suppose we stayed in the shop for half an hour, and though I watched everything as carefully as I could, I saw nothing wrong. The little man in the fez was patient and polite, and Thompson kept aloof from all the bargaining.

Jan was disappointed in the prices, and that surprised me, because I thought they were reasonable enough. She

looked at sapphires first, then at rubies, and finally asked
to see diamonds. I hoped that she wouldn't decide to buy a
diamond because they are the most difficult stone of all to
be sure about.

In the end, and partly due to my insistence, she bought
a small sapphire for ninety rupees. We thanked the proprietor and prepared to leave.

"Will you ride back with us?" Jan asked Thompson.

"No, thank you," he said. "I'm going the other direction."

He went out with us to call a carriage, and then said
goodbye. The whole episode left me completely baffled. I
had seen nothing wrong, and yet I had the feeling that
something was very wrong.

As we were riding back to the hotel, I asked Jan to let
me see the sapphire again. She opened her purse and gave
it to me, and I examined it carefully, rolling it around in
my palm. It had a good star, and though it was small, the
color was deep and blue and it was almost perfectly
shaped. I felt certain it was worth every cent she had paid
for it, maybe even more.

"Count your money again," I said. "See if he gave you
the correct change."

"It's all here," she said, thumbing through her bills.
"What makes you so suspicious?"

"I don't know. I honestly don't. I had a strange feeling
back there in that shop. Something fishy was going on, but
I can't figure out what it was. It was like watching a shell
game or a crooked poker hand. Know what I mean?"

"Yes," she said. "I think I do. I had that feeling myself."

When I looked at her I thought she had gone a little
pale.

Back in my room at the hotel, I poured a drink and went
out on the balcony to cool off. A moment later there was a
knock at the door and Jan came in. "Dad's still asleep,"
she said. "I thought I'd come down and have a drink with
you."

"Fine. I can give you scotch, but there's no ice."

"Mother India. Well, make it without ice and make it stiff. That jewel shop gave me the creeps."

She sat on the bed while I made the drink, and when I brought it to her, she asked for a cigarette to go with it. She had on a white linen skirt, but she had taken off the jacket she'd worn while shopping, and her blouse was open several inches down from the neck. I couldn't help noticing that she was not wearing a brassiere, but I put it down to the heat, and took a chair by the window where the view was not quite so distracting.

"You know," she said, "we've been together almost constantly for two weeks now, and you haven't even tried to kiss me."

"I'm a married man, I told you that. I've got a wife and kids at home, young lady."

She pursed her lips and gave me a reproachful look. "I didn't say I'd *let* you, but it's not very flattering when you don't even try."

"The trouble with you," I said, "is too much sun."

She laughed and got up. "I believe you're right. Mind if I go in and wash my face? I've felt positively dirty ever since that shop. I wish we hadn't gone." When she came out of the bathroom again, I noticed that the blouse was buttoned and I was relieved.

"What about dinner?" I said.

"We'll meet you in the bar at six. That is, if I can wake Dad. He was sleeping soundly a while ago."

When she was gone, I took a bath and shaved, and at six I went down to the bar to wait. I was still wondering about Thompson, but I couldn't find a flaw in it anywhere: Jan had got her money's worth in the stone; she had not been short-changed; the ever-obliging Thompson had departed without even hinting at a tip for his services. It was a bit thick, as the British would say. It didn't make sense, not in terms of what I knew about men like Thompson. But where was the catch?

I had a second drink as I mulled it over, and then all at

once I realized I had been waiting for quite a long time. It was six thirty now, and Jan and her father still hadn't showed up. I distinctly remembered hearing her say she would meet me in the bar at six. They were not the most punctual people in the world, but half an hour was a long time to be late and I felt sure they would have called down to tell me if something was delaying them. I began to be worried. So after a few minutes more, I decided to go back up to my room and give them a ring.

As I left the bar, I took a look around the lobby to make sure they were not waiting there by mistake, but there was no sign of them anywhere. I consequently went up the wide, red-carpeted stairs two at a time, feeling more worried with every step. The business with Thompson had set my mind in a high state of suspicion.

At the second landing, I turned left along the corridor and immediately saw that someone was in my room. The light was on and the door was open. When I reached the door, the first thing that caught my eye was my suitcase. It was lying open on the bed, and one of my cameras was lying beside it with the leather case taken off. The bed covers had been stripped from the bed and were piled in a heap on the floor, and several drawers of the dresser were hanging open. The next thing I saw was a little man in a black alpaca suit and a fez—the man from the jewel shop. He was standing in the bathroom door, looking over his shoulder at me in a rather surprised manner, and there was a pistol in his hand.

As he turned to face me, I took a step backward and dodged out of the door. I collided with a big man dressed in khakis and wearing a turban. The big fellow made a grab for me and caught my arm. When I tried to pull away, he gave my arm a twist. I swung around as far as I could in the other direction and hit him solidly in the mouth with my left fist. He let go and covered his mouth with his hands, and I hit him again, driving him back against the wall. But now another one had come up out of nowhere like the first—another big man dressed in what appeared to be a soldier's khakis. As I tried to go around him, he swung a short club at me. The blow missed my head, but hit my shoulder, and I went down to my knees, holding him around the waist. He swung again, and that's all I remember for quite a long time.

When I came to again, I was lying on my own bed looking up at the mosquito net, and the little man in the fez was bending over me with a wet towel. "We're sorry about this," he said.

"So am I." It was all I could think of at the moment.

He crossed the room and came back with my passport in his hand.

"We've checked all your papers and established your identity," he said. "We realize now that it was a mistake."

"I can agree with that. But what kind of a mistake?"

"We thought you were implicated with the girl. Now we have it straight."

"Jan?" I said. "Where is she?"

"They've both been arrested."

"Arrested? For what?"

"For the theft of several thousand dollars' worth of gems." He took a manila envelope from his pocket and emptied it into his hand. There were half a dozen rubies and pearls, an emerald and one large yellow looking diamond. "We found them in your bathroom," he explained. "Evidently she became suspicious after leaving the shop, and she brought them down here to hide."

"Wait a minute," I said, "I haven't kept up with you. Are you telling me you're a police officer?"

"That is correct, sahib," he said. "We were warned by the Bombay authorities to watch for these people; so when they arrived here, we prepared a trap for them. They've been working this system all the way from Hong Kong."

"What kind of system was it?"

"You see, they have synthetic gems. The girl substitutes a synthetic stone for a real one of similar shape and size wherever she finds it. Today, while you were with her, she obtained a ruby and this six carat diamond. She palmed off two synthetics, as you Americans would say."

I pulled myself up and let my feet down over the edge of the bed. My ears were ringing, and there was a terrific pain above my left ear. The big fellow with the turban was standing by the door with a swollen lip. He was a policeman all right.

"We're sorry about what happened in the hall," the man with the fez went on, "but there was much confusion and we still weren't sure who you were."

"What about Jan's father?"

The little man shook his head sadly. "I'm afraid the man wasn't her father, sahib. A most regrettable situation."

We were silent for a minute. My head was beginning to clear a little.

"Now about Thompson," I said. "He was your decoy, right?"

"I beg pardon?"

"He led us to the shop."

"Oh yes, Thompson." He smiled. "Thompson has been helpful to us on a number of occasions."

"But he's not a police officer?"

"Oh no. Thompson is—what would you call him? He does anything for a little money."

"A shady," I said. "I knew it all the time. Those people can't fool me for a minute."

T'ANG OF THE SUFFERING DRAGON

by James Holding

☐ LEANING OVER THE RANDOM SCATTER OF ANCIENT OBJECTS ON the table, Howard Mitchell was visited by the sudden, almost intolerable excitement of the avid collector who spots a treasure.

His heart lurched. He drew in a deep breath and leaned closer to the ceramic figure of the lute-player, breathing mental thanks to the clerk at his Hong Kong hotel who had directed him to Mr. Cheong's Emporium of the Suffering Dragon.

Mr. Cheong's antique shop presented a hodgepodge of supposed antiquities for sale to the credulous tourist, from Chinese weapons and armor to tatters of resplendent costumes once worn, no doubt, by noblemen and prostitutes before China became The New China.

Mitchell knew very little about antique armor or clothing but he did pride himself on a fairly broad knowledge of ceramics, and unless his eyes deceived him, he had discovered among the junk of Mr. Cheong's shop a true piece of ancient Chinese pottery. The lute-player was small—not more than six inches high—unglazed and dusty, but beautifully molded and fired. It was exactly the kind of piece originally placed in the tombs of prominent Chinese persons long ago.

How long ago? Mitchell leaned closer for better scrutiny. T'ang? Almost certainly, and that would make the little lute-player about twelve hundred years old, give or take a few. It would also make the lute-player a notable addition to the ceramic collection which occupied most of Mitchell's time and attention, now that his wife had died and left him alone with his money.

He became aware of shuffling footsteps and looked up to see an amiable Chinese gentleman regarding him. The shop's proprietor, if it were he, wore a shabby western business suit with vest, and looked every bit as ancient as his stock of merchandise.

"Very nice antiquities, sir," he said to Mitchell with the air of a man who has greeted ten thousand tourist shoppers with exactly those words. His English was excellent.

"Are you Mr. Cheong?" asked Mitchell.

Mr. Cheong bowed. "At your service, sir. Have you found something that strikes your fancy?" Mitchell noticed that under almost nonexistent lashes, Mr. Cheong's black eyes were shrewd.

Mitchell cleared his throat and tried to speak casually. "This . . . this ceramic figure," he said, indicating the lute-player with an index finger that trembled slightly with eagerness, "is it a genuine antique?"

"I have nothing but genuine antiques in this emporium," Mr. Cheong replied mildly, unperturbed by Mitchell's skepticism.

"Of what period is the figurine?"

"T'ang dynasty," Cheong said, spreading his hands in an Oriental gesture. "It is perfectly typical, I assure you."

"T'ang!" breathed Mitchell. He had been right. "How much do you want for it?"

Cheong smiled a faintly apologetic smile and shrugged his narrow shoulders. "It's a very nice piece, sir. Authentic T'ang in good condition is very hard to find these days, you know." He jerked his head in the general direction of the New Territories and Red China beyond them. "So I must ask a reasonably high price, you understand that."

"How much?"

"One thousand dollars," Cheong said.

Mitchell's excitement grew. "Hong Kong dollars?"

Again the faintly deprecatory smile. "Please, sir, American." He seemed amused, if anything, by Mitchell's question. "And I must warn you, sir, that it will do you no good to bargain with me. A thousand dollars is a very fair price. Ask anyone who knows antiquity values."

Mitchell felt a touch of self-consciousness. Haggling always made him uncomfortable. "I don't need to ask anyone, Mr. Cheong," he said. "I *know* it's a fair price."

As indeed he did. The going price for genuine T'ang figures, now very fashionable among the affluent citizens of the United States, was about two thousand dollars apiece. Only a month ago he had, himself, willingly paid a New York dealer thirty-one hundred dollars for a T'ang soldier not as perfect as this jewel of a lute-player.

For the first time, he reached out a hand and touched the figurine, lifting it tenderly from its perch among the welter of objects on the table. "I'll take it, please. Will you accept travelers' checks?"

Mr. Cheong bowed. Mitchell wasn't sure, but he thought he saw a lively pleasure in the black Chinese eyes. "Thank you," Mr. Cheong murmured. He took the figure from Mitchell's hand, leaving dust on his fingertips, and went behind a counter at the rear of the shop, where he proceeded to wrap the fragile lute-player in layer after layer of cotton and dirty newspapers. "Is there anything else my poor emporium can provide?" he asked with stereotyped Chinese humility as he worked. "I have other fine items, sir."

"That's all I want," Mitchell said. He was feeling very pleased with his luck. "Unless you have some more of those T'ang figures kicking around."

Mr. Cheong's hands grew still. He shot a glance at Mitchell. "Are you a dealer, sir?"

"Not a dealer, no. A collector. Of ceramics—Chinese, Etruscan, Persian. Only a beginner, but I'm learning." Mitchell gestured at the piece Mr. Cheong was now inserting in a sturdy cardboard box. "I recognized that one as a beauty, anyway."

Mr. Cheong finished wrapping the lute-player and watched quietly as Mitchell signed travelers' checks and passed them over to him. He put the checks in a drawer and turned back to Mitchell. He said, "A moment ago, I remarked that T'ang pottery is hard to find these days. I was telling the truth. But when one has the proper contacts in Red China, these things can be arranged."

Mitchell considered that oblique remark for a moment, then said, "Are you trying to tell me that you have contacts in Red China, Mr. Cheong?"

Cheong bowed.

"And that therefore you *do* have more of these T'ang figures available?"

Cheong repeated his bow.

"Well, I'll be damned!" blurted Mitchell. Excitement surged through him again, but caution overrode it instantly. He had seen too many fakes masquerading as genuine antiquities to rely on the word of a strange Chinese. Yet there was the lute-player. What harm could come of looking? "Where are they?" he asked. "Here in the shop?"

"Where else?" The Americanism sounded quaint from the mouth of the venerable Mr. Cheong, despite his western suit and vest which were now making him sweat. "Will you come along with me, please, Mr. . . . ?"

"Mitchell." He followed Cheong into a curtained alcove lined with wooden shelves. Cheong lit a dim bulb in the ceiling by pulling on a grimy string, and there, incontrovertibly, lined up at the back of one of the shelves among a miscellany of bangles, teapots, and jeweled chopsticks, stood a row of small ceramic figures that looked to Mitchell quite as authentic as the T'ang piece he had already purchased.

"I keep them back from the edge," explained Mr. Cheong, "to prevent accidents."

His heart beating fast, Mitchell's eyes rapidly traversed

the row of small figures: musicians, horses, soldiers—
twenty-eight of them, in prime condition. He picked up
one, went into the main shop, examined the figure by day-
light at the front window, and returned to Mr. Cheong.

Cheong smiled. "Authentic T'ang," he intoned earnestly.
"Very rare, very good condition, very cheap."

"*If* they're genuine," said Mitchell, unable to contain his
suspicion, now reawakened a hundredfold. "As I told you,
Mr. Cheong, I'm fairly new at this collecting business, and
not at all sure of my own ability to distinguish genuine
pieces from fakes. But you must realize," he jerked a
thumb at the row of figures, "that this is too good to be
true."

Cheong nodded. "I understand your feelings. But I told
you that I have good contacts."

"Good is too mild a word. Sensational would be better, I
think."

"These pieces are genuine," Mr. Cheong said mildly.
"You have my word." He dangled the carrot. "And only one
thousand dollars apiece. If you do not wish to own so many
T'ang pieces yourself, you could use them to trade with
fellow collectors for other ceramics, could you not?"

Mitchell struggled to retain his perspective. The figures
must be fakes, probably manufactured by the hundreds in
some hidden Hong Kong factory for the tourist trade. He
began to regret buying the lute-player.

Cheong seemed to read his mind. "You suspect these are
modern copies, Mr. Mitchell? Tourist souvenirs?"

"Yes. I'm sorry. But I do."

"Do not blame yourself. There are many such in Hong
Kong. I am aware of that. But not these. Why not assure
yourself of their genuineness?"

"How?"

"Submit them to a true expert in Chinese pottery, perhaps? For certification?"

"Whom do you have in mind?"

"You are American," said Mr. Cheong. "You live in New
York?"

"Yes."

"You know Philadelphia, then? In Pennsylvania?"

"Sure," said Mitchell, intrigued by the geographical turn of the conversation. "What about Philadelphia?"

"One of the greatest experts on Chinese ceramics in the world," Cheong said, "resides in Philadelphia. You could have him authenticate these figures as true T'ang pieces."

Mitchell said, "What good can your expert do me when he is in Philadelphia and these figures are in Hong Kong?"

"His evaluation of these pieces can be arranged without financial risk to you, if that's what you mean, Mr. Mitchell."

"Really?" said Mitchell. "How?"

"Suppose you were to pay me, today, the current souvenir price for these figures, as though they *are* copies? Then, after consultation with Dr. Kam Soon Fat in Philadelphia, if he finds the pieces genuine, you could mail me the proper price for them."

"You mean you'd *trust* me?"

Mr. Cheong bowed his amiable bow. "Thus you would risk only five American dollars for each of these T'ang figures, Mr. Mitchell, until you are satisfied they are authentic."

Mitchell said weakly, "But the matter of customs duty . . ."

"Declare the lute-player at its true value," Cheong suggested, "and declare these other twenty-eight figures as souvenirs at five dollars apiece. I shall give you a sales slip to that effect."

Mitchell was silent, considering wistfully the row of ceramic figures in a dusty Hong Kong shop, and thinking he'd like very much to own them, fakes or not—and they *must* be fakes. But if Cheong was willing to trust him, wouldn't it be very ungracious of him not to respond in kind?

He made one more cast before succumbing to the lovely temptation. "How do you happen to know this Dr. Fat—was that his name?—in Philadelphia?"

"I don't know him personally. Only his reputation as a preeminent Oriental scholar. Everyone seriously interested in Chinese art knows of him. He is head of the department of Oriental Studies at Widner College." Mr. Cheong paused and looked at Mitchell doubtfully. "If you collect Chinese ceramics, Mr. Mitchell, I am very much surprised that *you* haven't heard of him."

"I have," said Mitchell, smiling. "That's why I'm going to take you up on your offer, Mr. Cheong. I'll take all twenty-eight of these figures at five dollars a head, as you suggest, and I'll send you my check for twenty-eight thousand dollars if Dr. Fat certifies they are authentic. Thank you for selling them to me, Mr. Cheong. Whether they are copies or originals, they are still very beautiful."

Mr. Cheong bowed. "That is far more important than price, is it not?" Politely, he held out a fountain pen for Mitchell to use in signing two more travelers' checks.

Professor Kam Soon Fat, B.A., M.A., Ph.D., M.F.A., belied his name. In his mid-thirties, he was slender, almost emaciated, and his thin body gave no promise whatever of later obesity. His long-chinned studious face was saved from severity by his spectacles—half-moon reading glasses over which he peered genially at his visitor, like a mischievous teenager experimenting with granny glasses.

Mitchell sat down in the indicated chair beside Professor Fat's desk and held his leather case on his knees before him. "It was good of you to see me," he said. "I know you have a busy schedule."

"Never too busy to help a fellow-admirer of Chinese ceramics," said Dr. Fat. "Especially when I can earn a consulting fee by doing so." His English was fluent and unaccented. He gave Mitchell a quizzical look. "You see, I like money, as well as Oriental art."

"Who doesn't?" said Mitchell, amused at the frankness of this internationally-known scholar.

"Your letter mentioned T'ang figurines," said Dr. Fat. "You have reason to question their genuineness, you said."

"Yes. And I'm counting on you to tell me whether I have a treasure here or a set of fakes." Mitchell explained that he was a recent newcomer to the ranks of collectors and not yet confident of his own judgment. "Particularly," he said with a smile, "when quantity as well as quality is involved."

"Quantity?"

"I have twenty-nine pieces here," Mitchell said, opening his case and beginning to unwrap his figurines. "All acquired from a single source at the same time, in one transaction."

"I see. From a questionable source then, I take it?"

"Right."

"Almost any reputable dealer, or even collector," said Dr. Fat, "might come up with twenty-nine authentic pieces—"

"But not the obscure antique shop where I bought these," Mitchell interrupted.

"An American shop?"

"No, in the Orient." Mitchell saw no reason to be more specific. "The place catered largely to tourists. So it's stretching credulity a bit, in my opinion, to believe that all these figures are genuine."

As Mitchell removed the wrappings from each figure, he placed it on Dr. Fat's desk top. Over his spectacles, Dr. Fat watched with fascination as the collection of horses, soldiers, and musicians grew. "They are lovely, aren't they?" he murmured. His eyes caressed the figures. "Is that the lot?"

"That's it," said Mitchell. "Twenty-nine."

Dr. Fat regarded the figures on his desk for a moment without touching them. Then, slowly, he stretched out a lean hand and picked up one of them. He examined it carefully through his half-glasses, turning it this way and that, missing no tiny area of its surface. Then he took from his desk drawer a powerful magnifying glass and repeated the inspection, even more deliberately. Finally he set the piece aside and repeated the performance on a second figure, humming the while in a barely audible undertone, completely preoccupied. One after another, he scrutinized the twenty-nine pieces of pottery, while Mitchell sat quietly in his chair, too engrossed to venture even a single question.

When the specialist finished his inspection, there were twenty-eight figures at the right side of his desk, and at the left, a single ceramic figure of a trotting horse. Dr. Fat straightened, stretched, looked over his spectacles at Mitchell, and smiled. "That's the best I can do, Mr. Mitchell," he said. "There's not a question in the world about twenty-eight of your pieces." He waved at them.

Mitchell's heart sank. "Forgeries?" he asked.

"Not at all. Genuine T'ang, beyond any doubt. I'll gladly stake my reputation on them."

"That's wonderful!" Mitchell exclaimed. "They looked so right to me, and yet I couldn't quite believe it . . ."

"You can believe it now, I'm happy to assure you. You have twenty-eight authentic pieces here, Mr. Mitchell. As for this one . . ." Dr. Fat pointed to the trotting horse at his left hand, "I reluctantly must admit to uncertainty."

"You think that one's a fake?" Mitchell felt a faint relief that it wasn't his lute-player.

"It is possible, yes."

"What makes you think so? Isn't it just like the others?"

"Not quite. There's a minute variation in the clay which disturbs me." Dr. Fat offered his magnifying glass, and Mitchell examined the horse. He saw nothing remarkable about it except for a tiny chip in one hoof. Dr. Fat went on, "This piece could merely have been carelessly fired twelve hundred years ago. Or it could equally well be only twelve years old instead of twelve centuries." He smiled at Mitchell. "Which would make quite a difference in its value."

Yes, pondered Mitchell, how much would he pay Mr. Cheong at the Emporium of the Suffering Dragon for a possible fake? Five dollars . . . or a thousand? Or something in between? He said, "If *you* can't give that one a clean bill, I guess there's nobody who can."

"Not so," said Dr. Fat. "If you are willing to risk another hundred and fifty dollars on a possible fake, there *is* a way to determine whether this figure is genuine T'ang or not, a scientific certification."

Mitchell was surprised. "I thought you were the last word on that," he said.

Dr. Fat shrugged. "The last *living* word, let us say. There is a mechanical method, a new one, which can also separate the sheep from the goats. Infallibly."

"Infallibly?"

"Yes," Dr. Fat said. "Not many ceramics defy my own analysis; perhaps one in a hundred, like your horse here. But I am only human, therefore fallible. So in these rare cases, I recommend that this mechanical method be utilized to resolve the puzzle. The technique, I must say, is a remarkable example of the application of science to art, and recourse to it not only confirms or disproves my own judgment on a piece, but makes me feel much better about accepting a consultation fee for my advice." Dr. Fat put his fingertips together, steeple-shaped, and gave Mitchell a sudden boyish grin. "You're sitting there wondering why I didn't refer you to the infallible machine at once, aren't you?" he asked. "If it's so much more reliable than an expert's opinion?"

Guiltily, Mitchell said, "Well . . ."

"It is also very much more expensive," Dr. Fat said. "Each piece of pottery submitted to the process costs the owner a hundred and fifty dollars for its analysis—three times the amount of my consultation fee—in addition to a certain amount of inconvenience involved. Thus, I consider that only really questionable pieces merit the expense."

"Tell me about it," Mitchell said. "I've never heard of such a process."

"Few have. It's quite new, as I said. It was devised originally by a geochemist at UCLA, and perfected only very recently at the Research Laboratory for Archaeology and the History of Art at Oxford. So far, there are only a couple of laboratories in the world considered capable of doing it successfully. One of them is at Oxford, of course, and the other, happily for us, is at the University Museum right here in Philadelphia. The method requires a great deal of very expensive equipment, sophisticated instruments. That's the reason for the high charge per analysis."

"I see," said Mitchell. He was impressed.

"The method itself is based on the fact that all pottery contains at least some trace of radioactive isotopes, or atomic varieties, of such elements as uranium, thorium, and potassium. In the years after the pottery is fired, this radioactivity tends to damage the crystals of quartz, feldspar, and other minerals in the clay. Are you with me so far?" he asked Mitchell doubtfully.

"You lost me back there with the isotopes," Mitchell said. "My line was steel forgings. But please go on."

"Very well. If a piece of pottery is reheated years later, these damaged crystals in the clay give off a faint blue light, invisible to the naked eye, but readily detectable with special instruments."

"Reheat? How can they reheat a ceramic piece like my horse without ruining it?"

"They drill out a tiny sample from the base of your figure, where it doesn't show, and heat the sample up to 500 degrees centigrade. If cumulative radiation damage is present, the sample will emit the blue light. If the piece is a fake, of recent manufacture, the sample will emit no light . . . because there has not been enough radiation damage as yet."

"Sounds complicated to me," Mitchell said.

"It is. From the amount of light emitted, the date when the piece was fired can be roughly estimated. Not very precisely, but close enough to detect a recent copy at once."

Mitchell looked fondly at his ceramic horse which might be a fake. He said, "So it is possible to get an accurate answer about my horse, right here in town, for a hundred and fifty dollars? Then I'd be sure?"

Dr. Fat nodded. "And I heartily recommend it. Then you'd know what you've got, without question."

"You said this machine confirms or disproves your judgment on a questionable piece," Mitchell said. "What *is* your best guess on my ceramic horse?"

"Genuine," replied Dr. Fat promptly. "I'm sixty percent sure but forty percent doubtful."

Mitchell made up his mind. "Let's find out for sure, then. How do I go about it?"

"I'll give you a note to the director of the museum."

"Fine. And thanks for everything, Dr. Fat. I'll let you know the verdict on the horse."

"I'll be most interested," said Dr. Fat.

Two weeks later, Dr. Fat received a long-distance telephone call from Hong Kong. "Nephew?" inquired a thready voice above the satellite hum.

"Yes, uncle," replied Dr. Fat, recognizing the voice despite its distortion.

Mr. Cheong, venerable proprietor of the Emporium of the Suffering Dragon, switched to Mandarin. "I received a check in the mail today, nephew, for twenty-eight thousand dollars. From Mr. Mitchell. I thought you'd want to know. I shall bank your half as arranged."

"Good," said Dr. Fat with satisfaction. "Let us hope this is but the first of many such coups."

"I see no reason to doubt it. Did everything go smoothly?"

"Like clockwork. I solemnly certified the twenty-eight forgeries as genuine, and raised reasonable doubts about the only authentic T'ang piece, the horse, recommending he have it tested mechanically. Which reminds me, uncle. I *am* an authority on ceramics, you know. I can distinguish genuine T'ang figures without your help. The nick in the horse's hoof was almost flagrantly evident."

"Forgive me. That was merely double protection against error. It shall not happen again." Mr. Cheong paused. "Mr.

Mitchell did not question any of the forgeries? He had only the genuine piece tested?"

"That's right, uncle. And when the laboratory gave him the verdict on his horse, he couldn't thank me enough for being honest about my doubts of it."

Mr. Cheong laughed softly. "I expected as much." He controlled his merriment and continued, "The western mind is so illogical. It tends to jump to conclusions on insufficient evidence. For example: if one T'ang figure proves genuine, the twenty-eight others must be genuine also." He chuckled wryly.

"Your own conclusion, uncle, or something that Confucius say?" Dr. Fat laughed, too.

"Neither. I had a professor of anthropology at Stanford in my youth," said Mr. Cheong. "His favorite example of this western tendency to leap to conclusions dealt with an explorer who, returning from a trip through the North American wilderness, stated unequivocally that American Indians walked in single file. 'How can you be sure of that?' asked a friend, and the explorer replied, 'Because the only Indian I encountered was walking that way.' You see my point, nephew?"

Dr. Fat said, "I do indeed. May I ask another question?"

"Of course," said Mr. Cheong tolerantly. "It is proper that youth learn from age."

"How could you be sure that Mitchell would send you the money?"

"That same Stanford professor," said Mr. Cheong. "He made another pithy observation that I have never forgotten. It was to the effect that, in the American free enterprise system, no man can afford to be completely honest until he is financially independent. Yet when financial independence is achieved, most Americans are almost fanatically honest, to make up for early laxity, I presume. Thus, I felt that our Mr. Mitchell could be trusted."

"Because he is financially independent?"

"Of course."

"And how did you know *that*?"

Mr. Cheong chuckled. "Very simple, nephew. Your cousin, Hsien, who works as a clerk at the Hong Kong Hilton, looked Mr. Howard Mitchell up in *Who's Who in America* and *Dun and Bradstreet* before he sent him to my shop."

"Ah," said Dr. Fat admiringly. "You think of everything, uncle."

"*You* did very well for a first venture, nephew. Congratulations."

"Thanks. At least, let it stand to my credit that I *did* tell the unvarnished truth to Mr. Mitchell in one respect."

"Which was?"

"That I am fond of money, as well as Oriental art."

THE WESTERN FILM SCAM

by Francis M. Nevins, Jr.

❏ I PUT THE BOOK BACK ON THE STEEL SHELF, THREE FEET FROM the body, and listened. The storage room was empty except for the dead man and me; no sound but my own thundering heartbeat. I heard footsteps along some unseen corridor, maybe heading this way, I couldn't be sure. I knew I hadn't killed the man, and the reference book had confirmed my theory as to who had, but it still wouldn't do to be found in that film storage vault with a fresh corpse.

So I ran. Swiftly and silently as I could, like a poor imitation of an Indian. Back through the storage room and along the corridor to the loading-dock exit. Luck stayed with me. I met no one. I took out a handkerchief to avoid leaving prints, twisted back the lock, flung the door open, and leaped down to the Thirteenth Street sidewalk. Then I made myself slow down to a brisk walk and put as much distance between myself and the offices of KBMO-TV as my legs would allow.

West half a mile, then south to Olive where I caught a Bi-State bus that took me into the thick of the St. Louis business district where I could lose myself. Then I got off and walked aimlessly, wherever the crowds were. By now both the local cops and the Feds must be hunting me. I needed quiet time to sort out the mess.

So I turned in at Stadium Cinema II, a couple of blocks north of Busch Stadium, and bought two hours of peace.

The matinee attraction was one of those trendy older-woman younger-man romances, just the kind of film I could ignore completely as I leaned back in the well-upholstered theater chair and sent my thoughts returning to where it had all begun . . .

On that soft and quiet Los Angeles evening ten days after John West's funeral, despite smog and inflation and the energy crunch, I was at peace. The profits from my last adventure guaranteed three more months of ease, and I had nothing in mind but relaxation when my annunciator bloop-bleeped and a familiar if not totally welcome voice emerged from the machine's innards. "It's Louie. Just heard you were in town. Okay if I come up?" Without great enthusiasm I consented and crossed the living room of my hideaway apartment to lower the volume on the TV, which happened to be tuned to an old John West movie.

Of course half of the stations in the world were running West pictures that evening, and had been since a brain tumor had finally toppled the old oak two weeks before. The dozens of Westerns he'd starred in during his salad years, the war pictures, the macho action flicks—every station that could scrounge a West package from a distributor was blitzing the airwaves with the big rangy body, the king-of-the-hill walk, the drawl that had made John West a symbol of America for the world. So it wasn't really unusual that the booms and bangs of West's Korean War epic *The Beaches of Inchon* were providing background noise as Louie sat on my couch, downing a double jolt of my bourbon and trying to sell me his latest scheme.

Lou the Q—a short wiry-bodied lummox with arms as long as a monkey's and a face to match—had knocked around the fringes of scamdom for a dozen years under five dozen names. Rumor was that he'd been born Louis Quackenbush, which would explain his nickname. In Dallas he'd worked as Ithas Haggerson, in Minneapolis as J. Rudolph Klug; but no matter where he operated or what name he used, his scams had the same nasty habit of falling apart on him. He'd been slammered only once, however, and that time luck was his cellmate.

During the year he'd served at the Federal pen in Lexington, Kentucky, under the name of Harold O'Flynn, the cops never caught on that he was wanted in three other states under three other aliases. Since his release six months ago he'd been out of circulation, which wasn't surprising since most of us in the life considered him a jinx and wouldn't work with him. I had never pulled a job with him but I'd found him to be one of those dullards who inspire brightness in others, and a few of my past nifties had been conjured up during casual chats with him. Louie knew I owed him for those inspirations. That was why he was sprawled on my couch now, pitching an inspiration of his own.

"The guy in the cell next to me, he was a film pirate. One of those people who make duplicate prints or cassettes of movies and sell 'em to collectors. He was serving a year for criminal copyright infringement and I was bored in the slam so he said he'd teach me copyright law. Everybody else in the place was reading constitutional law and prisoners' rights stuff, I read copyright. Wild, huh?"

"Untamed," I murmured, sipping Early Times and wondering where this meandering monologue would end.

"And I watched a lotta shoot-'em-ups on the tube." Louie pointed vaguely across the room toward the flickers of colored light from my set. "He was my favorite—John West as The Rio Kid. God, I musta seen those Rio Kid flicks twenty times apiece when I was a boy. Did you know his real name was Adrian Jonathan Westmoreland and he was born in Mount Clemens, Michigan?" He scooped up last week's *Time* from the coffee table, the one with West's craggy face on the cover, and thumbed through the magazine for the lead story.

"Listen, Milo," he demanded, and began to read aloud from the obituary survey of the great Hollywood he-man's career. " 'For most of the 1930's he was confined on the open ranges of the low-budget Western film, starring in

some two dozen quickly lensed oaters as The Rio Kid, a
border adventurer who was the hero of countless pulp
magazine yarns by a long-forgotten hack named J. F.
Carewe. In later years an embittered and impoverished
Carewe made a sort of retirement hobby out of telling
interviewers how the movies had softened and sanitized
his authentic roughneck creation. Savants of horse opera
agree that the films resembled Carewe's stories only in
that the name Rio Kid was used for the hero, but they
rank these pictures, which gave West his first crack at
stardom, as among the finest series Westerns ever made.
The studio went bankrupt in 1949 and the Rio Kid movies
eventually fell into the public domain when no one bothered to renew the copyrights.' "

Louie rolled the magazine into a cylinder and aimed it
at the TV. "Get it, Milo? All the Rio Kid movies are in
public domain. You know what that means?"

"It means anyone can use the films as they please without paying any permissions or royalties," I hazarded.

Louie grinned like a monkey who's found an especially
tasty banana. "Not quite. There's a catch I learned from
that film pirate. A couple of cases say that if a public-
domain work is based on another work that's still in copyright, you infringe the other work if you use the public-
domain work. You see the plan now?"

"Vaguely," I told him. "Did J. F. Carewe renew the copyrights on his pulp stories?"

"You betcha. Like clockwork. And when he died in 1956,
a lonely old widower with everything he wrote long out of
print and forgotten, he left a very simple will. All his property including literary rights went to his only child, a
daughter named Carolyn Carewe who's now a spinster in
her seventies, living in a retirement home in northern
California."

I raised my hand to halt the flow of data. "Okay, time
out. Your idea is for us to contact this old lady, buy the
rights to the Rio Kid stories as cheap as we can, then

threaten to sue every station that runs those old movies unless they pay our price?"

"On the button, man," Louie nodded, and took a long swallow of bourbon. "You wanna be my partner or you wanna not?"

The more I tossed it around my brain pan the better I liked it, not least because technically it was legal. No wonder Louie had come to me: he needed a partner, and most confidence people wouldn't touch one of his scams with a mile-long pole. But this gem, if polished properly, had magnificent possibilities.

I answered his question with a definite maybe and watched him lurch hazily to my apartment door.

The next day I spent at the UCLA Law Library, checking out Louie's copyright theory in assorted treatises and journals, then reading the relevant judicial opinions as printed in the National Reporter System. By 6:00 P.M. I decided that the Kentucky film pirate had known his onions. The top legal scholars seemed to think the whole notion was silly—after all, if there are hidden patches of copyright in public-domain works, the basic concept and rationale of the public domain is destroyed—but just as one can make bread using an off-brand of yeast, I proposed to make bread using this quirk in the law. I called Louie late that evening and closed a deal with him.

Step Two took a few days and required the services of a lawyer. I needed to form a corporation to hold legal title to the rights we were going to buy from Carolyn Carewe. In due course Western Properties, Inc., was registered with the California Secretary of State. Its president's and vice-president's names were listed as John J. Terwilliger and August Lunt, since my rightful name and Louie's were too well known in certain official circles.

Step Three took no more than a phone call to Jock Schultz, the disembodied Dublin brogue that runs our profession's human supermarket. "That's the job description, Jocko. A woman who can persuade an old spinster to sign over some worthless literary rights her father left her. A woman who can talk convincingly about old Western novels and movies if she has to. Know anyone who can do it?"

"Call ye back in an hour," he promised. And true to his word, he had my lady for me in exactly 52 minutes. ". . . And ye get a bonus too, me bucko, in that she is a quintessential Ten. Her name is Becca Benbow. Tall, twenty-eight, form divine. She partnered with Fats Adamo last year in the Disco Cola thing."

"Speak no more," I told the Jock. "That's all the recommendation she needs. Can you set up a meet for me?"

He could and did, and that Friday evening I met her plane at L.A. International. She was honey-skinned and slender, with rich brown hair falling loosely below her shoulders. I felt like bending my knee and kissing her hand, for this lady was royalty in more than just looks.

Inside word had it that without her, Disco Cola would have been the world's fattest turkey instead of the superscam of the age. We found a dark corner in a quiet airport lounge, and as I unveiled the proposal to her she nodded and said "Uh-huh," her eyes glowing with the pure joy of the caper. "Equal split?" she asked at the end of my pitch.

I took a moment to ask myself if I could bulldoze Louie into accepting another partner, then nodded. "I wouldn't dream of offering you less," I replied, proud of my nonsexist approach to sharing the spoils. "Take a room at an airport hotel and catch PSA's first flight to San Francisco in the morning. Get cards printed up identifying you as, let's call you Roberta Ross, and your title will be Chief of the Purchasing Department, Western Properties, Inc. Then you rent a car and drive north to the retirement home where Carolyn Carewe lives. After you've signed her up, give me a call here and let me know how much I have to put in the corporate bank account to cover your check. The Rio Kid stories have been out of print for thirty years, so the price shouldn't be steep."

"And meanwhile what will you be doing?" Becca poked the ice in her Scotch-and-soda with a plastic swizzle stick. "Research," I said. "Pinpointing our first target."

For the next two days and evenings I sat in the Reading Room of the Los Angeles Public Library, hunched over the back files of numerous out-of-town newspapers, skimming the TV sections with my eyes keen for any station that ran old Westerns and the Rio Kid pictures in particular. On the second evening I went over my accumulated list and chose St. Louis, Missouri. Home of the Gateway Arch, the baseball and football Cardinals, the Anheuser-Busch Brewery, and, more to the point, the home of KBMO-TV, Channel 39, which, according to the *Post-Dispatch* and *Globe-Democrat* listings, broadcast an old horse opera every weeknight from 10:00 to 11:00 P.M.

I had some qualms about returning to the city where four years ago one of my juiciest scams had blown apart, leaving me with a pile of cash and the solution to an old murder case. But I was so excited over this new ploy— which, if it worked, could be replayed in city after city all over the land—that I told the voice of caution to be quiet.

Late that night back in my apartment, I was relaxing with a glass of white wine when the phone rang. Becca, my ESP told me, and when I lifted the receiver and cautiously helloed, sure enough it was she. "Got her!" she crowed. "And dirt cheap too. The poor bird's so grateful anyone still cares about her father's silly old stories she practically donated them to us." After we settled the financial details I gave her the next set of instructions. "Relax tomorrow and fly back in the evening. I'll pick you up at LAX. We'll get the transfers recorded with the Copyright Office. Then we pack our bags."

"Going where?" For a second I thought she was almost too eager to know. "A place with some good shopping centers?"

"Maybe," I said coyly.

No sooner had we broken connections than I fingered

the touch-tones myself, punching out Louie's local number. I caught him comparatively dry and reported his new-found partner's success. Then I gave him his travel orders.

"So it's meet me in St. Louie, Louie, heh?" he muttered. "Okay, I'll fly out tomorrow and start softening up the strike zone."

"And without liquid assistance," I warned sternly. "Have a smooth flight."

Then I settled back and killed the next day rereading books on the history of the Western film until Becca called me to pick her up at the airport.

We drove out to Tarzana for a delightful Japanese dinner at a place called Mon's, and over tempura and teriyaki I brought her up to date. ". . . He's in St. Louis by now, getting things ready for our arrival after we finish our paperwork."

Becca's lovely dark eyes clouded with hints of worry. "I'm frankly not crazy about this Louie with all his names." She sipped sake from a delicate white bowl. "He's a drunk and a jinx and he could mess things up royally."

"Granted. But, my sweet, he created this scam and we can't very well freeze him out at this stage. On the other hand, after we test-market the idea in St. Louis, I may want to buy out his share in the company and work the rest of the country just with you." I dazzled her with my most suggestive smile. "In fact, I'm quivering with delight over the prospect."

It was Sunday evening when a dour Lou the Q met us near the luggage carousels at Lambert-St. Louis International Airport. He lit up with momentary pleasure when he met his new partner, but something was clearly amiss with him and I couldn't tell whether it was sour stomach, shot nerves, or a hitch in the plans. He drove us in a rented car to our downtown headquarters at Stouffer's Riverfront Inn, less than a mile from KBMO's studios and offering fine views of the muddy Mississippi. Once unpacked and settled in, the three of us convened in my suite for drinks and a briefing. Louie's highball, carefully prepared by myself, was 99 percent mixer and ice.

"I got us a lawyer," the Q reported. "His name's Napoleon Jimson and he's young, mean, and black. He took a copyright course in law school, so he knows the game. And he's been involved in a lawsuit to take away Channel 39's operating license and give it to some black coalition, so he knows our pigeons."

"Sounds like a winner," I murmured, and Becca nodded solemn concurrence. "Tell us about the people who run the station."

"The place is a zoo." Before I could stop him Louie poured himself a too-generous slug of Early Times over rocks and shook the glass in his hairy paw to cool the booze down. "The station's owned by Blair Communications Company. That's a subsidiary of Blairco, the big conglomerate. The son of the president of Blairco is the station manager. Bradford Lockwood Blair the Second. The assistant station manager is a prune named Jerome McKenna who used to run the shop himself before Blair bought the station and put in his kid as head cheese. The program director is a guy named David Wilkes. He's been with the station about a year. The word is that he and the head of advertising and promotion, a fantastic blonde named Susan Otis, are the ones who persuaded young Blair to run those old cowboy pictures. I've also heard gossip that Otis and McKenna were a combo until Wilkes took her away from him."

"With all those undercurrents of emotion it's a wonder the station manages to broadcast anything," Becca remarked, strolling to the window with her drink to look at the lights twinkling on the river.

"Our office is all rented and ready," Louie went on after a long pull at his glass. "It's on the tenth floor of the Paul Brown Building over on Olive. An easy walk from here and from there to KBMO."

"Louie would have been a great White House advance man if he hadn't chosen another line," I told Becca.

She turned from the window and smiled at Louie's sim-
ian façade. "Teach me not to go by appearances. Milo, if
the game starts tomorrow I'm turning in right now." She
yawned lustily, swallowed the last of her drink, and
headed for the door. "Jet lag always knocks me out. Night,
guys."

A few minutes after her departure Louie got up and
started to take his own leave, until I halted him with a
traffic-cop arm motion. "Whoa! You don't sleep till I find
out why you look like the boy whose dog just died. What
haven't you told me?"

He shuffled back and forth, cracking his knuckles explo-
sively. "I woulda told you, Milo, only I didn't wanta panic
the chick."

"Ms. Benbow is a full and equal partner in this scam,
you chauvinistic porker," I reproved him. "Now cough up
the bad news."

"It mighta just been my imagination," he said furtively.
"You can never be sure about a thing like this. But the
other day, over on Twelfth a few blocks from KBMO, I saw
a guy on the street that I thought I recognized."

"Who was it?"

"That's what I don't know, but I think it was someone
from when I was working the South and calling myself
Hal O'Flynn. It mighta been one of the Feds who got me on
that rap. Milo, I swear it scared the stuffing outa me.
Every damn scam I'm on, something goes haywire. It's like
I'm planting trees and bushes in my yard and all the bagworms in the block pick my shrubs for their nests."

I shook him sternly by the shoulders, like a combat sergeant in a WWII flick bracing a fearful rookie before the
big battle. "Come on, Louie, knock it off. You are not a jinx.
You're letting your pessimism run away with you. Now go
get some sleep so we can get an early start. And no more
booze!"

He left, looking not the least reassured. It took me
longer than usual to drop off into slumberville that night,

and I couldn't help wondering if Louie's squeams were beginning to get to me.

The St. Louis headquarters of Western Properties, Inc., turned out to be a small but serviceable suite, with two side-by-side offices opening onto a reception room. Chauvinistically, we stationed Becca at the reception desk while Louie and I took the private rooms. Once we'd hung our office sign and a few framed cowboy prints and generally made ourselves at home, it was time for our first sortie against the target. This took the form of a phone call to KBMO, with me doing the honors since I was president of the company and—thanks to my Western Film Festival scam of glorious memory—knew the most about old shoot-'em-ups. I sat at my executive desk and made the pitch while Becca and Louie eavesdropped on extensions.

"May I speak to Mr. Blair, please . . . Well, if he's in conference I'll speak to Mr. McKenna . . . Good morning, sir. My name is John J. Terwilliger. I am president of Western Properties, Inc., a California corporation that owns the rights to the works of some of America's leading storytellers. Ah, have you heard of our company before?" I would have fainted from shock if McKenna had said yes, but his answer, in a decidedly prunelike voice, was that the name was new to him.

"Among the works we own," I went on, "are the original Rio Kid stories by the late J. F. Carewe." I went on with a concise statement of the copyright quirk which gave my company exclusive control over the public-domain Rio Kid movies starring John West.

A series of incoherent splutters from the other end had been punctuating my harangue, but finally Mac got a grip on himself and broke in, on my monologue. "Just who the hell do you think you are?"

"Your station has broadcast several hours of old Western films each week for the past nine or ten months, including the Rio Kid series. Since John West's recent death you've run a Rio Kid every weeknight. Miss Carewe could have sued you for copyright infringement at any time, and my company now stands in her shoes. Are you prepared to pay us a substantial cash settlement for prior infringements and enter into a licensing contract with us so that we will be paid royalties on all future broadcasts?"

"I'm prepared to kick you straight into hell," McKenna riposted furiously, and slammed down his phone with an eardrum-numbing clatter.

Having done likewise, though more sedately, I gave Louie and Becca thumbs-up. "The game's underway. Mc-Kenna's bound to report the call to Blair right away. Blair will consult the station's lawyers and the lawyers will order a copyright search to confirm that we own the rights. Then he'll be in touch with us," I predicted, "hat in hand."

"So what do we do until then?" Becca asked from her perch on the receptionist's desk.

"As you please, my sweet. Shop your heart out. But you, Louie, stay thirsty till I say you can drink. Understood?"

The three of us took turns manning, or should I say personing, the Western Properties office during the next week. It was a quiet, lonely existence. I bought a Japanese miniature TV, lugged it to the office, and caught up with an abundance of game shows and old movies during my tours of duty. Becca, judging from the classy outfits she wore to her shift each day, was buying clothes by the carload. Louie spent his off-hours God knows where, but his breath and walk satisfied me that at least it wasn't in bars.

Eight days after my phone call to KBMO, just when I was beginning to believe he was going to stonewall, he called. "This is Mr. Blair," he began in a deep operatic baritone. "Bradford Lockwood Blair the Second, general manager of Channel 39. Is this Mr. Terwilliger?"

I acknowledged that it was, my adrenalin pumping.

"I want to meet with you as soon as possible," he boomed. "We have business to discuss."

"My schedule's light this afternoon, sir," I replied with a

politeness that I hoped disguised my elation. "How would three P.M. be, here at our office?" It never hurts to lure the enemy onto your own turf—Milo's Maxim #43.

The reception committee that awaited its guest in the office at three consisted of Napoleon Jimson for legal advice, Becca for brightening the atmosphere, and me, the handsome one in the middle, for hard bargaining. Louie had been out of touch all day, even though I'd called the hotel and left him a message, and I was afraid he was prematurely celebrating with a bottle. We expected just the head honcho, not a war party, so I was rather floored when 3:06 brought a forceful knock at the outer door, and on Becca's call to enter, a quartet of determined faces and bodies trooped in.

Three were male and the unbelievably scrumptious fourth was female. Even before the introductions, carried out sans handshakes, I'd pinned the right name to each visitor. Bradford the Two was the tall thick-chested sandyhead in his early thirties who looked like the American Siegfried in a $500 suit. The fortyish one with the dyspeptic puss and the pipe never out of his mouth was obviously the ex-station manager, Jerome McKenna. The sex fantasy had to be Susan Otis, and the third man, the one she looked at with bedroom eyes when she thought no one was watching, I rightly deduced was her current lover, program director David Wilkes. We found chairs for the quartet, passed around coffee in styrofoam cups, and began haggling.

"Surely you know those Rio Kid films have nothing in common with Carewe's stories except the name," pruneface McKenna insisted as he refilled his pipe with cherry-flavored tobacco.

"And that is totally irrelevant to my client's position," thundered Napoleon Jimson. "Read the cases I cited. Personally I think the company should demand that those disgusting Rio Kid films be banned from the air." John West had not been known for sympathizing with civil-rights causes, and Jimson seemed to be enjoying the prospect of symbolically getting even. "Although my client will not go so far, when this matter is settled I may file another petition with the FCC to take away your license not only for discriminatory hiring and promotion practices but also for broadcasting racist movies."

A born diplomat, that lawyer of ours.

Suddenly David Wilkes, an obvious John West fan, lunged to his feet with his face rage-pale and took two steps in Jimson's direction. Bradford the Two flung an arm around his program director and tried to sit him down again. "Easy, Dave, we can handle it." And Wilkes roared, "That guy is pulling the same trick he tried in that other FCC thing," which in turn launched Jimson to his feet like a black torpedo aimed at Wilkes so that before mayhem erupted I had to fling an arm around my legal adviser. Just a nice friendly negotiating session. Blair finally sent Wilkes back to the station and I sent Jimson back to his office and an atmosphere of relative calm was restored.

"That outburst of Jimson's was a farce," Blair orated in his full-throated baritone. "He knows KBMO has the best equal employment opportunity figures of any station in the area. Blacks, women, ex-convicts, the handicapped— we've hired them all and we're proud of them all. Look, Terwilliger, we don't want protracted litigation over a bunch of old cowboy movies. Suppose the station pays you five thousand and you give us a release from all past claims and a license for unlimited future use of the Rio Kid package and any other public-domain films based on literary works you now or may hereafter own?"

I set down my styrofoam cup and pinned the bronze god with a businessman's stare. "Five thousand's fine for settling past claims, but we'll want three thousand a year to license future broadcasts." In my fantasies I looked ahead to the time when stations in a hundred or more cities would be shelling out that amount to our corporation, and I tried to suppress a beatific smile.

McKenna unmouthed his pipe and aimed the stem at

Blair. "Western Theater is pulling in the ratings now, Brad, but without the Rio Kid it could become a disaster."

"Figure a seven percent drop in total advertising revenues without them," Susan Otis chimed in. I attributed the worried look in her smoky blue eyes not to her prediction but to concern about Wilkes.

As the trio conferred I could almost see their brainwheels grinding. How much in legal fees would it cost the station if we sued for copyright infringement? Would a settlement keep Jimson from filing another petition with the FCC? Blair and Otis and McKenna huddled and conversed in whispers while Becca and I played pokerface. When the huddle broke up, Blair rose and approached our corner.

"Your terms are acceptable," he said, as gravely as Lee at Appomattox. Then he smiled at Becca, who had said not a word throughout the session, as if to thank her for breaking the impasse, and maybe—if I wasn't misreading his look—to suggest that he'd like to thank her in a more private and intimate way. "Of course, we'll have to consult again with our law firm in Washington before we sign anything. Look, why don't we meet at the station, say Friday at three P.M., and have a signing ceremony? Bring your standard contract and have all your officers present. Meanwhile I'll have Dave make a list of all the Westerns in our vault so we can add a rider to the agreement covering any other public-domain pictures based on prior literary matter. I don't want to go through this with you people again."

It all seemed so absurdly easy, I thought, now that it was over. We engaged in a round of handshaking as we parted and I noticed that young Siegfried seemed to hang onto Becca's dainty digits longer than the occasion called for. When they were gone we hugged each other in an ecstasy of glee. "We did it!" I crowed. "Easy Street from now on. Let's find a bar and toast the victory."

We made it a quick one, then headed back to the office to

call Jimson and report success. He agreed to join us at KBMO's offices at 3:00 P.M. Friday for the signing.

It wasn't until we were locking up that a sobering thought penetrated my buoyant mood. "Becca," I said as we waited in the corridor for a down elevator, "why did Blair want all of us for this signing ceremony Friday? As president of Western Properties I'm the only one whose signature's needed."

"I can't see any harm in it," she said brightly. "Maybe he wants to turn it into a media event." Then she bit down on her underlip as if she had thought of an even tougher question.

"Hey, Milo," she asked me worriedly, "what ever happened to our wonderful partner Louie?"

At exactly 5:14 the next morning by the traveling clock on my bedside table, her question was answered. I was jolted awake from lovely dreams by a loud tapping at the door, a frenzied tattoo that would have turned my nerves raw in two minutes. I cursed, kicked off blankets, and approached the door stealthily, knowing all too well who and what was on the other side.

"Let me in!" came Louie's unmistakable croak. Afraid his drum-beat would awaken everyone on my floor, I unbolted and dodged back as he lurched in.

"I don't have to ask where you've been," I said, sniffing his breath. "The meeting with Blair turned out to be a success, but we were lucky and your getting blotto could have blown the whole scam. I'll never work with you again."

"You only think you know where I've been," Louie muttered darkly. "Sure, I had some drinks this afternoon, maybe this evening. In fact, I was in the bar downstairs around eleven tonight. But I'll prove to you I wasn't drunk! You know who I saw sneaking out of the hotel about eleven thirty? Your little partner, that's who. So drunky Louie got suspicious and tailed her. She cabbed out to a luxury high-rise condominium in the Central West

End and took the private elevator to the penthouse." He
stopped for breath, eyed the unopened bourbon bottle on
my dresser top longingly. "Now guess who lives in that
penthouse?"

Given the sexy signals I'd witnessed during the afternoon's bargaining session, I hardly needed to guess.
"Young Beefcake. Bradford Lockwood Blair the Second," I
replied knowingly, a display that left Louie's mouth
agape.

"She stayed till half an hour ago," Louie went on when
he'd recovered. "I followed her back here just now. Oh,
God, why did I set up this scam? It's like the others, bagworms all over it."

"Calm down," I told him. "Look, so they get together.
They're young, single, and healthy. Why go puritan all of a
sudden?"

"The thing's coming apart," he mourned. "I feel it coming apart." He didn't stop prophesying doom until I'd fed
him three shots of bourbon and put him to sleep stretched
across a pair of armchairs. But his paranoia had infected
me, and I spent the tail of the night wide-awake.

A little before 11:00 A.M. I rang her room, one floor below
mine, and from the weariness in her hello I gathered I'd
awakened her. "Four hours to our date at KBMO," I said.
"Rise and shine. We have a problem I have to talk over
with you in a hurry. See you in half a minute."

I left Louie snoring on his armchairs, locked the room
door behind me, slipped down the firestairs, and tapped
gently at her door. She opened, wearing an ankle-length
caftan that concealed none of her attributes. "Okay, prin-
cess," I said once inside. "Level with Uncle Milo. Why did
you spend five hours at Blair's condo last night?"

A corner of her lovely mouth began to twitch. "Oh, that,"
she laughed softly. "Well, you must have noticed at the
meeting yesterday how he was sort of sending me signals.
And you must admit he's a gorgeous hunk of man, besides
being the son of a multimillionaire. He, ah, called me late
last night and invited me over."

"You were seen," I told her without explaining by whom, and gave her my businessman's stare. "Never again, kid. Understand? You've been in the life long enough to know it was a rotten idea. In a tender moment you might have let something slip that would have shot the scam to pieces."

Her deep brown eyes glazed over with a cat-full-of-cream look. "Milo, he is by far the best I've ever met," she said softly. "Oh, if there were only some way I could marry him I'd chuck the life and be happy ever after."

"Yeah," I said. "Until his old man had your background checked. Remember what I said—never again."

On that happy note a chastened Becca, a sullen Louie, and an increasingly apprehensive Milo picked up Napoleon Jimson at his Broadway office after lunch and made our way to the studios of KBMO-TV and our appointment with destiny.

It was a one-story tan-brick building a block west of Twelfth Boulevard, with a transmitting tower poking into the sky in its back yard. The receptionist deposited us in a parquet-floored waiting room where we sat in soft chairs and listened to the noisy electric wall clock. The hands showed 3:00. No one came to greet us. I picked up a discarded *Globe-Democrat* from a lamp table and read about how the secretaries in all the federal offices in St. Louis were staging a massive demonstration that afternoon, protesting having to make coffee for the men. The next most exciting story dealt with the annual meeting of the Mortgage Bankers Association which was to open that evening at the Cervantes Convention Center. Obviously a slow day for news.

The clock's hands reached 3:10, and still we sat. I began to feel a return of the squeams.

At 3:12 Jerome McKenna poked his pruneface and pipe-stem into the room. "Sorry for the delay," he said. "Dave's still working on that list of other public-domain Westerns and Brad's in conference with somebody. Okay if we make it three-twenty?" He didn't wait for answers or comments but ducked out again. Louie resumed his symphony for cracked knuckles, Jimson rose and stalked the room like a black tiger, and I started asking myself some unnerving questions. What was going on in this joint? Why was Blair with parties unknown when he should have been with us? Why had he insisted on all four of us attending this soirée? Why had Becca so unprofessionally spent most of last night with him? *Milo, Milo,* the voice of common sense reassured me. *Relax, man! This operation happens to be legal.*

And then, at 3:16 by the wall clock, I realized that on one hypothesis the deal was blatantly illegal, and my spine suddenly felt like an icicle in August.

That was when Louie jumped up and said he had to visit the men's room and walked out. Leaving three of us. Two minutes later Becca smiled, said something about locating a coffee machine, and walked out. Leaving two of us. At 3:23 Louie came back and as if on signal Jimson stormed out into the hallway, saying he would find Blair and demand that we be seen.

I had better do a spot of exploring myself, I decided. "Sit," I instructed a hand-wringing Louie, and went out to the hallway and very gingerly began walking. The place was a maze of corridors and cubbyholes. I followed what looked like a major artery, past a locked double door that seemed to lead out to a loading dock. Past a closed door marked *DAVID WILKES PROGRAM DIRECTOR,* with the johns right across the hall from Wilkes' cubicle. The corridor ended at a half-open door labeled *FILM STORAGE* but I could see another half-open door at the room's far end, so I started to walk through. I felt like a soldier behind enemy lines.

The film-storage room was crammed library-style with high steel shelves that bulged with cardboard cartons, each holding a 16-millimeter film print. The vault was stone-quiet, the narrow aisles between the shelves were empty.

Except the last one.

I threw a glance down that aisle. There was a man in shirt-sleeves lying on his side on the floor. He didn't look as if he were taking a nap. I tiptoed over and bent down to inspect the face. It was David Wilkes. The vacant stare of his eyes told me he was dead. A long sharp knife, the kind used as a letter opener, lay on the linoleum six inches from the body, the blade reddish-brown and sticky halfway to the hilt.

A ballpoint pen was clutched in Wilkes's right hand and a pile of white 8½ x 5½ halfsheets lay scattered around the body. I remembered McKenna's remark that David hadn't finished inventorying the Westerns—which suggested that pruneface had seen Wilkes bare minutes before the murder, or perhaps that he'd killed the program director himself—and looked down at the halfsheets again, forty or so in all. Ten or twelve looked blank. On each of the others that I could read without moving them, the title of a single horse opera was printed in sloppy block capitals. The one on which Wilkes's pen rested read MARSHAL OF LARAMIE. I noticed SMOKEY SMITH and WHERE TRAILS END on others nearby.

My thoughts, however, were not on old movies but new suspects. At first glance the likeliest candidate was McKenna, who had lost Susan Otis to the deceased. But it might also have been Ms. Otis herself—lovers do quarrel —or Bradford the Two, who might have wanted Susan for himself or might have blamed Wilkes, initiator of the idea for Western Theater, for the debacle with my company.

Then I glanced down again at the halfsheet directly underneath Wilkes's pen. And suddenly I didn't have to speculate further, because I knew.

By pure luck I found verification only a few feet away. One of the steel shelves in that aisle was being used as a sort of film-book reference library. I almost gasped with glee when I noticed among the twenty-odd titles Adams and Rainey's *Shoot-em-Ups,* a comprehensive listing of the casts and credits of every talking Western film ever made in the United States. With sweaty hands I thumbed through the alphabetical index of titles at the back of the book.

Marshal of Heldorado, Marshal of Laredo, Marshal of Mesa City—I was right. There was no such film as *Marshal of Laramie.*

Like an outlaw being chased by one of those marshals, I ran. Back through the storage room, along the corridor to the loading dock, out and away, until I'd lost myself in the cavernous darkness of Stadium Cinema II where I spent the rest of the afternoon.

When the show let out I did the only sensible thing left to me. I bought a cheap suitcase at Woolworth's, filled it with copies of the evening *Post-Dispatch,* cabbed back to Stouffer's Riverfront Inn, and—with the help of one of the paper identities I always carry for emergencies—checked in all over again where the cops would least expect to find me.

"And how long do you intend to stay, Mr. Rhodes?" the clerk inquired as she completed the registration card.

"Just for the meeting of the Mortgage Bankers Association," I said, taking the room key.

The weekend papers carried enough of the story to confirm my deductions all the way. The cops had Jimson and were investigating his role in the scam, but I was confident he could prove we had scammed him too. They didn't have Louie, who according to the KBMO receptionist had exited the waiting room and walked unopposed out the front door within a minute after I'd left on my own excursion. And of course they had Becca. But, as I explained Sunday morning over the lobby phone to the disembodied voice of Jock Schultz half a continent away, she didn't really count.

"Remember the ex-CIA spook I used to tap a phone on that scam I ran here four years ago? I had him bug the St. Louis FBI office Friday night. It cost me a pile but confirmed my suspicions all the way. Becca's not one of us. She's a sort of free-lance bounty hunter, working under a

deal that pays her so many thousand for each major operator she can hang a Federal rap on."

"Bounty hunter," Jock repeated thoughtfully. "Appro-
priate character in a Western film scam, wouldn't you
say?"

"I suspected something like that at the TV station Friday when I asked myself how our plan could possibly be
illegal. That was how I realized that if Becca had never
gotten Carolyn Carewe to sign over the rights to the Rio
Kid stories—say, if Becca had forged the old lady's name—
well, all she'd need to do later would be to testify at our
trial that the forgery was part of our scam, and Louie and
I would never be able to convince a jury it was she who did
it. They'd nail us for copyright fraud, wire fraud, conspiracy, and God knows what else.

"As soon as we hit St. Louis she contacted Blair, told
him what was up, and they worked out the charade to lure
us all to KBMO where the FBI would arrest us as soon as
we'd signed the contract. That's why she visited Blair's
condo Thursday night—strategy, not sex. If that Federal
secretaries' demonstration hadn't made the agents late for
their date to collar us at the station, Louie and I would be
in the slammer this minute. Thank heaven for militant
feminism!" I declaimed piously.

"So *that's* how the Feds got Fats Adamo for mail fraud
so soon after the Disco Cola scam," the Jock sighed. "Milo,
me buck, I feel devilish guilty that I recommended the
lady to ye and I'll make it up when the heat is lowered.
Now what about this Wilkes murder?"

"A mere bagatelle," I replied modestly. "I solved it thirty
seconds after I found the body. You see, all it took was the
tying together of five facts. One: Louie got out of the Federal pen six months ago. Two: Wilkes joined KBMO about
a year ago. Three: The station has a liberal policy about
hiring blacks, women, and *ex-convicts.* Four: Before Becca
and I flew here, Louie thought he saw someone he knew
from when he was in the South and calling himself Hal
O'Flynn—an encounter that took place on Twelfth Boule-

vard, a few blocks from KBMO. Five: At no time before our
Friday visit to the station had Wilkes set eyes on Louie in
this city. During the bargaining session which Wilkes attended, Louie was off somewhere getting plastered.

"It's easy enough to reconstruct what happened Friday
afternoon. On his way to the john Louie had to pass
Wilkes's office just as I did. It was both their misfortunes
that this time Wilkes did see Louie and recognized him as
a fellow Lexington alumnus. Now remember, Blair was
the only one at KBMO who knew about Becca's trap for us.
It's obvious from what McKenna told us in that waiting
room that he didn't know, and it's clear Wilkes didn't
know or he wouldn't have gone on inventorying those
Westerns as if they really mattered. So, Wilkes recognized
Louie and apparently inveigled him into the film-storage
room for a quiet chat.

"Louie was already nervous as a cat. Meeting a fellow
con in that station was the last straw. He panicked, saw
the paper knife they kept in the storage room to open
cardboard film containers, and used it. Then he went to
the john to wash the blood off his hands. But as soon as he
left the men's room he got his directions confused, wandered back into the storage room—and found that Wilkes
had not died instantly but had been able, after Louie left
for the john, to begin to write on a black halfsheet the only
one of Louie's many names he knew his murderer by, HAL
OFLYNN, with the apostrophe being omitted for obvious
reasons of haste. He'd gotten as far as the L of the last
name when he died.

"I give Louie credit for quick thinking under pressure.
He had only seconds to act. If he'd tried to flush the halfsheet down the toilet he might have been interrupted at
any moment. So instead he took Wilkes's pen and simply
added enough block capitals to each end of the dying message so that it would look just like the name of another
Western—MAR*SHAL OF L*ARAMIE!"

"He was a prophet in one respect at least," the Jock
pointed out. "The scam had bagworms all over it."

"A drunk, a jinx, a prophet, and for one split second a genius," I said. "I hope the poor schnook gets away."

Six months later—long after I had slipped out of St. Louis, sworn off John West movies, and retired to lick my wounds in solitude—I happened to pick up a copy of *Persons* in a New Orleans dentist's office. My eye was caught by a photo spread of a newlywed couple. The man was tall, thick-chested, sandy-haired, and resembled an American Siegfried. His bride was tall, in her late twenties, of form divine, smiling and radiant in white lace.

Son of a gun, I said to myself. She chucked the life and landed Young Beefcake after all.

HOSTILE TAKEOVER

by Robert Halsted

☐ AFTER WE ESCAPED FROM DOOLEYMONT, JOY SUE AND I GOT back on the interstate, crossed into the next state, and stopped for breakfast and some sleep. Whether her brother and boyfriend actually would have killed me to steal the Mercedes I'll never know for sure, but I was glad we hadn't stayed around to find out.

I was up and dressed and ready for lunch or whatever it would be when she woke around twelve. She looked so kittenish and cuddly when she stretched and yawned that I half regretted turning back the covers on both beds. But I like to get my projects thoroughly set up, let the customer feel confident, before I begin closing in for the kill. Besides, we were only thinking about a simple business partnership.

She was disoriented for a moment, then smiled when she remembered who I was. A very pleasant blue-eyed blonde kind of smile to start the rest of the day with.

"I ain't homesick any more," she said.

"You didn't seem very homesick last night."

"Well, I *have* been for nineteen years and some, but the further away I git from home, the less sick I am *of* it."

She walked away from her own punchline by getting out of bed, picking up her valise, and padding to the bathroom. Her pajamas, which looked like something her uncle might have worn as a boy and handed down to her, gave her an urchin look somewhere between pathetic and charming.

She came back in a little while fresh-scrubbed, wearing a gingham skirt, a top that almost matched it, and ankle-strap sandals.

"We'll have to get you a classier wardrobe," I said tactlessly.

She took it with a smile. "Ah'm available for fittin's. You talkin' about comp'ny money or my own meager funds?"

I pretended to consider her question. It sounded like an offer to let me off easier than I'd been prepared for. "Let's say half and half. As a business proposition, I'll front you office clothes and some travel stuff. You cover the, ah, more personal things and leisure wear." I cleared my throat. "I'd have to, ah, have some say in what you wear during business hours."

"Fair 'nuff. You feedin' me, too?"

"Customarily, the company pays for breakfast and dinner when you're traveling on company business."

She smiled the smile of someone who planned to make a quick study of expense account loopholes. As we walked to the restaurant, she put her arm through mine like a lady. I figured I could wait till later to tell her that I would personally cover lunch.

"My mamma must be envyin' me about now," she said as she was putting away amazing quantities of food for her size.

"I should think she'd be worried sick about you. If you were my daughter and disappeared in the middle of the night with a strange man—"

"But that's what *she* wanted to do. Just think, if she'da run off with that travelin' salesman like she wanted to do, I coulda grown up with my real father, and maybe been half civilized."

I started to say that I had her figured for just about that, and rather enjoyed her that way, but I didn't. "Well, maybe traveling with me you'll pick up some . . . sophisticated big city ways."

"I can hardly wait to see Noo York." I raised my eyebrows, and she went on: "I know you *told* 'em you were goin' to Noo York. And we're headin' east, not west, so you didn't mean California or Texas. So you musta been goin' to Florida, right?"

She was, I was beginning to decide, a pretty sharp cookie. I nodded in dazed agreement. Besides the correct conclusion, she was one of the few women I'd ever met for whom the points of the compass had any particular meaning.

"But I figgered I might could talk you into Noo York anyhow," she finished.

A nebulous plan began forming in my head. "Tell you what," I said, a little animated now that a plan was shaping up. "It wouldn't hurt me to drop by Delaware and check on my . . . *legitimate* business. Maybe we could fly up from there for a weekend, take in a stage play or musical, eat a couple of expensive meals, just so you can see the place and say you've been there."

I wasn't that crazy about New York. Criminal and con artist I may be, but I'm out of my class there, a small fox among wolves. When you talk economics in the Big Apple, Hobbes is a better reference than Locke. *Homo homini lupus,* and all that. Even the subway turnstiles are out to get you.

The compromise plan seemed to please her. We drifted eastward, spent nearly a grand on her wardrobe in Richmond, wandered around Williamsburg for a day. It amused but didn't impress her, and looked to me a lot more like an expensive stage setting and less like living American history than it had years before.

After that we went up the eastern shore to Wilmington. She was, I thought, terrified at going over and under twenty-odd miles of open salt water when we crossed Chesapeake Bay, but she was brave about it. My fingerbones healed in mere days, after she'd held my hand each time we went tunneling.

I drove straight to my apartment in Wilmington, a sort of glorified efficiency I used a few weeks out of the year, within walking distance of my office if the weather wasn't too east coastish. It was a good day, the wind off the Atlantic, and I opened all the windows.

"There's just the one king-size and it's my territory, not to be relinquished," I told her. "We can get you a rollaway if you want, or at your size you might be comfortable on the couch."

"You'd prob'ly be better huggin' than a ol' pillow."

"I might lose control."

"You will not lose control without ma permission."

We seemed to have made some usable definitions that we could live with for the time being.

After we were settled in and refreshed, I told her I was going to my office, a posh little private cubbyhole in a posh suite, with high-class generic receptionists. A lot of people who live somewhere else and own corporations in Delaware use a similar system.

"Kin I come?"

"Not in your lounging pajamas. If you show up at my office, it will be as my confidential secretary, appropriately dressed."

She changed quickly to a grey suit, medium black heels, and a prim-collared white blouse. I assumed she paraded back and forth in her underwear while getting ready because (a) it was a tiny apartment and (b) they probably always did it that way in the log cabin she grew up in. She didn't seem ill at ease or seductive about it—though I did more sidelong looking than I really felt was proper—but just matter of fact. When she was finished she still looked like a young sexy girl I'd picked up for reasons other than clerical. But less so than before.

When we arrived at 9100 Offices, I was wearing a double-breasted brown suit and rimless glasses, my hair an anonymous brown after I'd washed the darker rinse out. I introduced her to the head receptionist and took her into my private office.

In Wilmington, and hardly anywhere else, I am myself, and a totally respectable businessman doing odd jobs at a fair pay in the securities and corporate structure areas. Nothing big, on purpose. I am W. J. Brown, Ltd.—"Bill" to my associates—partly because the suffix has a transatlantic hint to it, and partly because limited partnerships invite a lot less official scrutiny than full-fledged corporations.

There was a laundry basket's worth of mail on my desk, after my weeks in Cinci. Anything important when I'm on the road gets to me by weekly phone calls I make, never disclosing where I really am.

I got her started on rough-sorting the mail while I made a few phone calls: "Hey, Jack, long time no see. . . . I've been on the road, cornering the market on ginseng futures. . . ." That sort of thing. A good bit of legitimate business comes my way in that kind of conversation. Both are boring, but necessary to my front.

I finished my duty calls and started the bird-dogging ones. On the third call I hit what seemed like a mild vein of paydirt—a broker with a client interested in a small block of stocks in an estate situation that I had an inside door to—so I agreed to meet him at our club.

"I'm going out for a while," I told Joy Sue. "If you need me you can reach me at the Bears Club. It's on the Rolodex. If you get bored, close the office and go shopping or something. I'll be back here about four. If you're not here, I'll go on home around five. Take what you need out of petty cash and leave a memo in the box."

I deliberately gave her the information rapid-fire to see how she handled it. Very well, apparently. She asked a couple of pertinent questions—like my home address and phone number—and took brief, cryptic notes on a scratch pad.

At the Bears Club I had a couple of drinks with Irving. It seems hardly worth mentioning, but I will mention it,

that the membership was one of the most bullish crowds
in town. Our deal was small stuff, to net us a couple of
hundred each for a few minutes' actual work, but little
deals like this accumulated to make up most of my legitimate income. Which had to be enough to screen my more
interesting work.

The club was mostly brokers, accountants, and lawyers,
with a few other shady types thrown in for variety. By the
time we'd worked out the terms of the deal, a general
conversation had grown up around us, and we joined in.

"What's the latest on Ulfsen?" one of them was asking
another. I pricked up my ears.

"Still quietly buying, last I heard," someone answered
him.

My radar antenna—also AM, FM, UHF, VHF, and so-
nar—started tingling. "What's the one-boy wrecking crew
doing this time?" I asked as casually as I could manage.

"Minicorp. He's got a way to go yet, but they're running
scared."

"I guess they would be. Getting raided by the Last of the
Vikings."

The conversation kept going, and I kept listening. I had
a phone brought and told Joy Sue to feed herself and take
a cab home. I nursed my third drink while they primed
and reprimed themselves, and learned a good bit. By the
time the crowd started breaking up and going home to
dinner, I had a nice plan forming.

Rolf Ulfsen was a classic case of something. Rags to riches
or virtue to vice.

The son of poor but thrifty immigrant parents, he had
decided when young not to make a living tilling the chilly
soil of Minnesota. He worked and wangled his way
through college to a B.S. in B.A., then got a graduate
scholarship to an Ivy League business school.

By age twenty-four he had acquired a number of things:
a reputation in the business world, his first million, a lot of
enemies, and epithets like "Super Yuppie," "Limo Surfer,"

"S.O.B.," and other worse ones. As Ulfsen made more money, it became apparent why he was making more enemies. By the time he had become enough of a public property to show up in the weekly scandal sheets, his M.O. was well known in the trade.

He started with a hostile takeover. If the tactic hadn't existed already, he would have invented it. As it was, he did some innovation in the field.

He was a genius at acquisition. The first few thousand shares more or less, especially if they're not voted in a boat-rocking way, are pretty much invisible. He held blocks that size in an indeterminate number of corporations, so many that it was pointless for management to worry until their own was singled out. And by then it was too late.

From that point, before they started worrying, he was discreet and subtle. In the course of normal trading, stocks would drift through brokerages, unknown individuals, small corporations, for a few months or a couple of years. Then they would all turn up in Ulfsen's hands.

Say you have a small corporation with a hundred thousand shares of voting common at ten dollars par. That million dollars' worth of stock may represent the power steering that controls millions upon millions of physical plant and other assets. The ratio between the face value of stocks and the liquidation value of the business is an excellent measure of the health of a corporation and is reflected, though not one-to-one, in the price of shares on the market. After that, it gets very complicated. But if you grab fifty thousand and one shares of that stock, the whole show is in your pocket.

Takeovers are common procedure. A rich dentist wants to fulfill a childhood dream of owning a golf club factory. Not having any idea how to put one together, he goes out and buys one, in the form of a majority of the shares. Normally it's no more disruptive or destructive than most other business procedures. Which is to say, usually the

boss doesn't botch things too badly for the guy with the
shovel to straighten them out.

Ulfsen, however, was of another breed. He didn't give a
holy damn about the fun, glamor, prestige, creativity, or
even the egotistic power trip of running a corporation. He
was out for money, pure and simple. One thing I'd heard
him called was "Spiderman": he caught it; he sucked it
dry; he threw the empty husk away. He spent some of the
money in intermittent flashy living, if you could believe
the tabloids, but he seemed to spend most of it escalating
the same game. He wasn't yet in the top ten of multibil-
lionaires, but he was working his way up steadily and not
too slowly.

By the time I got home I was weary of the business
world generally and of Ulfsen in particular. I put the
whole affair, for the moment, in the back of my mind and
shut the door.

Joy Sue hadn't eaten, so we went out to a nearby place
for a decent steak. She was cool throughout the meal without saying why. I have learned to let women have their
moods and not hasten trouble along before it's ready, so I
pretended not to notice.

Whatever was bothering her, it didn't affect her appe-
tite. Watching her surround thirty or forty bucks' worth of
quality cuisine as fast as it arrived, I considered the possibility that I'd unwittingly adopted a pregnant girl, but
decided she was just compensating for the times during
her childhood when the possum crop failed or something. I
plied her with port and cheese, then brandy with her coffee, and this seemed to have a mellowing effect. Except for
a tendency to hold her pinky out, she looked quite house-
broken. She didn't touch the flatware till she had watched
me.

I was still roadweary, and tired from the business day
as well. I showered and pajama'd myself as soon as we got
home, turned both bedlamps low, and staked out my side
of the bed by placing myself and a paperback there. In a
few minutes she changed to sexless, boyish pajamas, and

still looked like a sexy girl. I decided if the situation got too frustrating I'd simply get her a place of her own. Without discussing with myself why I was taking responsibility for her in the first place.

"You stay on yore side," she said as she got in bed.

"I plan to," I answered, smiling neutrally.

I lasted another five minutes, then put down the book and turned my light off. She was still reading a trade magazine she'd brought from the office. I didn't know whether she was doing her homework, trying to bore herself to sleep, or putting on some kind of act that went over my head.

During the night I felt something warm and soft molding itself against me. Whatever it was said, "Don't you go gittin' no ideas."

"Wouldn't think of it," I mumbled.

"Ah was just gittin' a little cool over there."

"You're better hugging than the pillow." Matter of fact, I had been hugging my pillow.

"You too. You're better huggin' than ol' Bobby Russell."

I lay awake for a while, enjoying the touch and warmth of her, realizing I was experiencing jealousy and possessiveness for the first time since college.

Despite the underlying distraction, I woke with a nicely formed plan. I basked for a moment in the tantalizing pleasure of holding Joy Sue, then disentangled myself, started the coffee, and sat at my desk with paper and pen.

I started to do some paperwork, then realized I didn't have the basic numbers to begin adding and subtracting. I did a couple of trial runs anyhow, with fairly credible maximum and minimum imaginary figures, and estimated my plan would work. Then, quietly, I slipped on slacks and sport shirt and made a quick trip to a private membership reference library, used their bound volumes and some computer time, and got much of what I needed.

When I got back to the apartment, Joy Sue had been out for groceries and was fixing breakfast.

"Just run off and leave me, why don't you?" she said, with identifiable asperity. "I was hopin' you'd be gone jess a little bit longer, so's I could feed you some cole bacon an' aigs."

"Petulance ill becomes you. I've been hard at work while you were getting your beauty sleep. Each of us contributing what we're best at." I gave her a playful kiss on the lips, which she accepted without comment.

She busied herself with breakfast, and I reviewed my notes till she called me to the table.

It was well set and well served, except for the flatware's being in random order. "Very elegant," I commented, not sarcastically.

"I used to help Grandmaw Dooley in the cafe," she said. "I'm pretty good at it. That, an' a lotta thaings." I thought there was a playful-malicious twinkle in her eye, but her face was harder to read than you'd think would be the case with a simple mountain gal lured away from her home by a city slicker. Besides which, I didn't lure her, she hijacked me, y'r honor.

Something interpersonal was poised on a brink, getting ready to happen. Till last night she had been all friendly and compliant, and now there was some kind of chip on her shoulder.

I decided to nip it in the bud. "Look, Joy Sue. I'm working on a *big* project, the biggest I've ever thought of, let alone tried. If you're angry at me, let's clear it up. If you regret coming with me, I'll fill your chubby little hand with cash and drive you to the bus station. I don't have the time and energy for games."

She sat on my lap, not so much the seductive female as a cat defining its territory. "Not angry. Jess a little insecure."

"Mmh. If this is insecure, I don't want to see you get mad."

She grinned, a Cheshire sort of grin. "That *is* a sight. Y'ever notice that little scar under m' brother's left eye?"

She studied her hands. Cat flexing its claws. I had noticed the scar. I hadn't noticed till then what nice nails she had.

We ping-ponged some shallow, low-key personal stuff back and forth for a couple of minutes, then she said out of nowhere, "Tell me all about this new scam you're workin' up."

"We don't use that word. Deal, coup, or even killing. Not scam." I frowned in thought. "Look, once I've told you about it, you're as guilty as I am. Accessory before the fact. Maybe the best thing would be for you to cut and run. Accept a grant from me for subsistence and education, go out and find your rightful place in the world." I had no idea why I was working so hard to send her away.

"You're not gonna get rid o' me that easy. Now jus' talk slow, an' explain the big words."

Explaining it to her helped clarify it for myself. She asked some dumb—no, naive—questions, and a couple of very sharp ones. What I told her was approximately this:

In the world of securities, one doesn't get sentimental about corporations. Unless, I suppose, it's your own. But Minicorp was a firm a lot of people, including myself, had friendly feelings for.

Minicorp was, interestingly, the brainchild of another Mid-western Scandinavian, John Stromquist. His life was pretty much an open book: high school football team, middle-aged now with a loyal dowdy wife and 3.2 children in high school and college, that sort of thing.

His parents had run a little neighborhood store in maybe Iowa or Nebraska, and it had slowly withered as the big chains drew away the clientele. When they finally folded, he was working his way through college.

He dropped out, went to work for a brokerage, and patiently put together a package to rescue the other mom-and-pop operations left in the world. It was a sentimental gesture, unrealistic, contrary to economic trends, and one he didn't have the experience or the backing to handle. And it worked.

Stromquist wasn't brilliant, but he was normally intelligent, plodding and persistent and committed. He did a few dumb things and some pretty smart ones, made some wrong guesses and had some keen intuitions, carefully corrected course when he saw the need. The operation he finally put together had the patchwork look of the British Parliament, and like it was good at muddling through.

He had four kinds of securities out: debenture bonds, preferred stocks, and two series of voting common. That had been one of his wrong guesses, but no Wall Street whiz kid could have told it was wrong till now. When he did it, it made sense. Most of your brilliant tycoons would have done the same without a second thought.

The junk bonds, everybody figured, people had bought because they thought he had an honest face, or let sentiment get in the way of common sense when he explained his goals. Nearly all the bearers were surprised when they turned out not to be junk. He'd put twenty percent of their face value in interest-bearing escrow to cover early dividends, then used that as collateral for working money. Every dividend was made on time, with a little extra from a bonus clause he'd not even made a point of.

You can imagine this made a lot of people happy and didn't hurt his image. A couple of cynics wondered if he was pyramiding, but his operation was so out in the open that nobody much took it seriously. Then, when he came out with his 6½% preferred stocks right after the second bond dividend, they sold.

By now his operation was rolling. There were Minit Marts across eight or nine states, franchised co-ops still mostly in the hands of the original Mom and Pop. They offered some of the services of convenience stores—with the help of a couple of other people, he'd done some really creative merchandising—and on a day to day basis were holding their own with supermarket chains on staples, though of course they couldn't match them in variety. But they stayed in business and made money. A decent living for the owners, better than they'd had as independents, and a small trickle back to Stromquist that added up.

His Series A common stocks had been part of the franchises fee, some of them on a dollar down, dollar a week basis. The outlet owners had often bought extra shares, less for the modest dividends than for a bigger piece of the action. His own block of shares were nearly all Series A.

Then, when he was ready to begin the Minit Meal operation, he went public. A normal thing to do. He overestimated the idealism of the SAP—Stockowning American Public—which isn't difficult to do. He wanted to give Americans the opportunity to invest in the American way of life. Supply quotes according to how cynical you are.

He could have made it non-voting, he could have issued more preferred shares. He could have sold a big issue of bonds by word of mouth, no promotion required, with his AAA-1 D&B rating and his track record.

But he issued Series B, and it sold. Series A was an open issue, more membership cards printed as more members joined. Series B was a limited edition, five million shares at five dollars par. He kept a few himself, sold maybe a hundred thousand to owners of Series A, and the rest went across the counter. The issue had sold out in two years, and it launched Minit Meal and strengthened Minit Mart by allowing expansion, though it was already solid enough. Later the two merged internally and became Minicorp. He bought out the dying Two Dollar Lunch chain and ran it as training outlets. Mom and Pop restaurants joined the way groceries had, and it was a moneymaker from the word go. He had first-rate consultants and some damn good ideas of his own. A lot of pre-prepared stuff, but shiptight quality control. Considerable local autonomy —he didn't set ceilings, he set floors—and freshness a must for all produce. He'd built his own trucking operation serving both the groceries and restaurants.

I'd eaten in Minit Meals more than once, and they were head and shoulders above any other fast and cheap places. Some of it that I knew had to be pre-prep I still couldn't help tasting as homecooked. I found out during the coming caper that none of the pre-prep came in a single package, one of his secrets. The final ingredients of his Salisbury steak (Wednesday Special) weren't added till minutes before serving started. And the beef inside them was real.

Joy Sue was taking notes, or maybe doodling. "So how many o' which is what? I think maybe you lef' me back there a ways." I wasn't sure I had.

"Okay, there's one million preferred at ten par, nearer fifteen market right now. Forget those, they don't vote. About two point three million Series A, nearly all in friendly hands, five dollars par, ten market. Probably a few thousand issued since last report, still friendly. Series B, five million in existence, same five and ten. Nearly one million known to be in hostile hands, Ulfsen and his identifiable fronts. Assume another million he's holding under cover. Say he has two million shares, the guys in the white hats have two point three million. That leaves three million running loose. It will take Ulfsen roughly one point eight million of those to take the company over. He's buying steadily, we have almost no idea how fast. If the Stromquist people can hold firm control over at least one point three million of Series B, they're safe. For a while."

"They all vote by the same rules?"

"One share of common stock is one vote, Series A or B. Both sides will get proxy votes, but we can't predict how many. Stromquist will have far more friends, but from what I know of Ulfsen he'd be willing to pay twenty dollars to vote a ten dollar share. Literally."

"An' this Woofson, he's not plannin' to expand an' improve, just suck the comp'ny dry?"

"Right."

"An' you're gonna just *hand* him a hunnert thousan' shares?"

"Not *hand* him. Convey at double the going market rate."

She stood up, eyes blazing. "Billy John Brown, you're *immoral!*"

"Honey chile, I told you I was a crook and a criminal and

a con man." If she could call me Billy John, I could call her honey chile. "If you don't want to play, you don't have to."

"Our bacon and *aigs* this mornin' come from a Minit Mart, an' they was nice as innythaing to me there though Ah was a stranger, an' you're plannin' to sell 'em down the *road*!" The more emotional she got, the more Appalachian she talked. "An' nice *fresh* aigs, too!" I reached toward her and she slapped my hand away. "Keep yore dirty hainds offa me!"

I breathed deeply and tried to look more patient than I felt. "Sweetheart, I'm not a county jail type of crook, I'm a federal pen type of crook. Now would you like to hear the *entire* plan?"

She continued glowering at me, crossed arms concealing lovely bosom, but her eyes were twitching.

Only Annette had ever known this much about one of my schemes, and that was when she had participated in the planning, after we'd been friends, partners, and lovers for a long time. Sure that I was being a damn fool, I told the hillbilly gal the whole basic plot, and part of the ornaments, while she cleared away the breakfast dishes.

"That could be kinda fun," she said when I'd finished. "Ah've decided maybe I do like you a little. Uncross your knees." She sat a soft warm cushiony sit on my lap. "Once I good 'n kiss a man, he's never the same after."

When the kiss was over a few minutes later, I believed her. I *haven't* been the same since. In the kissing department, she was born to be great.

It was all very Machiavellian, Byzantine, cloak and dagger.

First an anonymous typed letter to Ulfsen's corporate HQ, alerting him to expect a message in a week concerning a possible acquisition of great interest to him. Top security and total anonymity required. We marked the letter "Confidential—Executive Office Only" and mailed it from Philadelphia.

The next ten days—plenty of time for him to get the

message and for somebody in the office to be alert for a follow up—we did normal business things and made a few thousand legal bucks, enough to feed us and pay some overhead.

My confidential executive secretary showed great promise, at least. She kept the sweet warm Southern honey in her voice while managing to sound Eastern finishing school. A number of casual callers tried to date her, sight unseen. She took total care of the mail, was slow but conscientious in the little bit of typing required. Her spelling was, on the average, better than her pronouncing. She even took a little shorthand, her own hybrid system.

"Double-you Jay Brown, Limited," she answered the phone one day. "One moment, I'll see if he's in. May I say who's calling? . . . Well, I *know* he's sittin' right here in a li'l tiny room with me, but he won't be *in* till you tell me who you *are*. . . . Very well, Mr. Berlin, if you'll hold for a moment."

I winked at her and picked up. "Irv Cohen, what's up?"

"Oh, a little action here and there. Doing a small estate portfolio, and ran across some stuff you said to look out for."

That had to be Minicorp B. "Good. Can I afford it?" Both sides were paying well over twice par for it, the rare times it hit the open market. Mostly it was conveyed privately, more often than not in substantial blocks. If Ulfsen won the battle, people who were paying fifteen or twenty dollars for it now would be lucky to unload it at five, unless they were insiders in the conspiracy.

I paid Irv the going rate for the twenty shares. I'd have got them some other way, but this helped. We framed our second letter to Ulfsen. Joy Sue made a couple of useful suggestions, and we got it in the mail the next night. It stated that within six weeks, the writer expected to acquire from various sources as many as fifty thousand shares of Minicorp Series B Common Stock, and would Ulfsen be interested at market plus a fifty percent surcharge "for acquisition"? This time we used a fake name with a real P.O. box in Philly. It was a bit of commuting, but I stay dead legal around home base.

My palms began to sweat. I had decided to make it as much as that because I wanted to pull one million-dollar scam in my lifetime, just to know that I'd done it. Not to mention that the money would be useful. When the shares started going up, though, I'd retrenched from the planned hundred thousand shares. I just wasn't ready for that size operation.

I didn't know whether Joy Sue was so calm because she had nerves of steel or because it just wasn't real to her. If I hadn't been so edgy, I wouldn't have believed it was real to me.

It seemed time for a break, so I got some reservations for a New York weekend. We took a midday plane up Friday, went to a fair musical and an excellent restaurant, and then forgot the rest of our reservations and ate our meals in a posh little honeymoon suite at the Royal Wessex. I meant to do some business research while we were there, but it slipped my mind.

As our little commuter plane leveled off southbound Monday, she said with a weak grin, "Noo York shore is a sexy town." She hadn't even remembered to be scared taking off.

I kissed her fingertips. "Yeah."

We were basically silent for the forty-five minutes of the trip. Not a case of *omne animal post coitum triste,* but just that it was no longer a "hey, roommate, ol' buddy" situation. It was somehow a lot scarier than when Annette and I had more or less absentmindedly started doing the natural thing. I wished for Annette now, not to replace Joy Sue but somehow to protect me from her.

Tuesday we threw ourselves into our job and tried to work our buns off. Joy Sue was kind enough to wear something shapeless to the office, but on her it didn't take.

By then the time had come, and a little more, for me to

contact my printer. I hadn't been skittish about it since the second time, but this was bigger.

I've never met my printer, and hope I never will. There are probably about three layers of intermediary between us. What I do is put samples of what I want copies of in a double-sealed envelope and address it to a presumably fictitious person at an accommodation box in the office of a courier service. Instructions, simply coded, go in another envelope to another name at another courier service. I carry them by hand to a place that is not Wilmington.

In a week or so I get a billing, written to my own fictitious name, at the second courier service. The billing amounts to ten percent of a value somewhere between par and market, in the case of securities; I've never known his exact formula. For a relatively small extra charge he ages stuff with UV radiation and mild dirt. This is an option I often use.

Joy Sue and I spent a full day choosing serial numbers and degrees of aging for each block. We threw in a hundred or so odd-numbered singles.

I didn't tell her, but the seventy-five grand I paid the printer nearly cleaned us out. If the caper didn't work, the next issue we'd peddle would be pencils on the street. Assuming we were still running free.

While we waited for the printer, we typed out two listings of the stocks, one as an offer and one as a bill of lading. That was probably the riskiest moment in the whole operation. If they screened the serial numbers, they might find we were trying to sell them something they already had. The only safeguard I had come up with was to add an extra zero at the front to confuse the computers and/or hand checkers. They were all high numbers, and that would help muddle it a bit more.

"Makin' a killin' in the stock market's harder work than I'da thought," she said halfway through the second day of it. "You gotta pay me minimum wage anyhow if it don't work, don't you?"

I smiled wearily and kissed her forehead. "If it don't,

doesn't, work, we won't need to worry about that. They'll feed us in jail."

In due course we sent the inventory to the imaginary person who was middle-manning on Ulfsen's side. After that we checked the P.O. box in Philadelphia more often.

Things seemed to drag on interminably by the awkward system I'd set up. We needed safeguards, but I got awfully tired of the road to Philly. Air taxi, with hired ground transportation of one kind or another, wasn't much better.

And then one day the goods arrived. They were beautiful—that is, credible—and we wallowed in them for a while. We did a little more aging and dogearing of our own, for variety. One bundle, when we got through, even showed where a rubber band had been around it for years.

The next day I picked up the acceptance in the mail, with contact info and a New York phone number. I made the call from a WATS Line jack at the club with an old silicon-chip phoneset that made me sound like a sound-effects man at the bottom of a barrel. Just to be safe, I borrowed a little of Joy Sue's dialect on top of it.

That night, instead of a quick kiss and then returning to our own sides of the bed as we'd been doing since New York, we went to sleep hugging. Not for passion, but for comfort and reassurance.

The second day after, two people boarded a plane together in Wilmington, headed for Buffalo. A blowzily dressed frizzy redhead, a pale-blond guy—even blond eyebrows—gauchely attired in a padded-shoulder jacket and wide kelly-green tie right out of the fifties, or so. Their parcels were cardboard, carefully sealed with matte-surface tape. Her accent was nasal, vaguely working-class Northeast, his more Midwestern. You get the idea. We simply couldn't trust anyone else as courier, though we presumed Ulfsen had reliable hired hands to cover it. I'd have liked to see him up close, briefly, but didn't think it likely.

The short, fat, and swarthy man, accompanied by an

amorphous-looking assistant, with whom we spent an ago-
nizing hour in a nondescript hotel room was definitely not
Ulfsen, who had a Cassius' lean and hungry look. He laboriously examined the stocks and weighed them against
the tally sheet while we laboriously counted a little over
one and one half million dollars in U.S. banknotes, basically twenties and fifties. "We had to put in a few hundreds," he apologized. They were, however, old hundreds
with random serial numbers, like all the rest of the bills.
The money, stacked, would have been about forty-eight
feet high, but crammed into suitcases we could manage it.
It weighed less than a ton, at least early in the trip.

Bellhop, elevator, long wait for a cab. There was less
nervous sweat smell now that there were only the two of
us. Finally, ourselves in the cab and our fortune in the
trunk, the redhead leaned over to me and whispered, "Le's
go spend it." I kissed her and squeezed her hand so hard
she winced, then kissed it and apologized. We were both
near incoherence.

Skycap. Careful luggage checking, one carryon, the only
one small enough. Wilmington at last, reverse order sky-
cap/taxicab sequence. When we got home it was dark
enough not to worry about neighbors reporting a strange
couple entering my apartment.

"Go git us a bottle o' champagne while I slip into somethin' comfortable, sweetheart."

I kissed her tiptilted nose, still visible under the dis-
guise. "Do you mind if I take off this costume first?"

"Don't start undressin' yet. We'll never git the champagne if you do." I grinned, went to the fridge, and fetched
the bottle lying down on the back of the bottom shelf.
"Think you're pretty smart, don't ya?"

"You never doubted it, did you?"

"Not too long at a time. . . . Ah'd like a shower first.
Last one in is a rotten aig." She pulled off the ugly wig and
tossed it across the room. I decided to put off redyeing my
hair back to normal till morning.

It would have been a longer shower if the champagne

and money hadn't been waiting. But we washed the day's travel and stress off us, dried each other, and put on pajamas. Then we sipped champagne and looked at bundles of money.

"You could smooch me a little," she said as we were admiring a heap of approximately four hundred thousand dollars we'd poured onto the floor just to look at.

"What do you mean by 'smooch'?"

"Oh, hug me some an' cuddle me an' kiss me a little bit once in a while. If you're not still scairt."

"Not as scared as I was."

"Me neither."

In the small hours she shook me awake. I gathered her in and kissed her face, which felt pretty even in the dark. "Are you insatiable?" I demanded.

"That's not what I'm wakin' you for this time. I got a question."

"Mm-hm?"

"Where were you all them times you called in and said you's at your club or in somebody's office?"

"Where I said I was, of course. That's why I told you. So you could get in touch. If you needed to." I was still half asleep, and puzzled.

"You wasn't with another woman?"

I shook my head to clear it. "Uh-uh. God, no. There was already one woman too many."

"Who?"

"You."

"You mean that?"

"Of course. Can I go back to sleep now?"

"Uh-uh." She was silent for a minute. Then she asked, "Are you in love? A thaink Ah am."

" 'Fraid I am too."

"Whut we gonna do 'bout it?"

"I have no idea."

"Me neither. Gimme some more lovin's."

I gave her more lovin's, and got back better than I gave.

The sun was well up when I slipped out of bed, feeling half adolescent and half middle-aged, the regular me on vacation apparently. I stumbled over the heap of money on the floor, and wondered in awe at seeing myself leave nearly half a million unguarded overnight. Not to mention whatever we'd done with the rest of it.

I started the coffee, then on impulse went back to the bed. I pulled off the little bit of sheet that covered a little bit of Joy Sue and gazed down upon her. The lust, to my amazement, wasn't totally exhausted, though it had had every opportunity. But it was contaminated with something far more serious and fearsome.

I had to lighten my mood, so I picked up some bundles off the floor, broke the bands, and gently snowflaked the sleeping form of Joy Sue with ten grand in fifties. I didn't even care if a couple got lost in the laundry.

It seemed a fluke, but the fifty thousand fabricated shares apparently pushed Ulfsen up to the critical point. Less than a week after our delivery, rumors at the club were that he was calling for a major stockholders' meeting.

This accelerated our schedule considerably. We'd been going to prepare the letter at leisure and, if the fireworks hadn't started by the time we had somewhere interesting to go, mail it then.

So we framed the letter, informing Stromquist that Ulfsen had counterfeit shares and giving enough correct serial numbers to set off a thorough search. I also had some fairly reliable information on illegally obtained proxies, and we included that. We drop-shipped it to Stromquist via Fort Worth, dime store stationery we handled with gloves, and second carbon to render the typewriter unrecognizable if any one got hellbent on tracking us down, which was unlikely. We could have sent a copy to the SEC, but it seemed much better to let Stromquist wake the sleeping dogs if he decided it was needed.

"I think it's about time for a little trip to Jamaica," I told

Joy Sue when we'd done our duty by Stromquist and the American way of life.

"Ah'm willin'," she said. "Any p'tic'lar reason?"

"Do a little banking." I gestured at the linen closet, where we had stashed the boxes of banknotes. That's where she had put them when she vacuumed the carpet, and we decided it was as safe a place as any.

"How on earth you gonna git it 'crost the border? Won't they check it, an' all?"

"It won't go in this form. I deposit it over a period of time, several banks in several towns, in escrow accounts, so titled. Then I draw a cashier's check on the account made out to an imaginary client. I deduct one and a half percent, which I declare in my tax return as my commission. This keeps the Feds off me. It looks like somebody else's money. I've handled for them in a securities transaction. Then I deposit the checks in interest-bearing accounts here and there, mostly Jamaica. Jamaican banks, Swiss banks, British banks—they've all got branches there."

"How do you ever keep up with all yore names?"

"It's a challenge. . . . Joy Sue, do you want me to bank part of yours? There's a number of ways we can do it. I just have to be sure, for my own safety, the tax people don't investigate *you*."

Her eyes went blank. She had to trust me enough for me to keep us both out of trouble.

"What's the ten percent you promised me come to?"

I didn't think she hadn't figured it out already. "After deducting my expenses, which were around eighty thousand, that ten percent would be, roughly, a hundred forty-two thousand. But . . ."

"But there's somethin' in the fine print says I don't rilly git it?" Her eyes now reminded me of a set of blue and white glass marbles I'd played with as a child, cold and opaque, and her lips were set in a tight line, like the clasp of my grandmother's coin purse.

"No. Not that. Dammit, Joy Sue, I want you to have half of it."

She frowned, eyes still opaque. "How 'bout we put the ten percent in my name and the rest o' the half in a joint account?"

I didn't believe what was going on, what I was saying or the answers I was getting. I stood and pulled her up to me. "One or both of us need to have our heads examined."

"You could *start* there," she answered, and held her lips up to me, less like a coin purse now and more like a full-blown rose.

I humored her by examining her head for a minute, checking the various parts of it for kissability and such, and then held her at arm's length. "Jamaica's a safer subject."

The Hindu wiseman, or whoever it was, was right. Wealth is a burden. We worked ourselves ragged for a week and more. We went to banks in four states, invented firms, used all my available aliases. It was fun for a while, but it palled.

At last we had laundered all but a couple of hundred grand. I carefully took the toilet paper dispenser out and suspended the money between the wall studs. We just didn't feel like processing any more. When we finished the whole process, we had a bunch of cashier's checks and a residual deposit in some key accounts.

On a hunch I did an experiment as our plane took off. Before she got really phobic, I started smooching her and kept it up till we were well airborne. It not only averted the fear of flying, but it added something to the smooching.

Our stay of ten days in Jamaica was quite fraught. It was financial, erotic, at times frenetic and convoluted, beachy and nightlifey when we got tired of interesting things. We followed her 10/40/50 plan, part of it in her name and one female alias; the middle part in three joint accounts in our own names, no real tax problem in Jamaica though it would have been in the States; and the remaining half according to my own labyrinthine, Machiavellian, Byzantine system. It occurred to me then that I might be, like the rest of my species, mortal, and I decided to get a lawyer to help me set up a way for Joy Sue and Annette to split my funds if I should get myself deceased. Otherwise, without obvious heirs, I'd just be leaving it to a bunch of governments, Heaven forfend. I needed a Jamaican lawyer anyhow, so I lined up a fine old firm of solicitors left over from colonial days while we were down there.

There would be more trips to make before it was all ship-shape, but we decided after a week and a half we'd had all the fun we could endure, so we got ready to return to Wilmington and finish the job by mail.

"What kinda income is this gonna bring us in?" Joy Sue asked as I finished the arduous job of nibbling her left earlobe. It was certainly worth the extra ticket to have the three seats to ourselves.

"It's complex. But the simple answer is that, when we finish the job we've started, we can spend about a hundred grand a year between the two of us without depleting capital. If we keep working and let it sit there a while and maybe add to it now and then . . ."

"Yeah. Le's do that. But I druther do *small* stuff for a while."

"Yeah, me too." I smooched the inside of her wrist just to see if she would make a funny sound. She did.

When we got home we discovered that it had hit the fan.

Stromquist had challenged Ulfsen, apparently moments after we'd left the country. The SEC had jumped in with both feet; there were attorneys general of at least three or four states already involved and more on the way. It was shaping up to something much bigger and messier than a mere proxy fight. It was on front pages all over the country, hardly anything else was being discussed at the club, it was mentioned every time I picked up the phone.

Which by itself was a problem for Stromquist and Minicorp, but not insurmountable, and certainly better than being eaten alive as Ulfsen had planned. What was bad was that Wall Street had got a bad case of butterflies about the situation. People were unloading Minicorp Series B at an alarming rate, and it was rapidly dropping back toward par. Owners of A stocks were pretty much standing fast, and for the first time there was a big differential between the two issues.

There was no keeping it from Joy Sue, though I'd have liked to for several reasons. To help me along, good ol' Irv Cohen showed up at the office one day, which he almost never did, and he was full of it. Though it took him a few minutes to get around to it. He first inspected Joy Sue and offered me a partnership if I'd bring my executive secretary along.

"I *have* a partner, Irv. It'll be Brown & Witt, Ltd., as soon as we get her credentialed." I'd had no idea I was going to say something like that. She smirked the sweetest, smuggest little smirk I ever saw on an apparently innocent snub-nosed face.

Then, when he recovered from meeting Joy Sue, he had to start on Minicorp.

"They say Stromquist's having some credit problems. He's got reserve now, but if it keeps up he could be in trouble. Big legal fees. A couple of his high-level staff are quitting, somebody told me, I forget who. Suppliers are taking C.O.D. now, no thirty days—they're not sure Minicorp will be *around* in thirty days. A lot of rumors that he's got some counterfeit stuff of his own, overruns he's had tucked away."

"Don't believe it. You know how rumors fly. Stromquist has been straight arrow since his first corner grocery."

Irv frowned. "*I* don't believe it all, some of it maybe, but there's enough that do to make it a real bear market."

I leaned on the desk, experiencing one of my rare guilt

feelings. So much for good intentions. Joy Sue took it all in, eyes unreadable. When he left she said, "We sorta did that all by ourselfs, ditten we?"

"Not necessarily," I answered a little too hastily, and started to launch into a long and circumstantial explanation.

She interrupted me. "Billy, I want my, what was it, hundred and forty thousand. I'm gonna buy Minicorp stocks with it."

"Wait a week and maybe you can get it for a dollar or so."

"That'll be too late, an' you know it. Looky what happent in tin days."

I argued with her for a half hour or more before I realized that I was subtly and soulfully manipulating her, for a rarity, and it took even longer to realize that I had meant to.

"Billy John Brown," she finally said, "you're a stockbroker. Go out and buy me a hundred forty thousand worth of Minicorp, however you do it. You don't even hafta raid one o' your precious bank accounts, just take it out from behind the plumbin' and I'll sign you some Jamaican checks."

"Joy Sue, don't be ridiculous."

"Ridic'lous, am I? Ah'll do it myself, if you won't." She left in a huff. I'd been meaning to get her a car of her own, but a five block walk in heels wouldn't kill her.

I kept busy till quitting time, doing a lot of phone and telex work, including some to Jamaica. I hated to start taking down what I'd just set up, but at least it had been fun. And as good a moneymaking team as we were, it was only a delay and not a defeat of my early-retirement plans.

When I got home the dispenser had been put back in crooked. I undid her job, counted the conscientious sixty thousand left in the baggie, and put it back right.

She had already eaten, she informed me curtly when she got home that evening. A *gentleman* had taken her out to dinner. I'd heard Irv called a lot of things before. At least I *hoped* it was Irv. As much as I missed her on the far side of the king-size, I was glad it wasn't the Atlantic. When I woke I found stone-cold bacon and eggs on the table for me. Not as food, as a message.

When I got to 9100 Offices, the generic receptionist signaled me to pick up my phone. I quickly unlocked the office and answered it.

"Bill, what the *hell* is going on here?" It was, as I'd expected, Irv, the only other broker she knew to speak to. "Your secretary comes in with a wad of bills to choke a hippopotamus and tells me to buy Minicorp—"

"You know how sentimental women can get. You know, family business, American way of life. . . ."

"Bill, you're not telling me something you know."

"Not free to, Irv. I have to talk with my lawyer on an ethics matter before I can say anything. She's exempt, of course, from the, uh, restraints that might possibly affect me."

Forty-eight hours, I figured. I pointedly got rid of Irv after he told me he'd sold her twenty-eight thousand shares on a fifty-point margin, figuring he was safe any way it went.

Not being spoken to for two days, let alone touched in any way whatever, was a desolate experience, but my optimism remained unflustered. I started buying cautiously at 9¼ the next day, and the second day I plunged at 5½.

Then I met Irv at the club for a drink. There were many eyes on me, and ears seemed to be stretching my way. *"Now* can you talk?" he demanded. The nearer ones started edging in.

I smiled smugly. "I had some dope from so near the horse's mouth that I wasn't sure it wouldn't be considered insider stuff."

"Well, what the hell *was* it?"

"They've got the serial numbers of every phony Minicorp share." If that wasn't true, it would be by the time FedEx made the afternoon delivery. "Ulfsen has them all, the

Feds are going over him with a microscope, and he's practically indicted. Rumor has it, though I can't verify it, they're going to nail him for more than just the Minicorp bit." That was a skilled guess, and one I wouldn't mind betting on.

"So you bought, and didn't tell me?"

"So I'm telling you now. You can still get it for a good price. By morning it'll be near normal, I'd predict, and plateaued a couple of points above that by the end of the week."

There were listening ears all around us. Irv downed his drink and headed back to his office. He wasn't the only one.

The rally had begun. Irv got his at 7⅜. Next morning it opened at 10¼. New York prices were running about three hours behind ours.

When I got back to the office she was filing her nails. To a very sharp point, it seemed to me. I leaned over to kiss her. She didn't stab me in the eye with the nail file, but she glared daggers at me as she recoiled. "Please do not touch me. Mr. Brown, after careful consideration, I am tendering my resignation. On the basis of incompatibility and irreconcilable differences. I believe that I have approximately two thousand dollars still due to me. If I may have that, I will stop darkenin' your *door!*" She was near tears.

"What are these 'irreconcilable differences,' Miss Witt?"

" 'Cause you're just lettin' li'l ol' Minicorp *sink,* after you *sunk* it, you ol' stinker!" One of the tears trickled out of her eye and she tried to twitch it back in with a corner of her cheek.

"Before you make final plans, how are you going to cover the margin on the twenty-eight thousand shares you bought?"

"Irvin' said he'd see I dittin git burnt or stung or bit or whatever it was he said. He *also* said if you wasn't treatin'

me right I could work for him an' come live at *his* house.
He has a *big* place."

Good ol' Irv. I'd have done the same for him, if the girl
had been in the Joy Sue class. "Well, before we split the
quilt, we'll have to agree on the disposition of our joint
holding of a hundred thousand shares of Minicorp B." I
showed her the faxes confirming the purchases. "Your
twenty-eight thousand, after a normal delay, started the
rally. Irv spread the rumor we had inside info. Then I
added more rumors, and started buying myself. Including
some purchases made through other brokers. They didn't
know what the hell I was doing, but they were glad to take
the commission. And they talked. This started a bull market in Wilmington, which quickly spread to New York.
Then I placed a couple of phone orders in Chicago, just to
be sure the Midwest would get the idea."

She was standing close and smiling. "You mean you
meant all along to ressacue 'em?"

"Not till you kicked me in the conscience."

She studied my face. "Did you do it for your conscience,
or to git me back?"

"I have to live with my conscience. I don't have to live
with you. Unless, of course, you insist."

"Conscience like yours, it needs a fulltime keeper jess to
stay awake."

"Are you volunteering for the job?"

She was silent so long I was sorry I'd asked. Finally she
spoke. "Ah'm gonna move into a bigger place. Since you're
payin', you might as well come along. Just to keep your
conscience on the straight an' narrow."

"If I won't be in the way."

"Not atall. Ah might find a use for you, now'n then."

My proposal that night late, as we snuggled and
smooched in the warm dark, pleased her more than it
surprised her. The scam I proposed, though much smaller
than the Minicorp caper, was in a way even more outra-
geous. But that's another story.

A LEFT-HANDED PROFESSION

By Al Nussbaum

☐ HE WAS A BIG, RED-FACED MAN WITH A NOSE THAT WAS TOO large and eyes that were too small, and I never heard a grown man whine so much. He sat at the bar, surrounded by flunkies, and didn't shut up for a moment. To hear him tell it, and no one in the lounge of the Buena Vista Casino heard much else that afternoon, he hadn't made a nickel's profit in years. Taxes had left him with nothing.

He might have convinced the Internal Revenue Service, but he didn't convince me. His English leather shoes, hand-tailored suit and wafer-thin wristwatch all said he was a liar. So did the large diamond he wore on the little finger of his right hand—the hand he gestured with—and the thick roll of currency he carried.

From where I sat with my back to the wall, I had a good view of both the bar and the entrance. I watched Benny Krotz nervously make his way across the casino floor, past the crap tables, blackjack dealers and roulette wheels. He paused in the entrance for a moment, blinking his eyes rapidly to adjust them to the reduced illumination. When he spotted me, he came over and dropped lightly into the seat beside me. Benny was a gambler who believed in flying saucers and luck, but he'd never seen either one. A loser if I'd ever seen one, not that my white hair and conservative clothes made me look like a world-beater.

I nodded toward the bigmouth at the bar. "Is that the mark?" I asked.

Benny hesitated, afraid of giving away the only thing he had to sell. Finally he acknowledged, "Yeah, that's the guy. How'd ya make him so fast?" His expression was glum.

"I'd have to be deaf, blind and have a cold to miss him," I said quietly.

"A cold?"

"Even if I couldn't hear him or see him, his smell would give him away." I allowed myself a brief smile. "He smells like money."

Benny brightened. "He looks good to ya, huh?"

"He looks almost perfect. He's a liar who lives well, so he's probably dishonest and greedy. There's no better target for a con game. There's only one trouble."

"One trouble?" Benny echoed.

"Uh-huh—this town is crawling with hustlers. If I can spot that guy in less time than it takes to light a cigarette, others have done it, too. He's probably been propositioned more times than the chorus line at Radio City Music Hall. And, considering the type of person he is, he's probably already fallen for more than one con game and is extra cautious now. That's right, isn't it?"

"Yeah," Benny admitted. "That's right. He's been burned."

"Badly?"

"Yeah, pretty bad. He's been taken in card games, crap games and a bunch o' con games, already."

I finished my drink and signaled for the waitress. When she had taken our order and left, I turned back to Benny. "What kind of con games?" I asked.

"All the usual—phony stock, underwater real estate, cheap stolen goods that turned out to be perfectly legitimate factory rejects. And Red Harris took him for twenty thousand about six months ago with a counterfeit money swindle. Red gave him fifty brand-new twenties, telling him they were samples of the stuff he had for sale. He let him try them out all over town, then sold him a wrapped-up telephone book and made a nineteen-grand profit."

I laughed and looked over to where the mark was sitting. "That must have hurt his pride," I said. "How about his wallet? What kind of shape is that in?"

"Good shape. Very good shape. That's Big Jim Thompson, the drilling contractor. He has about half a hundred rigs working throughout the Southwest, and he gets paid whether they hit anything or not."

"That's fine," I said, smiling again. "It would ruin my Robin Hood image to take money from a poor man."

The waitress brought our drinks and I paid for them while Benny fumbled politely in his empty pockets. Because my money clip was already out, I removed three $100 bills and passed them to Benny. "For your help," I said.

"You're satisfied with him?" Benny asked, snatching up the money. He couldn't conceal his surprise. "He's gonna be mighty cautious."

I shrugged. "I don't think that will be a problem. Can you introduce us?"

"Yeah, sure." Benny started to push his chair back. "What's your name? For the introduction?"

Benny had been recommended to me as a source of information. Since he was in the business of selling what he knew about people, I hadn't given him any more about me than he needed to know, which was nothing. I had been in the game too long to make that kind of mistake. Now I gave him a name. "William Henk," I said, but I didn't move to get up. "There's no hurry, Benny. Finish your drink, then we'll go over."

Benny could have had ten more drinks; it wouldn't have mattered. Big Jim Thompson was firmly ensconced at the bar. He was still holding court over his followers when we walked over to them a few minutes later, and he gave every impression of being there for hours to come. He glanced contemptuously at Benny, then he noticed me and his small eyes narrowed.

"Mr. Thompson," Benny said, "my friend William Henk wants to meetcha."

Thompson swung around on his stool, but he didn't extend his hand, and I didn't offer mine. "Why?" he challenged.

"Because I've been hearing a lot about you," I said.

"What have you been hearing?"

"That you're a real sucker for a con game," I answered, and Benny looked as though someone had just kicked him in the stomach.

Thompson's face started to go from red to purple. "What business is it of yours?"

"I might have a deal for you."

"*Might* have?" Thompson snorted disdainfully.

"OK, *will* have. Tomorrow. Meet me here at this time and I'll tell you about it."

"What makes you think I'll be interested in any deal of yours?"

"It will give you a chance to get even for your losses. Maybe get a little ahead. You'd like that, right?"

"So why wait till tomorrow?"

I nodded pleasantly at all his friends. "The audience is too big, and I have someone waiting for me. There's no rush. This is no con game," I said, then turned on my heel and walked away. I could feel their eyes on me, but I didn't look back. I had sunk the hook into Thompson. Now I could reel him in—carefully.

I bought a stack of out-of-town newspapers, then drove back toward the hotel where I was staying. I made a lot of unnecessary turns to be sure I wasn't being followed and put the rented car in a lot a block away. I could hear the shower running when I opened the door of the suite, and my wife Margie's soft voice floated out to me. She was singing an old folk song, but she'd forgotten most of the words.

I slipped out of my suit coat, kicked off my shoes, and sprawled across the bed with the newspapers. I read all the crime news I can find. Doctors read medical journals; I study newspapers. Both of us are keeping abreast of the changes in our professions.

Margie came out of the bathroom wrapped in a yellow robe. Her long chestnut hair was freshly brushed and shiny. She sat on the edge of the bed and kissed me. "Anything new in the papers?" she asked.

I'd married Margie because she was beautiful and young, and made me feel young, too. Later I noticed I had received a bonus—no one ever looked at me when we were together.

"Not much," I answered. "A couple of bank robberies in New York City—amateurs; a jewel robbery in Miami that has the police excited; and the Los Angeles cops are still hunting for the four men who held up the armored car three days ago."

"Do you think they'll catch them?"

"Probably. Men who have to make their livings with guns in their fists will never win any prize for brains," I said.

Margie stood up and started to unpack more of our clothes. I stopped her. "Don't bother," I said. "We won't be here as long as I figured. I've found a live one."

"Are you going to tell me about it?"

"When it's over. I'm still working it out in my head."

The next afternoon, Thompson was waiting for me in the lounge of the Buena Vista Casino when I arrived. He was alone and seemed smaller. He was one of those people who needs an audience before he can come alive.

"What've ya got to sell?" he asked, bypassing all small-talk preliminaries.

"Counterfeit," I answered, handing him a single bill.

Thompson stood up without another word and headed for the entrance. I followed him across the casino floor, and into the coffee shop. There were a couple of customers at the counter, but that was all. Thompson went to the last booth along the wall and sat down, waving away a waitress who started toward him. I took the seat opposite his and waited.

He pulled a ten-power jeweler's loupe out of his pocket, screwed it into his right eye, and examined the $50 bill I had given him. I knew he was studying the portrait of Grant, the scrollwork along the borders, and the sharpness of the points on the treasury seal—and he was finding everything perfect.

"You must think I'm a real fool," he said with a nasty smile. "This ain't counterfeit."

"You don't think so, huh?" I handed him another $50 bill. "What about this?"

He was a little faster this time, but his verdict was the same. "It's real."

"And this one?"

A look, a feel, a snap. "Good as gold."

"Nope." I shook my head. "Counterfeit."

He pointed a blunt finger at the center of my chest. "Listen, punk, I know genuine money when I see it. Whatever you're planning ain't gonna work, so forget it."

"You can be sure of one thing."

"What's that?"

I gave him a nasty smile. "I won't try to sell you a twenty-thousand-dollar telephone book."

His jaw tightened.

"Instead," I continued, "I'm going to give you the chance of a lifetime. Those bills *are* counterfeit. In fact, these samples have one major flaw that the rest of my stock doesn't have."

I took the three bills out of his hand and lined them up on the table between us. Then I added three more fifties to the row. "Unlike genuine currency," I told him, "all six of these bills have the same serial numbers."

Thompson's eyes jerked back to the bills, and he snatched up two of them. He held them up to the light and studied them, frowning. After that he compared two more and sat staring at the six identical Federal Reserve notes.

"Do you still think they're real?" I taunted.

"I've never seen anything like this," he said in an awed tone. "These bills are perfect."

"*Almost* perfect," I corrected. "But I'll deliver brand-new, absolutely perfect bills."

He started to scoop up the money from the table, but I put my hand over his. "Where do you think you're going with that?" I asked.

He gestured toward the gaming tables. "Out into the casino to test some of this."

"Not without paying for it first. I don't give free samples, mister. I don't have to. I've got the best queer there is, and I get fifty cents on the dollar for *every* dollar. That three hundred will cost you one-fifty."

"That's pretty steep for counterfeit, isn't it?"

"You said yourself, you've never seen anything like it. I've been in business for five years and not one bill has ever been questioned, let alone detected. It's not every day you get a chance to double your money."

Thompson gave me a hundred and fifty from the roll he carried, then took my six identical bills into the casino. I ordered a cup of coffee and a hamburger, and settled down to wait for him. I was drinking my second cup of coffee when he returned.

He looked a little stunned by his success. "Not one dealer so much as blinked an eye. I've had 'em look closer at good money," he said.

I didn't have to give him any more of my sales pitch. He was selling himself. I sat back and sipped my coffee.

He didn't keep me waiting long. "Tell ya what, I'll take twenty-five thousand worth."

I shook my head.

"That too much?" he asked.

"Too little. You've seen the last samples you ever will. From now on I sell nothing smaller than hundred-thousand-dollar lots."

He did some mental arithmetic. "That's fifty thousand to me, right?"

"No. The hundred thousand is what *you* pay. In exchange, I give you two hundred thousand in crisp, new tens, twenties and fifties. Each bill with a *different* serial number."

He didn't say anything right away. I gave him two full minutes to think about it, then slid out of the booth and stood up. "Hell, I thought you were big time," I said disdainfully, then started to walk away.

Thompson called me back, as I knew he would. He was as predictable as a fixed race. "OK," he said. "You've got a deal, but you better not be planning a rip-off."

"How can there be a rip-off? You're going to examine every bill before you pay me, and you can bring all the help you think you'll need. And I'm not worried about being hijacked by you because I'll tell some friends who it is I'll be doing business with. If anything happened to me, you wouldn't be hard to find."

"So we understand each other," he said. "OK, when can we complete the deal?"

"The sooner the better," I said. "The sooner the better."

Four hours later, Margie and I were on our way out of town with Thompson's hundred grand. We were in the rented car because I figured we'd better leave before there was any chance of Thompson getting wise to how I'd tricked him. I could return the car to the agency's office in L.A. or Frisco.

"You're really something," Margie said, hugging my arm while I drove. "When you bought the loot from the armored car robbery in Los Angeles, you paid ten cents on the dollar because all the money was new and the numbers had been recorded. You said it was so hot you'd be lucky to get fifteen or twenty cents on the dollar, and then only after you located the right buyer."

"That's what I thought until I met Thompson."

"Didn't he know the money was stolen?"

"No. He thought it was counterfeit. I showed him six perfect fifties, all with the same serial numbers." I told her what had happened in the coffee shop.

"Where did you get counterfeit money?" she demanded.

"I didn't. It was good. Part of the armored car loot, in fact."

"You must think I'm stupid," Margie said. "I know good money doesn't have the same serial numbers."

I stopped for a traffic light, then got the car rolling again after it changed. "It does if you take half a dozen consecutively numbered bills and erase the last digit."

Margie's mouth opened in surprise. "You can do that? You can erase the numbers?"

"Easier than you'd think, and without leaving a trace, either."

We rode in silence for a few minutes, then Margie said, "Why didn't you erase the first digit on all the bills? That way they'd all be good to spend and you'd have gotten one hundred cents on the dollar?" She was smart as well as beautiful.

"Because the risk of detection was very slight with only six bills, but some smart teller would surely have noticed if I'd tried to change the numbers on every bill. Then it would have been you and I back there, trying to explain where we got the money, instead of Big Jim Thompson."

JUST THE LADY WE'RE LOOKING FOR

Donald E. Westlake

◻ THAT MORNING MARY CLEANED THE KITCHEN, AND AFTER LUNCH she went shopping. It was a beautiful sunny day, but getting hot; the lawns and curbs and ranch-style houses of Pleasant Park Estates gleamed and sparkled in the sunlight, and in the distance the blacktop street shone like glittering water.

Mary had lived here barely five weeks now, but one development was very like another, and in her seven years of marriage to Geoff she'd seen plenty of them. Geoff transferred frequently, spending six months here, eight months there, never as much as a year in any one location. It was a gypsyish life, but Mary didn't mind: we're just part of the new mobile generation, she told herself, and let it go at that.

All the stores in the shopping center were air-conditioned, but that only made it worse when Mary finally walked back across the griddle of a parking lot to the car. She thought of poor Geoff, working outdoors 'way over at Rolling Rancheros, and she vowed to make him an extra-special dinner tonight: London broil, a huge green salad, and iced coffee. In fact, she'd make up a big pot of iced coffee as soon as she got home.

But she didn't get the chance. She'd barely finished putting the groceries away when the front doorbell sounded.

She went to the living room, opened the door, and the man smiled, made a small bow, and said, "Mrs. Peters?"

He was about forty, very distinguished-looking, with a tiny Errol Flynn mustache and faint traces of gray at his temples. His dark suit fitted perfectly, and his black attaché case gleamed of expensive leather. He said, "I wonder if you could spare five minutes, or should I call back later?"

Mary frowned. "I'm sorry," she said, "I don't under—"

"Oh! You think I'm a salesman!" He laughed, but as though the joke were on himself, not on Mary. "I should have shown you my identification," he said, and from his inside coat pocket took a long flat wallet of black leather. From it he plucked a card, and extended it to Mary, saying, "Merriweather. Universal Electric."

The card was in laminated plastic, the printing in two colors. There was a photo of Mr. Merriweather, full face, and his signature underneath. The reverse side gave the office locations of Universal Electric in major cities.

Mr. Merriweather said, smiling, "You *have* heard of Universal Electric, I hope."

"Oh, of course. I've seen your ads on television."

Mr. Merriweather accepted his card back. "If you don't have time now—"

"Oh, I have time. Come on in."

"Thank you." He wiped his feet on the mat, and entered. "What a lovely home!"

"Oh, not really. We just moved in last month and it's still an awful mess."

"Not at all, not at all! You have charming taste."

They sat down, Mary in the armchair and Mr. Merriweather on the sofa, his attaché case beside him. He said, "May I ask what make of refrigerator you now have in your home?"

"It's a Universal."

"Wonderful." He smiled again. "And how old is it?"

"I really don't know—it came with the house."

"I see. And a home freezer unit, do you have one of those?"

"No, I don't."

"Well, fine. You may be just the lady we're looking for." Taking his attaché case onto his lap, he opened it and began removing brightly colored sheets of glossy paper. "A part of our advertising campaign for—"

Now she was sure. "Excuse me," she said, and got to her feet. Trying to smile normally and naturally, she said, "My groceries. I just got home from the store and nothing's put away yet. Your talking about the refrigerator reminded me."

"If you'd prefer that I come back la—"

"Oh, no." No, she didn't want to frighten him away. "This won't take a minute," she assured him. "I'll just put the perishables away, and I'll be right back."

He got to his feet and smiled and bowed as she left the room.

Her heart was pounding furiously and her legs didn't seem to want to work right. In the kitchen she went straight to the wall phone and dialed Operator, her hand trembling as she held the receiver to her ear. When the operator came on, Mary said, keeping her voice low, "I want the police, please. Hurry!"

It seemed to take forever, but finally a gruff male voice spoke, and Mary said, "My name is Mrs. Mary Peters, two-twelve Magnolia Court, Pleasant Park Estates. There's a confidence man in my house."

"A what?"

Didn't this policeman watch television? "A confidence man," she said. "He's trying to get money from me under false pretenses. I'll try to keep him here until you send somebody, but you'll have to hurry."

"In five minutes," the policeman promised.

Mary hung up, wishing there was some way to call Geoff. Well, she'd just have to handle it herself. Generally speaking, confidence men avoided violence whenever they could, so she probably wasn't in any direct physical danger; but you could never be sure. This one might be wanted for other more serious crimes as well, and in that case he might be very dangerous indeed.

Well, she'd started it, so she might as well see it through to the end. She took a deep breath, and went back to the living room.

Mr. Merriweather rose again, polite as ever. He now had the coffee table completely covered with glossy sheets of paper. She said, "I'm sorry I took so long, but I didn't want any of the food to spoil."

"Perfectly all right." He settled himself on the sofa again and said, "As I was saying, Universal Electric is about to introduce a revolutionary new type of refrigerator-freezer, with an advertising campaign built around the concept of the satisfied user. We are placing this refrigerator-freezer in specially selected homes for a six-months' trial period, absolutely free, asking only that the housewife, *if* she loves this new product as much as we are convinced she will, give us an endorsement at the end of that time and permit us to use her statement and name and photograph in our advertising, both in magazines and on television."

What would a housewife say who hadn't seen through this fraud? Mary strove for a suitably astonished expression and said, "And you picked me?"

"Yes, we did. Now, here—" he pointed to one of the papers on the coffee table "—is the product. On the outside it looks like an ordinary refrigerator, but—"

"But how did you happen to pick me?" She knew it was a dangerous question to ask, but she couldn't resist seeing how he would handle it. Besides, if she acted sufficiently naive, there wouldn't be any reason for him to get suspicious.

He smiled again, not at all suspicious, and said, "Actually, *I* didn't pick you, Mrs. Peters. The names were chosen by an electronic computer at our home office. We are trying for a statistical cross-section of America."

It was time to leave that, and become gullibly enthusiastic. She said, "And you really want to *give* me a refrigerator for six months?"

"Six months is the trial period. After that, you can either keep the unit in payment for your endorsement, or return it and take cash instead."

"Well, it sounds absolutely fantastic! A brand-new refrigerator for nothing at all."

"I assure you, Mrs. Peters," he said, smiling, "we don't expect to lose on this proposition. Advertising based on satisfied customers is far more effective than any other sort of campaign." He flipped open a notebook. "May I put you down as willing?"

"Yes, of course. Who wouldn't be willing?" *And where in the world were the police?*

He started to write, then suddenly cried, "Oh!" and looked stricken. "I'm so sorry, there's something I forgot, something I should have told you before. As I explained, you have the option either to keep the unit or return it. Now, we want to be sure our trial users won't harm the units in any way, so we do request a small damage deposit before delivery. The deposit is automatically refunded after the six months, unless you wish to return the unit and we find that it has been mistreated."

Would the unsuspicious housewife become suspicious at this point? Mary wasn't sure. But if she seemed *too* gullible, that might be just as bad as seeming too wary. So she said, guardedly, "I see."

"I'll give you a receipt for the deposit now," he went on glibly, "and you show it when the unit is delivered. It's just as simple as that."

"How much is this damage deposit?"

"Ten dollars." He smiled, saying, "You can see it's merely an expression of good faith on your part. If the unit *is* mistreated, ten dollars will hardly cover its repair."

"I'm not sure," she said doubtfully. She *had* to act more wary now, if only to stall until the police got here. "Maybe I ought to talk it over with my husband first."

"Certainly. Could you phone him at work? I do have to

have your answer today. If you elect not to take the unit, I'll have to contact our second choice in this area."

"No, my husband works outdoors. I wish I *could* phone him." There was nothing to do now but pay him the money and pray that the police would arrive in time. "All right," she said. "I'll do it."

"Fine!"

"I'll just get my purse."

Mary went back to the kitchen and looked longingly at the telephone. Call the police again? No, they were surely on the way by now. She got her purse and returned to the living room.

It seemed to take no time at all to give him the money and get the receipt. Then he was rising, saying, "The unit should be delivered within three weeks."

Desperately, she said, "Wouldn't you like a glass of iced coffee before you go? It's so hot out today."

He was moving toward the door. "Thank you, but I'd better be getting back to the office. There's still—"

The doorbell chimed.

Mary opened the door, and Mr. Merriweather walked into the arms of two uniformed policemen.

The next five minutes were hectic. Merriweather blustered and bluffed, but the policemen would have none of it. When Mary told them his line, they recognized it at once: complaints had been coming in from swindled housewives in the area for over a month. "There's always a couple of these short-con artists working the suburbs," one of the policemen said.

But Mr. Merriweather didn't give up until one of the policemen suggested that they phone the local office of Universal Electric and verify his identification. At that, he collapsed like a deflated balloon. Turning to Mary, he said, "How? How did you know?"

"Women's intuition," she told him. "You just didn't seem right to me."

"That's impossible," he said. "What did I do wrong? How did you tumble to it?"

"Just women's intuition," she said.

The policemen took him away, shaking his head, and Mary went back to the kitchen and got started on dinner. She could hardly wait for Geoff to get home—to tell him about her day.

Geoff came in a little after five, his suit and white shirt limp and wrinkled. "What a scorcher," he said. "If it keeps up like this, we'd better move north again."

He pulled a handful of bills from his pockets, fives and tens, and dumped them on the dining-room table. As he counted them, he said, "How was your day?"

"Got rid of some of the competition," she told him. "Guy working the Free Home Demonstration dodge. Get that grift off the table, I have to set it for dinner."

THE CACKLE BLADDER

by William Campbell Gault

◻ THE LAST TIME I SAW PARIS, HE DIDN'T LOOK LIKE THIS. HE'D always been a snappy lad when it came to clothes and he'd never been at a loss for words, as they say.

This gloomy Monday I was sitting in Monte's, watching the rain hit the front windows and trying to find a mudder in the Form. I was low on scratch, and drinking beer when this—this apparition walked in, wringing wet.

I figured Monte would give him the heave, but good. Monte don't like no bums cluttering up the place.

But Monte just sighed and said, "Morning, Paris."

If this was Paris, I was Pittsburgh Phil. Then I looked more closely. No teeth in this wretch, pale as snow, wearing stinking rags, but it was Paris, all right.

I looked at him and thought of the last time I'd seen him. He'd been with Joe Nello, then, working the short-con together. Paris had taught the kid everything he knew.

He was looking at me now. "Hi, Jonesy," he said.

"Hello, Paris," I said, and nodded to the chair across the table. "It's been a long time. Sit down and have a drink."

He sat down, and Monte brought over a big tumbler of fortified wine. I knew then that Paris was on the way out. That comes just before your toes curl, fortified wine.

I took the chance and said, "How's Joe Nello?"

He wasn't looking at me; he was looking through me. "Would you really like to know?"

I nodded. "That's why I asked."

This is what he told me . . .

Joe and I, he began, were pretty thick, as you know. I mean, we worked all right together. I made the guy; he wouldn't have been nothing without me. He had the looks, sure, but he was kind of soft, you know, at first. He had a lot to learn about taking care of himself in this damned world.

Times I was discouraged about Joe, but he knew what was important, really. I mean, down deep, he understood there's nothing like a few bucks to make people notice you. Lot of talk about the worthwhile things, but name me one you can't buy.

Anyhow, we were working Iowa with the short-con, everything from hog cholera tonic to three-card monte, and Joe was catching on. So many honest people in that state, they should have a closed season on the suckers. Begging to be taken, those rubes.

And the girls? They believe anything you tell them. *Anything.* Few tears when you leave them, but you don't always have to tell them you're going, not when you're on the move all the time.

We made a small pile in the tank towns and holed up in Des Moines for a while. We bought a convertible and enjoyed life. We didn't work the town; it's a wrong town. We just had ourselves a time.

That's where this Judith comes in. That's the babe that almost kept Joe from amounting to anything. I met her first, in the lobby of the hotel where we were staying.

She was a hostess for the tea room in the hotel, and in town on her own. Her folks had a farm about eighty miles into the tall and uncut.

She was maybe twenty-two, and slim, but not slim where she shouldn't be. She had blue-black hair and deep blue eyes. An innocent, if I ever saw one. But ready, I could tell. Bored, and ready.

She was sitting near the front windows, watching the traffic, a magazine in her lap, the first time I saw her.

I took a chair nearby and said, "Things can't be that bad."

She looked over, startled, and she smiled. She seemed about eighteen when she smiled. "Was I looking as bored as I feel?" she asked.

"I don't know how bored you feel," I answered. "Haven't I seen you around here before?"

"I work in the tea room," she said. "I'm the hostess. I went to school, and now I'm a hostess in a tea room and I can write testimonials for the school. I'm a success."

Then Joe came along. Her eyes went past me, and they seemed to come alive when she looked at Joe. He was staring, too.

He grinned then and said, "Is this gentleman annoying you, miss? And if he is, can I help him?"

Joe was going under the name of Jim Kruger at the time, and I said, "Jim, I'm sure you have something to do. There are lots of interesting things to do in this town. Goodbye, Jim, old pal."

"Now I know he's annoying you, miss," Joe said. "He has evil intentions, despite his age. And if there are so many things to do, can't we do them together?"

That crack about age wasn't so hot, I thought.

Joe said, "Run along, now, Don, or I won't give you any more of my old suits."

Sharpie, he was getting to be. I said, "Why don't the three of us go out together? Then the lady will be safe, and we'll all have a good time."

"All but me," Joe said, and looked at her. "However, if that's the only way, I'm for it. You don't think we're bold, do you?"

"I think you're fun," she said, "and my sales resistance is at an all-time low. I'm sold."

I never had a chance; this one was Joe's right from the

start. We went to a spot on the edge of town where the lights were low and the liquor bonded.

They danced, and I drank. They danced and danced until you'd think Joe would develop a charley horse. Young they were, and graceful, and they danced awful close, but good. People gave them room, and some stopped to watch and this Judith ate it up and got flushed and prettier than ever.

Joe's old man had been a hoofer, and Joe had started dancing when he was four. He was really going good that night.

I drove, going back. The car purred along and I kept my eyes on the road ahead, and they didn't say anything.

In the room, while we were getting ready for the hay, Joe said, "This Judith, she's different, Paris."

"Not in any place I could notice," I said, "though my eyes aren't so good, now that I'm *old.*"

"Aw, Paris," he said, "you know what I mean."

"I wish I did," I said.

"I mean, she's—she's a decent kid, and only a kid. She's different."

You see what I mean? I'd worked on the boy. He knew the difference between a wolf and a lamb, I thought, and now he gets all mixed up with a lamb who's ready and he's got to go soft. What could I tell him, if he wouldn't learn?

Love . . . How many pitches have gone wrong because some guys think it's love? Love's all right, if you want to call it that, but you don't have to buy a ring to prove it.

And that's what this punk meant to do. All the babes he'd run around with, and he's talking marriage.

"Her dad," he says one night, "has got three hundred and twenty acres of the finest corn land in Iowa, Paris."

"That's the guy you should be hanging around, not the daughter, then," I said. "Maybe we can touch him for a couple grand."

He didn't even seem to hear me. "She wants me to settle down. She wants me to take a winter course at Iowa State and learn to run those three hundred and twenty acres."

"That's the wrong side of the fence, Joe," I told him. "You're no yokel and you couldn't learn to be one."

He laughed at me. "What have we got? A couple grand. Small-time grifters, working the short-con. I could have done this good in the five-a-day."

I was glad then that I had the telegram in my pocket. Lou Pettle had sent it from K.C. and I hadn't shown it to Joe yet. I did, now.

He read it and said, "Lou Pettle . . ." like a yokel would say "J. P. Morgan." Lou was just as big a man, in his field.

"Lou Pettle," I agreed. "The biggest operator in the country. This is the chance we've been waiting for. This is where we move up, Joe."

He shook his head and blew out his breath. "A fortune. Lou Pettle. Golly, Paris."

"Well," I said, "are you going to buy the ring?"

He laughed and shook his head. Then he grinned at me. "But give me a couple days. Let me get her out of my system."

I couldn't blame him for that. He could have a lifetime without meeting another like Judith. I said, "I'll wire Lou we've some unfinished business, but to expect us."

He did buy a ring, though. Nice big Mexican diamond that must have cost him well over two bucks.

He spent most of the two days with her. She had a vacation coming and she took it, and where they went I couldn't swear to in court. I know I didn't see much of Joe.

Then, one afternoon, he comes into the lobby looking like a cat that has just polished off a quart of Grade-A. "When do we leave?" he said.

"Congratulations," I said. "Any time you're ready."

"Now," he said. "Judith's gone out to bring her dad to town. He wants to meet me." He seemed a little nervous. "We haven't got too much time."

We had less than that.

Joe was out getting the car gassed up when Judith comes into the lobby, this stout gent in tow.

He didn't look like a farmer. He looked like a banker—

that's the kind of moola there is in that Iowa soil. She introduced us and asked, "Where's Jim?"

"He'll be back," I said, watching her face.

Her face was thinner, but her eyes were starrier than ever. Golly, she was a looker! I'll never forget it.

Her dad went over to buy a paper, and she said, "He will be back, won't he, Don? I suppose that's a silly question, but he's so . . . I mean, it's hard to believe, even now, that he's all mine. Oh, you must think I'm a perfect idiot. Only—"

"Easy, baby," I said. "Of course he'll be back. You go over and sit in that big chair, and I'll try and locate him."

She was trembling like a bride at the altar.

I got hold of him at the service station. I said, "You'd better steer clear of the hotel. There's no shotgun in sight, but there could be one around. I'll pack your stuff, and you pick me up near that restaurant where we ate the first day. Got it?"

I came out of the booth, and she was standing about five feet away. I walked over, and she put a hand on my arm.

"Don, there's something wrong."

"Nothing, nothing," I said. "Jim's trying to land a customer that will net us eighteen thousand dollars, Judith, and I'm not going to bother him now. He'll be here at six to clean up. Or, if you'd rather, he'll meet you at the Golden Pheasant. He's arranged a dinner for the four of us out there. He said this is the biggest evening in his life."

She smiled. "Did he say that?"

"His exact words."

Now she looked calm. "I'm going out and buy the nicest dress in town. We'll meet you here at seven, Don."

"We'll be here," I said.

They went out, and I went to the desk. I paid our bill and told the clerk, "Any mail that comes to either of us, you could send to General Delivery, in Kansas City."

He grinned at me. "Sure thing. Don't tell me Mr. Kruger is walking out on our Judith."

I was glad now we hadn't used our right names. All these squares work together.

I said, "Your memory isn't much good, is it?" I laid a twenty on the desk.

"I don't know from nothin'," he said, and that twenty just disappeared.

"Send for the cab, then," I told him, "and have the cabbie come up for our luggage."

Joe was waiting with the car in front of the restaurant, and we piled the luggage in the back.

Joe said, "How'd it go?"

"We're taking them to dinner at seven," I said. "Judy's out, buying a new dress."

Joe chuckled and shook his head. "Squares," he said. "Kansas City, here we come."

I was proud of him. I'd got him past this one, and I knew he wasn't going to get on the wrong side of the fence again. That was his graduation, you might say. From then on, I knew there was no danger of Joe getting simple. We were going places.

Two days after we started to work for Lou, I went over to the post office and picked up our mail. There wasn't much —a couple letters and a copy of the Des Moines paper. That was probably the clerk's idea, sending that paper along.

There was a picture of Judith on the front page. It didn't say it had been suicide. It just said she'd taken an overdose of sleeping tablets which had proved fatal. There was an unfounded rumor of an unhappy love affair, but neither of her parents would comment on that. She'd died clutching an immense imitation diamond ring in her left hand.

That's a square for you. I mean, he hadn't taken a nickel from her. As a matter of fact, he'd spent his own money on her and she hadn't lost a thing. What'd she have to beef about?

I threw the paper away. I didn't want to annoy Joe when he had his big chance, like this.

Kansas City was right. Lou was an operator and the fix was solid, and he ran enough steerers to keep him busy. Lou handled the inside, of course, and I watched him close. That's what I wanted, the inside job. That's where the moo was.

Lou had ulcers and was due to retire soon. I watched and learned, and we salted it, Joe and I. I rode the trains in from the West and he rode them in from the East, and Lou plucked them clean as a whistle, those marks we brought in to the store.

Store is just a con-name for the front we were using, an imitation bookie joint that could have been staged by a Broadway producer, it was that authentic. He had shills that looked like millionaires and he had shills that looked like playboys and shills that looked like retired farmers, but none that looked like shills.

Lou's ulcers got worse, and Joe and I began to take him out on parties, here and there, and raise hell with him generally.

Then one day Lou said to me, "Paris, I can't take any more. The fix is still solid, and the store is a mint, but a man has got to think of his health. You wouldn't be interested in the inside job, would you?"

"Not for me," I said. "I'm a simple, happy man."

"There's no one else could handle it in the organization," he said. "I wouldn't expect you to shell out; all I want's a percentage. And you'd be handling the money, Paris, remember. You'd get yours."

"And you'd get yours, with me handling it," I said, "but how much?"

We finally agreed on what I should send him. I argued so long he must have thought he was actually going to get it.

So we didn't use a dime of our money. We had seventy grand, Joe and I, in a joint account. That's how I trusted him.

Well, Judith had been one milestone, and this was likely to be another. The inside man, you know, is the boss and not always popular, because he's got the chance to knock down some personal moola at the expense of the others. If Joe and I got through this, we were solid; there wasn't any limit to the long green we could garner.

I knew that by now I could handle anything Lou had handled, and I didn't have ulcers.

It was Joe who brought me my first mark in the new job. Joe phoned me from the Alcazar and said, "Kind of a young guy, Paris. But he's got forty grand salted, right here in town. He wants to go into business here." Then he paused. "Husky, though. Might be rough to cool out."

"We'll use the cackle bladder," I said. "I've got a new poke already made and I'll send it over to you. I'll get a suite at that hotel, and you can bring him up right after lunch tomorrow." And then I said slowly. "No mistakes, though, Joe. The gang all think nobody can take Lou's place, and we've got to show them how wrong they are."

"Lou," Joe said, "was a piker and an amateur."

I got the best suite in the house and I was sitting in it the next afternoon, smoking a dollar cigar, when they rapped at the door.

I went to the door and opened it. I said, "Well?" sounding annoyed.

Joe said, "Are you Mr. Walters?"

"And what if I am? I suppose you—you gentlemen are reporters?"

"No, sir," Joe said.

"Well, then, speak your piece. You're selling something? A man purchases privacy, you know, when—"

"You've got us wrong," Joe said. "We're here to return something of yours, Mr. Walters, something we found in the dining room." He had the poke I'd sent over yesterday.

I threw the door wide open. "Gentlemen," I said, "forgive me. You've found my wallet."

While I said this, I was sizing up the mark. He must have been about twenty-six, a scrubbed-looking guy in a neat blue suit. He sure didn't look like forty grand to me.

"I *think* it's your wallet," Joe said. "You'd be willing to identify it, of course, Mr. Walters."

"A few hundred dollars," I said, "and some membership cards. One for the Pegasus Club, one for the Civic Betterment Club, a couple telegrams and"—here I paused—"and a code sheet."

Joe nodded and handed it over. "Correct, in all details. Mr. Walters, this is a recent acquaintance of mine, Mr. George Apple. And my name is Delsing, Carlton Delsing."

I shook their hands. "It's a distinct pleasure and a memorable occasion," I said. "I insist you have a drink on me."

"Don't mind if I do," Joe said, and Mr. Apple nodded and sat down. He wasn't missing a thing; he watched me like I was the President.

When I handed them their drinks, Joe said, "There was one thing you forgot to mention, Mr. Walters. You mustn't be so modest."

I looked blank.

"That newspaper clipping in your wallet," Joe went on. "It described you as the Pittsburgh Phil of our era, the greatest plunger the track has ever known."

"Oh, that," I said. "You mustn't believe everything you read, Mr. Delsing." I smiled at him. "Income tax, you know. The less publicity, the better."

The mark sort of stirred in his chair. "You mean—this money you win isn't taxable? I mean, it really is, but you don't declare it. Isn't that dishonest, Mr. Walters?"

That wasn't good. A guy should have a little larceny in him to make the perfect mark. There's an old saw that you can't cheat an honest man. But this was important, this fish, and I barged ahead.

"Dishonest?" I said. "I have certain expenses, and the possibility of loss in other lines. Is it dishonest to build up a reserve against that contingency, Mr. Apple?"

"Well, no," he said. "I see what you mean. I'm all for the private enterprise system, myself, Mr. Walters, and I know that we have to protect ourselves against government greed, but, well, I mean—"

"We aren't under the private enterprise system at present, Mr. Apple," I told him coolly. "But there'll be a change, one of these days. There's got to be a change, or the system is dead." I sighed. "I don't worry about myself. I've made mine. This track plunging is a sort of hobby with me. It's the young people I worry about, the young lads with gumption enough to go out on their own."

He sort of flushed, as though I'd been talking about him, which I had.

I smiled at him and said, "What's your line of business, Mr. Apple?"

"Well, nothing right now." He sure was an easy blusher. "I came out of the service and bought some land in the Everglades. I put it all into celery, and I—well, I did all right. I put away forty thousand dollars in three years, and then decided to come up to Kansas City and get into business here. Mom's waiting down in Florida until I can get established up here."

"Beautiful climate, Florida," I said.

He nodded. "I liked it. But it's kind of hot for Mom in the summer, and that's one reason I'm moving north. If I don't find what I want here, I'm going up to St. Paul."

"Forty thousand of risk capital," I said, "is a nice little sum for a young man to have, and a war veteran to boot. You're one of a kind I thought was missing in America these days, Mr. Apple."

"I've always made my own way," he said, and looked at his hands. "I don't mind work, but I sure hate a time clock."

Now Joe came in. "Speaking of risk capital, Mr. Walters, I guess you've found a way to take the risk out of it."

I gave him a knowing smile. "I don't quite understand you, Mr. Delsing."

"That code sheet," Joe said. "I'm no gambler, but I've played the ponies enough to know a code tip when I see one."

"You're an astute young man, Mr. Delsing," I said. "Have a cigar."

He shook his head, and Mr. Apple declined, and I changed the subject. "I was in Washington just last month on some legislation and . . ."

I went on and on, tossing the big names around, giving this punk a picture of corruption and finagling that was bound to turn his stomach. A veteran, see, and still with some old-fashioned ideas in him, and I had to make him see it wasn't cheating, keeping the money out of the hands of those power-mad, greedy, corrupt officials.

I had to get him partly on our side of the fence, and make him forget mama, sweltering down in Florida. I had to make the rube forget all those things Mom had told him.

They both listened, Apple politely, like he'd been taught, and Joe with evident irritation. Joe was starting the switch right then, the sense of allegiance from him to me. Joe was to be the goat, and the mark was going to have to dislike him, or the blowoff might go sour.

When I'd finished, Joe said impatiently, "To get back to that code sheet, Mr. Walters—"

The apple looked at him, and then at me. "I suppose we're prying, but that remark of Mr. Delsing's—I mean, am I to assume that some horse races are . . . fixed?"

"Some?" I smiled at him. "Quite a few. Though very few that I don't know about, Mr. Apple. I think I can honestly say there are none at the major tracks that I don't know about—and well in advance of the running."

The square jaw of this young mark was set, and I could see the wheels turning in his thick skull. He was remembering the picture I'd painted of Washington, and at the same time the fine words about my generosity he'd read in that newspaper clipping. Here I was, an esteemed man, and a wealthy one, not looking like a crook at all. I could almost see his ideas change.

He nodded, and his voice was quiet. "Well, as Mr. Delsing said, that certainly takes the risk out of it."

I puffed the dollar cigar and shrugged. I frowned and picked up my wallet. "Which reminds me, gentlemen. I'd like to give you a little token of my gratitude." I pulled out the three hundred from the poke. "This you won't need to declare in your income tax, and it might pay the hotel bill."

Both of them shook their heads, and Apple said, "It's enough of a reward for me just to meet a man of your caliber, Mr. Walters." He looked uncomfortable. "How do you know in advance which races are fixed?"

I smiled. "That's almost an impertinent question, young man. But if I'd lost that code, and those telegrams . . ." I took a breath. "I know in advance because I work with the organization that fixes them. As I said, it's just for fun, and most of the money I make goes to various charitable organizations. And it gives me an excuse to travel from town to town, seeing this country I love."

Now Joe said, "If you really feel indebted to us, Mr. Walters, we'll settle for the name of a horse."

"I'll do better than that," I said. "I'll make a small wager for both of you this afternoon." I rose. "And now, gentlemen, if you'll excuse me, I have to make a call to Washington. How about dinner tonight in the dining room here? I'll have your winnings with me."

"It will be an honor, Mr. Walters," Apple said. He was still looking thoughtful.

They left, and I stayed there, waiting for Joe's call. He called at three.

"You sold the jerk, I think," Joe said. "Made to order, isn't he?"

I thought of that square jaw and those wide shoulders, and a punk that could take forty grand from Everglade muck. I said, "He could wind up a beefer, Joe. He might be rough to cool off, once he gets a chance to think it over. It'll be the cackle bladder, for sure."

"Right," Joe said. "Mama's boy and I will see you at dinner. He's beginning to get bored with me already, after your personality, Paris."

* * *

At dinner I gave each of them a hundred and fifty dollars. I gave Joe a card to the Pegasus Club.

I said, "If you'd like to risk that capital again, gentlemen, this is as good a place as any. You won't be bothered with riff-raff."

Joe looked at the card, and Apple looked at the money, as though wondering if it was right to pocket it.

Joe said, "If we're going to wager, it would only be on your advice, Mr. Walters. Nothing I love more than a sure thing. But we won't ask any more favors."

I could see the apple was about to say something, but he must have changed his mind. He pocketed the hundred and fifty. I could see he was starting to simmer. This was better than celery.

Joe kept yak-yaking all through the meal, and I could tell the apple didn't like it. Joe can talk awful damned foolish when he puts his mind to it.

When we were finished, I excused myself. "I have a rather important engagement with Senator Cormack," I apologized, "or I'd break the date." I looked thoughtful. "It so happens I'm going over to the Pegasus Club tomorrow afternoon. If you're both there, I might have something for you."

Joe called me that night. "I've been telling him what a gang of racketeers these bookies are. I've got him convinced it wouldn't be dishonest to take advantage of them. He's getting to think he's Robin Hood, instead of Galahad."

"I'll see you at the club," I said. "I think he's ripe."

Lou had really done a job on that Pegasus Club. It was a super-streamlined, high-class bookie joint that would have fooled anybody. And the shills could have stepped right out of the Blue Book. The wire service was the regular service—with one small change.

Lou had records made of the results as they came in, and it was the records that came out of the loudspeaker— a half hour after the race was over.

That way, if any mark happened to check the race results in the paper next day it would all be the quill.

I had the results of the third at Tanforan when the pair of them came in next afternoon.

The apple's eyes got big and bright when he saw the fancy company around. Some of them were lined up laying their bets, and the thousand-dollar bills were like push-notes in that big room. Old Judge Brewer stepped up and laid down a stack an inch high.

What the apple didn't know was that all the bills were singles on the inside. It looked like a good half million in cash being waved around that room; there was really about twenty thousand.

They came over to me, and I gave them the winner of the third at Tanforan. "He'll be odds-on," I told them, "so a small bet isn't going to do you any good."

"There's nothing small about me," Joe said. "I'm betting the whole hundred and fifty."

Apple's look was full of scorn. "Mr. Walters' gift. I'm willing to bet some of my own money on his word."

Joe looked away.

"I'm going to bet two thousand," Apple said, "of *my* money."

"Gentlemen," I said, "let's not quibble. The line is forming."

The announcement was coming through the speakers, and the winners of the second had been called off.

Joe managed to get in line before Apple did, shoving him as he did so, and not apologizing. It was a long line, but moving pretty well—until it got to Joe.

Joe mumbled and fumbled when it came his turn. The apple fidgeted and I could almost feel him burning. Joe finally stepped away from the window, and the cashier shrugged as the PA barked, "They're off!"

"Sorry, sir," the cashier said to the mark, "but the betting closes with that." He turned away and didn't even glance at the crummy two grand lying on the counter.

I thought Apple was going to swing on Joe right there.

And when the horse came home, the horse I'd given him, I waited for the melee. He'd paid three for two and Mr. Apple had been stalled out of a fast thousand dollars.

He just stood there, white in the face for a second, and then he began to use some language he must have picked up in the fields under that Florida sun.

Joe took it, and a few of the shills gathered around to see what was going on and the manager came over.

Horny Helmuth is the manager and he made it look like the McCoy. "I'll have to ask for your guest card, sir," he said quietly to Apple. "We don't tolerate that kind of language in the Pegasus Club. This is a gentlemen's club."

"Gentlemen?" the apple said evenly. "I can see that most of them are, sir, but I think you're making a mistake in this—this—" He couldn't finish.

"Mr. Apple," I said soothingly, "you have a just complaint, but I'm sure you didn't mean to lose your temper. You've been robbed of a few dollars, but there'll be other days."

Horny says, "These men are known to you, Mr. Walters?"

"I'll vouch for both of them," I said.

Horny practically crawled into the thick carpeting. "I—I didn't mean to intrude in a personal misunderstanding. I'm sincerely sorry, Mr. Walters."

He walked away.

Joe said, "I guess I am kind of jerk, at that. I only bet him to show. He certainly won't pay much to show."

"To show," I said, and smiled at the apple. "To show." I started to chuckle and slapped the apple on the back. "Isn't he terrific?"

The apple half grinned. He looked at Joe and then over at the windows where the Judge was collecting what looked like a quarter million, at least.

The apple said, "You'd better get over there, Mr. Delsing, before they run out of money."

We both got a laugh out of that, as Joe went to the window.

I said to Apple, "The pikers we will always have with us. The men who haven't the guts to take a risk. He's a good example."

Apple nodded. "Well, he's young, and maybe he never had to make his own way, like I did." He smiled. "I guess he'll never be bothered with income tax, like you, Mr. Walters."

"No," I said, "he sure won't."

Now the rube blushed again, and said quietly, "I—it's not right for me to ask it—but you wouldn't have another winner for today, would you?"

I shook my head sadly. "Not today, no." I frowned. "I—ah—shouldn't mention it. But call me this evening, around seven thirty."

He said humbly, "Thank you, sir. I certainly will."

"And another thing," I cautioned him, "don't antagonize your young friend. After all, Mr. Delsing does know about me now, and he could cause me some trouble in New York. I made nearly a million dollars in undeclared income last year, Mr. Apple, and it's not a source of revenue I'd relish losing because of a personal animosity. You can see how it is."

"I'll get along with him," he said. "I'll stay right with him and see that he doesn't blab to anybody. But I wish he wasn't always running everybody down."

"Including me?" I suggested.

"Let's forget it," he said. "I should shut up."

I shook his hand and left him. I was a little leary of his temper. We'd had some trouble with a couple of widows I'd brought in for Lou, and he'd cleaned them all the way, and the fix was kind of wary of any big beefs right now. Forty grand would make a big beef.

I knew how I was going to play him. He wouldn't need the big convincer; he believed in me now. I knew just how the "mistake" was going to be made, and how I was going to cool him out after the touch. Cooling him out right would save the fix a lot of trouble.

With a temper like young Apple's the cackle bladder was the only sure way.

He phoned at seven thirty, this Apple did, and I said, "Can you shake Delsing for an hour? I'd like to talk to you here."

He was over in ten minutes. I mixed him a drink and put him in a chair away from the light. I wanted the light on me, so he could see how sincere I was.

I took a sip of my drink and looked at him for a couple seconds. "Tomorrow night I'm leaving for Denver. Tomorrow afternoon I'm hitting the Pegasus Club for the Allenton Stakes, and I'm hitting them hard. I don't think they'll be happy to see me after that. I've won quite a lot this past week and they don't like consistent winners."

He was staring at me. "You've got the winner of the Allenton Stakes tomorrow?"

"Not yet," I said. "But I'll have it in the morning. I'm not going to be a pig. I figure to bet fifty thousand, collect my winnings, and take the first train out."

"And make a big profit in a few minutes." He must have been thinking of the difference between this and a celery farm.

I nodded. "In cash money. Now, because of the—the unfortunate bungling of our mutual friend this afternoon, you were cheated out of a tidy sum. Mr. Delsing seems to be something of a piker, so I prefer not to tell him of this. However, I'll be glad to wager any amount for you that you care to. Frankly, Mr. Apple, young men of your stature are rare these days and I have a great regard for you."

He said softly, "But won't the organization find out about it if you bet more than you declare to them? Won't they be suspicious?"

"Of a few extra thousand? Why should they?"

He gulped and looked at me hard. "I—I wasn't thinking of just a few thousand. I was thinking of betting it all, the whole forty thousand. Then I could buy the kind of business I want."

I frowned. The phone rang, and I went to answer it. Joe

was always a good man on his timing. He told me who he was and didn't say another word.

"New York?" I said. "I'll hold the wire." Then after a couple seconds, "Hello, hello—P.J.? I can hear you fine. Sure, everything's under control. How's your asthma, P.J.? Too bad. And the kids? Fine. No, no, not yet. Well, no later than noon. By the way, I'd like to take a little flyer myself on that one tomorrow. Need some traveling money, you know, and I eat pretty well."

A pause, a long pause, and I said, "Oh, maybe an extra forty or fifty."

Another pause, and I laughed. "No, not millions. I haven't got your kind of money, P.J. Okay? Thanks. It's a pleasure to work with you, P.J. Remember, it's Denver, tomorrow night. And my regards to your wife."

When I turned from the phone, I said, "That was New York. That was a man who really has trouble with his income tax."

"He said it was all right?"

I nodded. "Now, not a word of this to Delsing. He could spoil the whole deal, you know."

"Not a word," he agreed. "I'll stay with him. You'll be here the rest of the night, Mr. Walters?"

I nodded. "Why?"

"I'll want to phone you, in case Delsing gets out of hand. I wouldn't want him to cause you any trouble with his talk."

"Well," I said, "I'll be here." I finished my drink and shook his hand. "I'll see you in the morning, down in the grill."

He went out.

I checked my money, stacking it to look like fifty grand. I checked the revolver I'd inherited from Lou. It was clean and loaded—with blank cartridges.

I started to get sleepy, and I couldn't figure it. I don't usually hit the kip before two, and it wasn't even nine now. I was sound asleep by nine thirty.

* * *

I was still pounding the pillow at eight, next morning, when the phone rang. It was the apple, and he was waiting in the grill.

I told him I'd be right down.

Over ten hours, and I'd slept like a baby all through it. This one was working like a dream.

When I came into the grill, the apple looked unhappy. "I don't know where Mr. Delsing's gone to," he said apologetically. "You don't think he's out somewhere—"

"Shooting off his mouth? We can hope he isn't. I wish I hadn't given him that guest card to the club. You and he . . . quarreled?"

He nodded. "Nothing serious. He talks and talks and talks."

I sat down at the table. "Well, I'm not without influence in this town. It isn't as though we were cheating any honest citizens, you know. The authorities would like to see the Pegasus Club out of business." Which was no lie.

After breakfast we sat in the lobby for a while, and then I went with him to the bank. He drew out the forty grand, and we returned to the hotel.

We sat there, waiting for the code telegram that was going to make us our pile. He didn't have much to say. He'd sweated for that forty grand, and he might have been thinking of the risk, even on a sure thing.

The telegram came just before lunch, and I excused myself while I decoded it.

At lunch he said, "Well, Mr. Delsing hasn't appeared as yet. It looks like we'll be spared his company."

"It looks that way." I chewed my lip. "There's some trouble in New York. We may have to settle for second place today. We know what horse is going to finish second, and that should give us a reasonable return, if we bet to place, but I'm still waiting for word of the winner. Of course, it will depend on the final odds. The second place horse may even pay better. We'll see what develops."

Mr. Apple said earnestly, "All I expect is a reasonable

return, Mr. Walters. It's very seldom a fellow gets a sure thing."

"We'll wait," I said, "and see."

We waited and waited and waited after lunch. Finally, I went to the booth and pretended to put in a call to New York. I really put in a call to Horny, at the club.

When I came back, I said, "We'll have to settle for second. I hope it's going to be all right with you, Mr. Apple, if we make only an ordinary profit today."

He nodded, watching my face.

I let him simmer for a few seconds, and said, "Honey Boy to place, and it's in the bag."

Outside, I gave the cabbie a twenty and said, "Don't spare the horsepower."

He didn't. We got to the Pegasus Club in five minutes and hurried up to the second floor.

The place was as busy as ever. They were calling off the entries for the Allenton, and the line was forming. At the board the results of races all over the country were being chalked up.

The line was starting to stretch out, and Horny was there, getting it orderly. He smiled at me and said, "Some of you aren't going to make it for the Allenton, I'm afraid, Mr. Walters."

I could see the impatience in the mark's eyes. I could see him remembering yesterday and how he'd been robbed of an easy grand.

His eyes moved along the line, measuring it, and then he said quickly, "There's Delsing, right up near the front. Do you think? I mean—"

"Let him place it?" I asked. "Is that what you mean?"

Joe saw us and waved. I waved back and looked at the punk. "I guess we'll have to. I'll make it clear to him that he's not to increase his own bet too much. That wouldn't sit well with New York."

Apple said, "He hasn't got the money to hurt us. We'll just have to take the chance, Mr. Walters. Of course, it's really your decision."

I stepped out of the line. I had the apple's forty grand and my phony fifty. I handed it to Joe and said clearly, "Here's ninety thousand dollars. On Honey Boy, to *place*. Have you got that straight?"

"I certainly have," he said. "Only I'm going to add my hundred dollars to it now."

The apple and I went over to sit down. He had the shakes and his face was like snow. He said, "It's only justice that he helps us out now, after what happened yesterday."

Joe just made it. The PA started to bawl right after he left the window, bringing the tickets with him. He'd bought two, one for him and one for us.

He showed us his first. "I still haven't got the faith I should have, Mr. Walters. I bet him to place, for myself."

"For yourself?" I said. "How did you bet him for us? I said to *place*."

Joe looked stubborn. "You said straight, Mr. Walters."

I held my breath until my face was good and red. "I asked if you had it *straight*. But I distinctly told you to bet Honey Boy to place. You damned fool, you—"

My voice was loud, and Horny came over. "Gentlemen, gentlemen," he said quietly.

"Mr. Nelson," I said in a lower voice, "a mistake has been made and I'm sure it's not too late to correct it. I asked this young man to purchase a place ticket on Honey Boy, in the Allenton for me. He misunderstood and purchased one to win. I haven't that much faith in the horse. I'd like to exchange it."

Horny frowned and said, "There really isn't much time. However, for you, Mr. Walters—"

And then the call came over the system, and he smiled and said, "I'm afraid your request came just a few seconds late, Mr. Walters. Well, perhaps Honey Boy will win."

He walked away and I looked at Joe, and he backed away a step, looking belligerent.

"Ninety thousand dollars," I said. "Young man, that horse had better—"

Apple was white and talking to himself, and I thought he was going to hang one on Joe. Then the account of the running came, and we stood up. In the excitement I saw Joe slip the cackle bladder into his mouth.

It's a rubber dingus, you know, like a syringe, filled with blood, usually chicken blood, and it's the big part of the act.

Honey Boy was leading at the five-furlong post, and he was going away, and the apple almost looked human for a change. I started to talk to myself, and then the challenge came.

Into the last turn it was still Honey Boy, but Velveteen was coming up now on the outside, making the big bid, and Velveteen was the odds-on favorite in this one.

Velveteen was moving, moving up, moving past, going away in first place as she hit the wire. It was Honey Boy second, paying a bundle to place.

I saw Apple look at Joe and start to get up, but I was there in front of him, and I had Joe by the neck, shaking him, and his face started to get blue.

The shills were hollering and Horny was making his way through the crowd, and Apple was trying to get in with a slug or two of his own.

I slammed Joe's jaw, and he went to his knees. I stepped back, pulled the gun from my pocket, and now the apple looked scared.

I fired three times, at point-blank range, and it made one hell of a racket in that noisy room. The chicken blood just squirted from Joe's mouth, and he crashed forward on his face.

A couple of the shills started hollering, "Police!" and Horny had me by the arm.

"My God, Mr. Walters, you've killed him! Here, follow me!" He turned to Apple. "You too, sir. This will ruin us." Now he had us both by the arm and was pushing through the room toward his office.

He closed the door behind him there and took us to

another door, leading out the back way. "I wouldn't do this for anyone in the world but you, Mr. Walters. Go—hurry."

The apple and I clattered down the steps and through the short alley to the street. There was a cab waiting, one of our shills.

I put the apple in and handed him a couple hundred dollars. I said, "The Rockland Hotel, in Denver. Don't even go back to the hotel. I'll meet you there."

"But you—" he said, scared.

"I've got to see our local attorney," I said. "Remember, if I'm not there tomorrow; don't wire. I'll get in touch with you. Take a plane. Goodbye."

In Monte's, the rain was still hitting the front windows, and Paris finished his fourth glass of the fortified.

"Smooth as silk," I said. "You've got the touch, and you've got him cooled out and blown off. In Denver he gets a wire to go to Frisco, because the law is hot and he's an accessory. In Frisco he gets a wire telling him you're leaving for Europe to avoid the chair, because Mr. Carlton Delsing, alias Joe, is dead."

Paris was staring past me at nothing, the same thing he'd been staring at when he came in.

"Joe was dead," he said, without looking at me. "He lived for two hours, and I didn't go up for murder, though I got quite a jolt. But he had three slugs in him—three slugs *I* put there." Now he looked at me. "My boy, you understand. I made him. I killed him."

Monte was listening to it all. Monte came over and filled Paris' glass. "On the house," Monte said.

"The mark," Paris went on. "That night in my room, while I was pretending to talk to New York, he drugged my drink. While I slept, he changed the bullets from blanks to real slugs. He knew enough about the big con to guess we'd use the cackle bladder. And Joe was the boy he wanted dead."

"But why?" I asked. "Forty grand he drops, and gets involved in a murder. Why?"

Paris reached a dirty hand into a pocket and pulled out a torn, much-folded piece of paper that had once been a letter. I read:

Dear Grifter:

You'll want to know why, and maybe you won't remember back those years to Des Moines—and Judith. But I'll remember her. That wasn't Florida money I flashed, that was Iowa money, from selling my farm. I knew Judith since she was twelve and we were engaged before your buddy came along. She sent me a picture of him when he gave her that phony ring, and I studied it a long time until I knew it. I learned the big con from Mike Joaquin, and I rode the trains for a long time waiting for the guy in the picture to pick me up. I figured you'd use the cackle bladder, and I was glad he was the outside man. Because you made him, grifter, and you should destroy him.

"A nut," I said. "Forty grand, just because he was sold on the dame. Of all the lop-eared—"

But Paris wasn't listening. Paris' head was on the table; the fifth glass of fortified was empty near his dirty outstretched hand.

The rain was letting up a little, and I went back to the Form, trying to find a mudder.

THE MESSENGER

Jacklyn Butler

◻ JAKE LEFT THE BUSINESS AND ALL HIS MONEY TO HIS PARTNER Rodney, which would have been nice of him except there was so little of either. Rodney sat in the hole-in-the-wall office south of Market Street where he and Jake had scrounged out a living and thought about Jake's working his butt off for fifty, sixty years only to disappear without a trace. It didn't take Rodney long to decide that wasn't going to happen to him. He figured on using the next ten, fifteen years to make a bundle.

He used some of the money to buy enough shirts so he could wear a clean one every day, closed up the office, moved to a bigger one in a better neighborhood, and raised his rates. Until he could afford to hire a girl, he engaged an answering service to handle calls when he was out. The new office had a door with an opaque glass panel on which gold letters announced PRIVATE INVESTIGATIONS, and smaller black letters, below and to the right, ENTER. In the middle Rodney hung a cardboard clock with movable hands and a sign that read BACK AT. He put Jake's big desk facing the door and got rid of the clutter by getting four three-drawer filing cabinets. Two would have been enough right now, but he had hopes, and anyway it gave the place an air. He completed the desired ambience by getting a fax, a copy machine, a coffeemaker, and a three compartment desk organizer which he kept full but not messy. He'd have to hustle like crazy, but it was going to be worth it in the long run. He'd retire and have time to think about who he was and what it all meant. For the time being he'd forgo one luxury Jake had insisted on: the privilege of refusing to work for anybody he didn't particularly like.

He was just breaking even after a month. He looked around for a gimmick, some stunt that would bring people in, and got an inspiration reading funeral notices in the paper one Monday morning. He called both the *Chronicle* and the *Tribune* and placed an ad to run for three days in their personals section:

CONTACT DEPARTED LOVED ONES
Arrangements will be made for a terminally ill person to carry a short message to the other side. Call Rodney, 555-5698.

When he got to his office on Tuesday, he took the clock sign down, plugged in the coffeemaker, turned up the ventilating system, and lit his first cigarette before opening the papers. His ad, buried in the middle of the classifieds, was set apart by a box and its capitalized caption. He knew a lot of people would see it. In the *Chron* his ad was right under one that started out: GIRLS! GIRLS! GIRLS! and the one just above his in the *Trib* began with ARE YOU POURING MONEY INTO YOUR BANK?

Sure enough, his first nibble was there before he finished his cigarette. Young fellow, in his twenties, probably a college graduate, trying to be nonchalant but obviously a little uncomfortable as he looked around the office before sitting down in the chair beside the desk.

"I got your address from your answering service," the man said. "Nice place. I imagine you charge plenty."

Rodney was glad he'd got the extra filing cabinets. "Like they say, you get what you pay for," he said. This young man was not like his usual customers, but Rodney knew he'd seen him before. Probably a picture in the paper. Maybe on TV.

"What do you mean by a 'short message'?" the man asked.

"Ten words or less," Rodney replied. "The messengers are not in very good shape, of course. The current one will probably die before the week is out. Can't expect him to learn anything long or complicated." He watched the man take a ballpoint out of his pocket and click the point out.

"How do you give him the message?"

"I visit him every day, during visiting hours." Rodney pushed a notepad toward the man.

The man looked at the pen in his hand as if surprised to see it there. He put the pen back in his pocket. "How much for a ten word message?" he asked.

"Five hundred dollars."

"Phew! How much of it do you keep?"

"One hundred."

"And the terminal person gets four hundred? What's he gonna do with it, bribe the Almighty?"

"Poor fellow has used up most of his money on a long illness. I've promised to slip it to his daughter."

"Isn't that illegal?"

"Not on my part. By the way, which paper do you work for?"

"The *Trib*—hey, howdya know—"

"It's my business, son," Rodney said. "Now, suppose you tell me about yourself. What's your name, and what can I do for you? I charge a hundred an hour, starting now." He crushed the stub of the cigarette and picked up a small clock. He pushed a button on its side.

"You charge a hundred an hour to give you one of these messages? In addition to the five hundred?"

Rodney smiled. "No. That's for interviews. You have a message, the fee includes everything."

"Okay. My name is George Watkins. I'll give you a message."

Rodney nodded and stopped the timer. "The *Trib* gonna pay for it?"

"Maybe. Five hundred bucks, huh? You take a credit card?"

"Of course."

"Can I give any message I want?"

"Not quite. There are some restrictions. No messages that request information, like where did you hide the insurance papers."

"How will I be sure it's been delivered?"

"You'll feel a great relief."

"Relief from what?"

"From the guilt that makes it worth five hundred dollars to send the message."

"What about confidentiality?"

"That's one of my specialties. Nobody on earth but the messenger will ever know what your message is, or that you even sent it. You write it out, and I'll pass it on to him. Nothing in my files." He indicated the pad and lit another cigarette.

"I'll have to think about how to word the message. I'll come back later. Maybe tomorrow."

This was more than Rodney'd dared hope for. An article in the *Trib* would attract a lot of attention.

At a quarter to two, Rodney set the clock on his door to show he would be back at three and left to go to San Francisco State Hospital. He drove carefully, trying not to hurry, making it easy for the car that was following him to keep up. He parked in the section reserved for patient families; there were always plenty of vacant places. The car that was following him parked close by; George got out just as Rodney reached the elevators. Rodney avoided the elevator that was just leaving, waiting for the other one to descend from the top floor. He punched a button just as George started through the revolving door of the lobby.

Andy was noticeably paler than he had seemed on Rodney's first visit. He seemed tired, more listless.

"No business yet?" He sounded discouraged.

"Not yet, but I expect to have at least one message for you tomorrow," Rodney said.

"And you'll give Susan some money for each one I memorize?"

"Absolutely."

"It gives me something to think about," Andy said, closing his eyes.

"A man was asking about you," the head nurse told Rodney as he left.

"I know," he said. "I hope you answered all his questions."

"He asked mostly about Andy. Wanted to know if he was really terminal. I told him we don't discuss our patients."

"Did he ask to talk to Andy?"

"No."

"Well, if he does, be sure he keeps it short."

Rodney stopped in the lobby for a cigarette before leaving the hospital. The place depressed him, but he had to cover his ass by visiting somebody there. His stomach had begun to hurt, and so did his jaw. He hoped he wasn't getting a toothache. He reached in his pocket for a Tums. The problem was, he'd had no lunch. The hospital cafeteria was getting ready to close, but he managed to get a burger and fries.

When he got back to his office at three fifteen, George was waiting for him.

"You back already?" Rodney said.

"Yeah. Don't worry about my article. You'll get some good publicity."

"You got a message?"

"Yeah. I was gonna give you a phony, but now I think it's on the square—this is for my brother, Walter." George wrote on the pad: I'm sorry I beat you up. I love you. George. "It's hard to say much in ten words. I sure didn't mean to hurt him." He handed Rodney his credit card.

Now Rodney remembered where he had seen George. His picture had been in the papers some years before, when his brother had died from injuries received in a fight they'd had over some trivial matter; a high school date or something.

"We'd been fighting like that all our lives. I just didn't realize how much bigger I was—"

Rodney handed George the receipt. "As soon as Andy dies, I'll call you so you'll know your message has been delivered."

"Do I get my money back if I don't feel this great relief?"

"Let's discuss that when the time comes."

The five hundred bucks, less the fee for using the credit card service, would more than pay for the ad. But the best part of it was that George's article appeared in the morning paper, right above the obituary section. Almost as good as the front page. Rodney saved some money by canceling the last day of his advertisement. Another customer came in the afternoon, just as he was getting ready to leave.

The woman was not young, hair obviously tinted, could be a schoolteacher. He told her it would cost two hundred.

She gave her name only as Marcia. Rodney did not press for more information. If she wouldn't tell him, she'd have to pay cash.

Marcia demanded details. Rodney explained about Andy.

"If there is an afterlife, he will deliver it."

"But—how will I even know?"

"It becomes a matter of faith," Rodney said.

"Will I meet the messenger?"

"He's too sick to have visitors."

"Then how will he get the message?" Rodney could tell she was wavering.

"I have permission to see him once a day. I'll drill him on the message. He'll have it by heart before he dies." Rodney could see how much she wanted to believe him. He handed her the pad.

Thank you, Daddy, for paying my way through school, she wrote. She looked up at Rodney. "I—I never even asked him over, after I graduated. He—he was a garbage collector. I didn't realize how hard it must have been until my son started going to the university."

Rodney became businesslike. "We have to have some way to be sure it gets to the right person," he said. "There are a lot of people in heaven, I'm sure."

Marcia thought for a while. "Daddy always remembered my birthday," she said. "Even when I forgot to thank him for the presents. Just say Marcia who was born on May 19, 1930."

She counted out ten twenty dollar bills; she had a couple left in her wallet. Rodney didn't expect her to be back, but she might mention him to some of her friends.

Andy was definitely on his way out, a stick figure of a man, the ghastly pallor gradually turning to yellow. He tried to memorize the messages but kept stumbling. Rodney would have told him to forget it, but he thought he'd seen George's car in the parking lot so he better keep it up a while longer. "I haven't gotten any sleep," Andy said.

Rodney found it painful to listen.

"Don't they give you something to help?"

"Oh, yeah. But I never take that stuff."

"You should use everything they give you." Rodney hated the hospital. He wanted to get out of there as fast as he could.

James Cravey was the third person to answer the ad. He was casually, expensively dressed; the business card he handed Rodney showed that he was a software engineer. He frankly admired the office.

"They say there are two kinds of lawyers," he said. "The kind with fancy offices and fancy prices, and the kind willing to operate in a dump and charge moderate rates. I guess the same goes for private eyes, huh? So, what's the tab?" Rodney said it was a thousand dollars. Cravey smiled. "How much do you give the messenger?" he asked.

"I agreed to give his daughter nine hundred dollars per ten words," Rodney said.

"So you keep one hundred?"

"That's right."

"Pretty generous of you. Why not keep it all? Who'd ever know?"

"Yeah. I started by offering him only five hundred. But every time I talk to the poor fellow I get demolished." Rodney was proud of the smooth way he said it.

"You better hope he kicks it soon. You'll be losing money if you keep this up."

"He's entirely helpless," Rodney explained. "So anxious to earn a bit of money for his family! It's all he has to live for."

Cravey was going for it, hook, line, and sinker. "I know this is some kind of scam," he said, "but it's worth a try. I have a message for a fellow who'd be about my age, name is Carl Hughes." He wrote on the pad, printing block letters: You were the lucky one after all, you big stiff. "Poor Carl shot himself when he heard his wife was having an affair with me. It was a big scandal. I married the girl, and boy oh boy was that a mess! I'm finally divorced, broker, wiser, and happier. But I can't put all that into a message."

He wrote Rodney a check, decorated with a Picasso.

"By the way, is this message stuff a big part of your business?"

"Not really. I do surveillance, stakeout, undercover stuff."

"I should have hired you before I married my ex. Might have saved myself a bundle of grief."

Rodney put the check in his wallet. Enough to keep the office for a while longer. And this bozo might need some help with his next divorce.

That afternoon Andy was so weak he could not sit up. They'd stopped the I.V.'s because his veins were gone. To wake him, Rodney put his hand on his shoulder but drew it back quickly. His bone was right under the skin, hard and sharp, like a knife edge.

"I'm dying, Rod."

"We're all dying, pal."

"They say it isn't so awful," Andy whispered. "You see this bright light and pass through a tunnel. Everybody will be waiting for me—" He clutched Cravey's message tightly. "Gotta do this for Susan. It's all I can, now—"

Later, in his office, Rodney received a visit from the pastor of one of the nearby churches. The minister accepted a cigarette, looking around as if to see if anyone noticed before he lit it.

The minister said he was appalled at what Rodney was doing.

"Communicating with the dead is not exactly a new idea," Rodney said. "It wouldn't surprise me to learn that Eve tried to contact Abel. Though I suppose the Bible would have mentioned it if she got through."

The minister was not amused. "What you are doing is cruel and dishonest," he said.

"No, no! First of all, it is not cruel. I am giving a little meaning to the last moments of a painful death. That's a helluva lot more than this man's priest has done for him, believe me. And I am taking a load of guilt off the people who send the messages. What's wrong with that?"

"You're taking money under false pretenses. You know these messages will never arrive."

"I don't know that. I'm going to send one myself, in fact."

At the time, he only said it to get the minister off his back, but after he'd gone Rodney began to think about his late partner, Jake. These were the kind of people Jake would've refused to work for. Rodney could almost hear him: "They're guilty," he'd have said. "They deserve to feel uncomfortable. I'm not gonna help 'em unload." By now maybe Jake realized it was a mistake to have so many scruples. Rodney wrote a message on the pad: Don't you wish you'd thought of this one, you jerk?

* * *

He found Andy's bed empty.

"He died last night," the nurse told him. "I think he left you something. Ask the orderly." She turned her back to him.

The orderly was in the lobby.

"Yeah, they don't want to talk about it. They could get disciplined. Guy'd saved up his sleeping pills, probably took eight or ten. He a relative of yours?"

Rodney felt lightheaded. "No. A friend is all."

"Well, they won't order an autopsy; he was due to kick the bucket any minute anyhow."

"She said he left something for me?"

"Oh, yeah. These slips." He handed Rodney the three messages, wrinkled up from being clenched in a bony hand. "He talked to me just before he cashed in. He said something like he couldn't even do this much for Susan." The orderly stared at Rodney. "Look, mister, don't feel bad about it. It isn't your fault. These terminal cases get like that."

Just to be sure he was covered, in case George followed up and inquired about him at the hospital, Rodney asked the nurse at the desk for the address of Andy's next of kin. She wrote it on a slip of paper, frowning the whole time. Probably thought he was going to investigate the death. Make a stink about all those sleeping pills.

He thought about looking Susan up, passing her a few bucks, but decided that was silly. After all, Andy had failed even to try to deliver any messages. Back in his office he threw Susan's address in his wastebasket.

He knew them by heart, but he spread the notes out on his desk and reread them anyway. He wondered if any of the suckers would dare demand a refund—

He felt a sharp pain in his left lung. Damn, he'd forgotten lunch again. He pushed the messages aside and picked up a cigarette, but before he lit it he felt in his pocket for his Tums. The pain crushed his chest and burst loose, spreading down his left arm and around his back. He tried to reach for his phone but stopped as he saw a bright light at the end of a dark tunnel and heard voices calling him and all the pain stopped.

The janitor found the body facedown on the desk. There was no evidence of foul play, so nobody paid much attention to the scribbled notes on the papers clutched in the hand of the corpse.